THE BORROWERS
THE BORROWERS AFIELD

MARY NORTON

THE BORROWERS
THE BORROWERS AFIELD

Illustrated by Diana Stanley

Orion
Children's Books

First published in Great Britain in two separate volumes:

The Borrowers
First published in 1952 by J M Dent Ltd
Text copyright © Mary Norton 1952
Illustrations copyright © Diana Stanley 1952

The Borrowers Afield
First published in 1955 by J M Dent Ltd
Text copyright © Mary Norton 1955
Illustrations copyright © Diana Stanley 1955

The moral rights of the author and illustrator have been asserted.

This 2-in-1 edition first published in 2011 by Orion Children's Books
a division of the Orion Publishing Group Ltd
Orion House
5 Upper St Martin's Lane
London WC2H 9EA
An Hachette UK Company

1 3 5 7 9 10 8 6 4 2

The Orion Publishing Group's policy is to use papers
that are natural, renewable and recyclable products and
made from wood grown in sustainable forests. The logging
and manufacturing processes are expected to conform to
the environmental regulations of the country of origin.

A catalogue record for this book is available from the British Library

Printed in Great Britain by Clays Ltd, St Ives plc

ISBN 978 1 4440 0581 3

www.orionbooks.co.uk

CONTENTS

THE BO-------

THE BORROWERS

for
SHARON RHODES

CHAPTER ONE

It was Mrs. May who first told me about them. No, not me. How could it have been me—a wild, untidy, self-willed little girl who stared with angry eyes and was said to crunch her teeth? Kate, she should have been called. Yes, that was it—Kate. Not that the name matters much either way: she barely comes into the story.

Mrs. May lived in two rooms in Kate's parents' house in London; she was, I think, some kind of relation. Her bedroom was on the first floor, and her sitting-room was a room which, as part of the house, was called 'the breakfast-room.' Now breakfast-rooms are all right in the morning when the sun streams in on the toast and marmalade, but by afternoon they seem to vanish a little and to fill with a strange silvery light, their own twilight; there is a kind of sadness in them then, but as a child it was a sadness Kate liked. She would creep in to Mrs. May just before tea-time and Mrs. May would teach her to crochet.

Mrs. May was old, her joints were stiff, and she was—not strict exactly, but she had that inner certainty which does instead. Kate was never 'wild' with Mrs. May, nor untidy, nor self-willed; and Mrs. May taught her many things besides crochet: how to wind wool into an egg-shaped ball; how to run-and-fell and plan a darn; how to tidy a drawer and to lay, like a blessing, above the contents, a sheet of rustling tissue against the dust.

'Where's your work, child?' asked Mrs. May one day, when Kate sat hunched and silent upon the hassock. 'You mustn't sit there dreaming. Have you lost your tongue?'

'No,' said Kate, pulling at her shoe button, 'I've lost the crochet hook.' They were making a bed-quilt—in woollen squares: there were thirty still to do. 'I know where I put it,' she went on hastily; 'I put it on the bottom shelf of the book-case just beside my bed.'

'On the bottom shelf?' repeated Mrs. May, her own needle flicking steadily in the firelight. 'Near the floor?'

'Yes,' said Kate, 'but I looked on the floor. Under the rug. Everywhere. The wool was still there though. Just where I'd left it.'

'Oh dear,' exclaimed Mrs. May lightly, 'don't say they're in this house too!'

'That what are?' asked Kate.

'The Borrowers,' said Mrs. May, and in the half light she seemed to smile.

Kate stared a little fearfully. 'Are there such things?' she asked after a moment.

'As what?'

Kate blinked her eyelids. 'As people, other people, living in a house who . . . borrow things?'

Mrs. May laid down her work. 'What do you think?' she asked.

Kate looked away. 'I don't know,' she said, pulling hard at her shoe button. 'There can't be. And yet'—she raised her head—'and yet sometimes I think there must be.'

'Why do you think there must be?' asked Mrs. May.

'Because of all the things that disappear.   Safety-pins, for instance.   Factories go on making safety-pins, and

every day people go on buying safety-pins and yet, some-how, there never is a safety-pin just when you want one. Where are they all? Now, at this minute? Where do they go to? Take needles,' she went on.   'All the needles my mother ever bought—there must be hundreds—can't just be lying about this house.'

'Not lying about the house, no,' agreed Mrs. May.

'And all the other things we keep on buying.   Again and again and again.   Like pencils and match-boxes and sealing-wax and hair-slides and drawing-pins and thimbles——'

'And hat-pins,' put in Mrs. May, 'and blotting-paper.'

'Yes, blotting-paper,' agreed Kate, 'but not hat-pins.'

'That's where you're wrong,' said Mrs. May, and she picked up her work again.   'There was a reason for hat-pins.'

Kate stared.   'A reason?' she repeated.   'I mean—what kind of a reason?'

'Well, there were two reasons really.   A hat-pin is a very useful weapon and'—Mrs. May laughed suddenly—'but it all sounds such nonsense and'—she hesitated—'it was so very long ago!'

'But tell me,' said Kate, 'tell me how you *know* about the hat-pin.   Did you ever see one?'

Mrs. May threw her a startled glance.   Well, yes——' she began.

'Not a hat-pin,' exclaimed Kate impatiently, 'a—whatever-you-called-them—a Borrower?'

Mrs. May drew a sharp breath.   'No,' she said quickly, 'I never saw one.'

'But someone else saw one,' cried Kate, 'and you know about it.   I can see you do!'

'Hush,' said Mrs. May, 'no need to shout!'   She gazed downwards at the upturned face and then she smiled and her eyes slid away into distance.   'I had a brother——' she began uncertainly.

Kate knelt upon the hassock.   'And he saw them!'

'I don't know,' said Mrs. May, shaking her head, 'I just don't know!' She smoothed out her work upon her knee. 'He was such a tease. He told us so many things—my sister and me—impossible things. He was killed,' she added gently, 'many years ago now, on the North-West Frontier. He became colonel of his regiment. He died what they call "a hero's death" . . .'

'Was he your only brother?'

'Yes, and he was our little brother. I think that was why'—she thought for a moment, still smiling to herself—'yes, why he told us such impossible stories, such strange imaginings. He was jealous, I think, because we were older —and because we could read better. He wanted to impress us; he wanted, perhaps, to shock us. And yet'—she looked into the fire—'there was something about him—perhaps because we were brought up in India among mystery and magic and legend—something that made us think that he saw things that other people could not see; sometimes we'd know he was teasing, but at other times—well, we were not so sure. . . .' She leaned forward and, in her tidy way, brushed a fan of loose ashes under the grate, then, brush in hand, she stared again at the fire. 'He wasn't a very strong little boy: the first time he came home from India he got rheumatic fever. He missed a whole term at school and was sent away to the country to get over it. To the house of a great-aunt. Later I went there myself. It was a strange old house. . . .' She hung up the brush on its brass hook and, dusting her hands on her handkerchief, she picked up her work. 'Better light the lamp.' she said.

'Not yet,' begged Kate, leaning forward. 'Please go on. Please tell me——'

'But I've told you.'

'No you haven't. This old house—wasn't that where he saw—he saw . . .?'

Mrs. May laughed. 'Where he saw the Borrowers? Yes, that's what he told us . . . what he'd have us believe. And, what's more, it seems that he didn't just see them but that he got to know them very well; that he became part of their lives, as it were; in fact, you might almost say that he became a borrower himself. . . .'

'Oh, *do* tell me. Please. Try to remember. Right from the very beginning!'

'But I do remember,' said Mrs. May. 'Oddly enough I remember it better than many real things which have happened. Perhaps it was a real thing. I just don't know. You see, on the way back to India my brother and I had to share a cabin—my sister used to sleep with our governess—and, on those very hot nights, often we couldn't sleep; and my brother would talk for hours and hours, going over old ground, repeating conversations, telling me details again and again—wondering how they were and what they were doing and——'

'They? Who were they—exactly?'

'Homily, Pod, and little Arrietty.'

'Pod?'

'Yes, even their names were never quite right. They imagined they had their own names—quite different from human names—but with half an ear you could tell they were borrowed. Even Uncle Hendreary's and Eggletina's.

Everything they had was borrowed; they had nothing of their own at all. Nothing. In spite of this, my brother said, they were touchy and conceited, and thought they owned the world.'

'How do you mean?'

'They thought human beings were just invented to do the dirty work—great slaves put there for them to use. At least, that's what they told each other. But my brother said that, underneath, he thought they were frightened. It was because they were frightened, he thought, that they had grown so small. Each generation had become smaller and smaller, and more and more hidden. In the olden days, it seems, and in some parts of England, our ancestors talked quite openly about the "little people."'

'Yes,' said Kate, 'I know.'

'Nowadays, I suppose,' Mrs. May went on slowly, 'if they exist at all, you would only find them in houses which are old and quiet and deep in the country—and where the human beings live to a routine. Routine is their safeguard, and enables them to organize their borrowing. They must know which rooms are to be used and when. They do not stay long where there are careless people, or unruly children, or certain household pets.

'This particular old house, of course, was ideal—although as far as some of them were concerned, a trifle cold and empty. Great Aunt Sophy was bedridden, through a hunting accident some twenty years before, and as for other human beings there was only Mrs. Driver the cook, Cramp-furl the gardener, and, at rare intervals, an odd housemaid or such. My brother, too, when he went there after rheumatic fever, had to spend long hours in bed, and for those first weeks it seems the Borrowers did not know of his existence.

'He slept in the old night-nursery, beyond the school-room. The schoolroom, at that time, was sheeted and shrouded and filled with junk—odd trunks, a broken sewing-machine, a desk, a dressmaker's dummy, a table, some chairs, and a disused pianola—as the children who had used it, Great Aunt Sophy's children, had long since grown up, married, died, or gone away. The night-nursery opened out of the schoolroom and, from his bed, my brother could see the oil-painting of the battle of Water-loo which hung above the schoolroom fire-place and, on the wall, a corner cupboard with glass doors in which was set out, on hooks and shelves, a doll's tea-service—very delicate and old. At night, if the schoolroom door was open, he had a view down the lighted passage which led to the head of the stairs, and it would comfort him to see, each evening at dusk, Mrs. Driver appear at the head of the stairs and cross the passage carrying a tray for Aunt Sophy with Bath Oliver biscuits and the tall, cut-glass decanter of Fine Old Pale Madeira. On her way out Mrs. Driver would pause and lower the gas jet in the passage to a dim, blue flame, and then he would watch her as she stumped away down-stairs, sinking slowly out of sight between the banisters.

'Under this passage, in the hall below, there was a clock, and through the night he would hear it strike the hours. It was a grandfather clock and very old. Mr. Frith of Leighton Buzzard came each month to wind it, as his father had come before him and his great-uncle before that. For

eighty years, they said (and to Mr. Frith's certain knowledge), it had not stopped and, as far as any one could tell,
for as many years before that. The great thing was—that
it must never be moved. It stood against the wainscot,
and the stone flags around it had been washed so often that
a little platform, my brother said, rose up inside.

'And, under this clock, below the wainscot, there was
a hole. . . .'

CHAPTER TWO

IT WAS Pod's hole—the keep of his fortress; the entrance to his home. Not that his home was anywhere near the clock: far from it—as you might say. There were yards of dark and dusty passage-way, with wooden doors between the joists and metal gates against the mice. Pod used all kinds of things for these gates—a flat leaf of a folding cheese-grater, the hinged lid of a small cash-box, squares of pierced zinc from an old meat-safe, a wire fly-swotter. . . . 'Not that I'm afraid of mice,' Homily would say, 'but I can't abide the smell.' In vain Arrietty had begged for a little mouse of her own, a little blind mouse to bring up by hand—'like Eggletina had had.' But Homily would bang with the pan lids and exclaim: 'And look what happened to Eggletina!' 'What,' Arrietty would ask, 'what did happen to Eggletina?' But no one would ever say.

It was only Pod who knew the way through the inter-secting passages to the hole under the clock. And only Pod could open the gates. There were complicated clasps made of hair-slides and safety-pins of which Pod alone knew the secret. His wife and child led more sheltered lives in homelike apartments under the kitchen, far removed from the risks and dangers of the dreaded house above. But there was a grating in the brick wall of the house, just below the floor level of the kitchen above, through which

Arrietty could see the garden—a piece of gravelled path and a bank where crocus bloomed in spring; where blossom drifted from an unseen tree; and where later an azalea bush would flower; and where birds came—and pecked and flirted and sometimes fought. 'The hours you waste on them birds,' Homily would say, 'and when there's a little job to be done you can never find the time. I was brought up in a house,' Homily went on, 'where there wasn't no grating, and we were all the happier for it. Now go off and get me the potato.'

That was the day when Arrietty, rolling the potato before her from the storehouse down the dusty lane under the floor-boards, kicked it ill-temperedly so that it rolled rather fast into their kitchen, where Homily was stooping over the stove.

'There you go again,' exclaimed Homily, turning angrily; 'nearly pushed me into the soup. And when I say "potato" I don't mean the whole potato. Take the scissor, can't you, and cut off a slice.'

'Didn't know how much you wanted,' mumbled Arrietty, and Homily, snorting and sniffing, unhooked the blade and handle of half a pair of manicure scissors from a nail on the wall, and began to cut through the peel.

'You've ruined this potato,' she grumbled. 'You can't roll it back now in all that dust, not once it's been cut open.'

'Oh, what does it matter?' said Arrietty. 'There are plenty more.'

'That's a nice way to talk. Plenty more. Do you realize,' Homily went on gravely, laying down the half nail scissor, 'that your poor father risks his life every time he borrows a potato?'

'I meant,' said Arrietty, 'that there are plenty more in the store-room.'

'Well, out of my way now,' said Homily, bustling around again, 'whatever you meant—and let me get the supper.'

Arrietty wandered through the open door into the sitting-room. Ah, the fire had been lighted and the room looked bright and cosy. Homily was proud of her sitting-room: the walls had been papered with scraps of old letters out of waste-paper baskets, and Homily had arranged the hand-writing sideways in vertical stripes which ran from floor to ceiling. On the walls, repeated in various colours, hung several portraits of Queen Victoria as a girl; these were postage stamps, borrowed by Pod some years ago from the stamp-box on the desk in the morning-room. There was a lacquer trinket-box, padded inside and with the lid open, which they used as a settle; and that useful stand-by—a chest of drawers made of match-boxes. There was a round table with a red velvet cloth, which Pod had made from the wooden bottom of a pill-box supported on the carved pedestal of a knight from the chess-set. (This had caused a great deal of trouble upstairs when Aunt Sophy's eldest son, on a flying mid-week visit, had invited the vicar for 'a game after dinner.' Rosa Pickhatchet, who was housemaid at the time, gave in her notice. After she had left other things were found to be missing, and no one was engaged in her place. From that time onwards Mrs. Driver ruled supreme.) The knight itself—its bust, so to speak—stood on a column in the corner, where it looked very fine, and lent that air to the room which only statuary can give.

Beside the fire, in a tilted wooden book-case, stood Arrietty's library. This was a set of those miniature volumes which the Victorians loved to print, but which to Arrietty seemed the size of very large church Bibles. There was Bryce's *Tom Thumb Gazetteer of the World*, including the last census; Bryce's *Tom Thumb Dictionary*, with short explanations of scientific, philosophical, literary, and technical terms; Bryce's *Tom Thumb Edition of the Comedies of William Shakespeare*, including a foreword on the author; another book, whose pages were all blank, called *Memoranda*; and, last but not least, Arrietty's favourite Bryce's *Tom Thumb Diary and Proverb Book*, with a saying for each day of the year and, as a preface, the life story of a little man called General Tom Thumb, who married a girl called Mercy Lavinia Bump. There was an engraving of their carriage and pair, with little horses—the size of mice. Arrietty was not a stupid girl. She knew that horses could not be as small as mice, but she did not realize that Tom Thumb, nearly two feet high, would seem a giant to a Borrower.

Arrietty had learned to read from these books, and to write by leaning sideways and copying out the writings on the walls. In spite of this, she did not always keep her diary, although on most days she would take the book out for the sake of the saying which sometimes would comfort her. To-day it said: 'You may go farther and fare worse,' and, underneath: 'Order of the Garter, instituted 1348.' She carried the book to the fire and sat down with her feet on the hob.

'What are you doing, Arrietty?' called Homily from the kitchen.

'Writing my diary.'

'Oh,' exclaimed Homily shortly.

'What did you want?' asked Arrietty. She felt quite safe; Homily liked her to write; Homily encouraged any form of culture. Homily herself, poor ignorant creature, could not even say the alphabet. 'Nothing. Nothing,' said Homily crossly, banging away with the pan lids; 'it'll do later.'

Arrietty took out her pencil. It was a small white pencil, with a piece of silk cord attached, which had come off a dance programme, but, even so, in Arrietty's hand, it looked like a rolling-pin.

'Arrietty!' called Homily again from the kitchen.

'Yes?'

'Put a little something on the fire, will you?'

Arrietty braced her muscles and heaved the book off her knees, and stood it upright on the floor. They kept the fuel, assorted slack and crumbled candle-grease, in a pewter mustard-pot, and shovelled it out with the spoon. Arrietty

trickled only a few grains, tilting the mustard spoon, not
to spoil the blaze. Then she stood there basking in the
warmth. It was a charming fire-place, made by Arrietty's
grandfather, with a cog-wheel from the stables, part of an
old cider-press. The spokes of the cog-wheel stood out
in starry rays, and the fire itself nestled in the centre.
Above there was a chimney-piece made from a small brass
funnel, inverted. This, at one time, belonged to an oil-
lamp which matched it, and which stood, in the old days,
on the hall table upstairs. An arrangement of pipes, from
the spout of the funnel, carried the fumes into the kitchen
flues above. The fire was laid with match-sticks and fed
with assorted slack and, as it burned up, the iron would
become hot, and Homily would simmer soup on the spokes,
in a silver thimble, and Arrietty would broil nuts.

How cosy those winter evenings could be.
Arrietty, her great book on her knees,
sometimes reading aloud; Pod at
his last (he was a shoemaker, and
made button-boots out of kid
gloves—now, alas, only for
his family); and Homily,
quiet at last, with her
knitting.

Homily knitted their
jerseys and stockings
on black-headed pins,
and, sometimes, on
darning needles. A
great reel of silk or

cotton would stand, table high, beside her chair, and sometimes, if she pulled too sharply, the reel would tip up and
roll away out of the open door into the dusty passage
beyond, and Arrietty would be sent after it, to re-wind it
carefully as she rolled it back.

The floor of the sitting-room was carpeted with deep
red blotting-paper, which was warm and cosy, and soaked
up the spills. Homily would renew it at intervals when
it became available upstairs, but since Aunt Sophy had
taken to her bed Mrs. Driver seldom thought of blotting-
paper unless, suddenly, there were guests. Homily liked
things which saved washing because drying was difficult
under the floor; water they had in plenty, hot and cold,
thanks to Pod's father who had tapped the pipes from the
kitchen boiler. They bathed in a small tureen, which once
had held *pâté de foie gras*. When you had wiped out your
bath you were supposed to put the lid back, to stop people
putting things in it. The soap, too, a great cake of it,
hung on a nail in the scullery, and they scraped pieces off.
Homily liked coal tar, but Pod and Arrietty preferred
sandalwood.

'What are you doing now, Arrietty?' called Homily from
the kitchen.

'Still writing my diary.'

Once again Arrietty took hold of the book and heaved
it back on to her knees. She licked the lead of her great
pencil, and stared a moment, deep in thought. She allowed
herself (when she did remember to write) one little line on
each page because she would never—of this she was sure
—have another diary, and if she could get twenty lines on

each page the diary would last her twenty years.   She had
kept it for nearly two years already, and to-day, 22nd
March, she read last year's entry: 'Mother cross.'   She

thought a while longer then, at last, she put ditto marks
under 'mother,' and 'worried' under 'cross.'

'What did you say you were doing, Arrietty?' called
Homily from the kitchen.

Arrietty closed the book.   'Nothing,' she said.

'Then chop me up this onion, there's a good girl.
Your father's late to-night. . . .'

CHAPTER THREE

SIGHING, Arrietty put away her diary and went into the kitchen. She took the onion ring from Homily, and slung it lightly round her shoulders, while she foraged for a piece of razor blade. 'Really, Arrietty,' exclaimed Homily, 'not on your clean jersey! Do you want to smell like a bit-bucket? Here, take the scissor——'

Arrietty stepped through the onion ring as though it were a child's hoop, and began to chop it into segments.

'Your father's late,' muttered Homily again, 'and it's my fault, as you might say. Oh dear, oh dear, I wish I hadn't——'

'Hadn't what?' asked Arrietty, her eyes watering. She sniffed loudly and longed to rub her nose on her sleeve.

Homily pushed back a thin lock of hair with a worried hand. She stared at Arrietty absently. 'It's that tea-cup you broke,' she said.

'But that was days ago——' began Arrietty, blinking her eyelids, and she sniffed again.

'I know. I know. It's not you. It's me. It's not the breaking that matters, it's what I said to your father.'

'What did you say to him?'

'Well, I just said—there's the rest of the service, I said—up there, where it always was, in the corner cupboard in the schoolroom.'

'I don't see anything bad in that,' said Arrietty as, one by one, she dropped the pieces of onion into the soup.

'But it's a high cupboard,' exclaimed Homily. 'You have to get up by the curtain. And your father at his age——' She sat down suddenly on a metal-topped champagne cork. 'Oh, Arrietty, I wish I'd never mentioned it!'

'Don't worry,' said Arrietty, 'papa knows what he can do.' She pulled a rubber scent-bottle cork out of the hole in the hot-water pipe and let a trickle of scalding drops fall into the tin lid of an aspirin bottle. She added cold and began to wash her hands.

'Maybe,' said Homily. 'But I went on about it so. What's a tea-cup! Your Uncle Hendreary never drank a thing that wasn't out of a common acorn cup, and he's lived to a ripe old age and had the strength to emigrate. My mother's family never had nothing but a little bone thimble which they shared around. But it's once you've *had* a tea-cup, if you see what I mean. . . .'

'Yes,' said Arrietty, drying her hands on a roller towel made out of surgical bandage.

'It's that curtain,' cried Homily. 'He can't climb a curtain at his age—not by the bobbles!'

'With his pin he could,' said Arrietty.

'His pin! I led him into that one too! Take a hat-pin, I told him, and tie a bit of name-tape to the head, and pull yourself upstairs. It was to borrow the emerald watch from Her bedroom for me to time the cooking.' Homily's voice began to tremble. 'Your mother's a wicked woman, Arrietty. Wicked and selfish, that's what she is!'

'You know what?' exclaimed Arrietty suddenly.

Homily brushed away a tear. 'No,' she said wanly, 'what?'
'I could climb a curtain.'

Homily rose up. 'Arrietty, you dare stand there in cold
blood and say a thing like that!'

'But I could! I could! I could borrow! I know I could!'

'Oh!' gasped Homily. 'Oh, you wicked heathen girl!
How could you!' and she crumpled up again on the cork
stool. 'So it's come to this!' she said.

'Now, mother, please,' begged Arrietty, 'now, don't
take on!'

'But don't you see, Arrietty . . .' gasped Homily; she
stared down at the table at loss for words and then, at
last, she raised a haggard face. 'My poor child,' she said,
'don't speak like that of borrowing. You don't know—
and, thank goodness, you never will know'—she dropped
her voice to a fearful whisper—'what it's like upstairs. . . .'

Arrietty was silent. 'What is it like?' she asked after
a moment.

Homily wiped her face on her apron and smoothed back
her hair. 'Your Uncle Hendreary,' she began, 'Eggletina's father——' and then she paused. 'Listen!' she said.
'What's that?'

Echoing on the wood was a faint vibration—the sound
of a distant click. 'Your father!' exclaimed Homily.
'Oh, look at me! Where's the comb?'

They had a comb: a little, silver, eighteenth-century
eyebrow comb from the cabinet in the drawing-room
upstairs. Homily ran it through her hair and rinsed her
poor red eyes and, when Pod came in, she was smiling and
smoothing down her apron.

CHAPTER FOUR

Pod came in slowly, his sack on his back; he leaned his hat-pin,with its dangling name-tape, against the wall and, on the middle of the kitchen table, he placed a doll's tea-cup; it was the size of a mixing-bowl.

'Why, Pod——' began Homily.

'Got the saucer too,' he said. He swung down the sack and untied the neck. 'Here you are,' he said, drawing out the saucer. 'Matches it.'

He had a round, currant-bunny sort of face; to-night it looked flabby.

'Oh, Pod,' said Homily, 'you do look queer. Are you all right?'

Pod sat down. 'I'm fair enough,' he said.

'You went up the curtain,' said Homily. 'Oh, Pod, you shouldn't have. It's shaken you——'

Pod made a strange face, his eyes swivelled round to-wards Arrietty. Homily stared at him, her mouth open, and then she turned. 'Come along, Arrietty,' she said briskly, 'you pop off to bed, now, like a good girl, and I'll bring you some supper.'

'Oh,' said Arrietty, 'can't I see the rest of the borrow-ings?'

'Your father's got nothing now. Only food. Off you pop to bed. You've seen the cup and saucer.'

Arrietty went into the sitting-room to put away her

diary, and took some time fixing her candle on the up-turned drawing-pin which served as a holder.

'Whatever are you doing?' grumbled Homily. 'Give it here. There, that's the way. Now off to bed and fold your clothes, mind.'

'Good night, papa,' said Arrietty, kissing his flat white cheek.

'Careful of the light,' he said mechanically, and watched her with his round eyes until she had closed the door.

'Now, Pod,' said Homily, when they were alone, 'tell me. What's the matter?'

Pod looked at her blankly. 'I been "seen,"' he said.

Homily put out a groping hand for the edge of the table; she grasped it and lowered herself slowly on to the stool. 'Oh, Pod,' she said.

There was silence between them. Pod stared at Homily and Homily stared at the table. After a while she raised her white face. 'Badly?' she asked.

Pod moved restlessly. 'I don't know about badly. I been "seen." Ain't that bad enough?'

'No one,' said Homily slowly, 'hasn't never been "seen" since Uncle Hendreary and he was the first they say for forty-five years.' A thought struck her and she gripped the table. 'It's no good, Pod, I won't emigrate!'

'No one's asked you to,' said Pod.

'To go and live like Hendreary and Lupy in a badger's set! The other side of the world, that's where they say it is—all among the earthworms.'

'It's two fields away, above the spinney,' said Pod.

'Nuts, that's what they eat. And berries. I wouldn't wonder if they don't eat mice——'

'You've eaten mice yourself,' Pod reminded her.

'All draughts and fresh air and the children growing up wild. Think of Arrietty!' said Homily. 'Think of the way she's been brought up. An only child. She'd catch her death. It's different for Hendreary.'

'Why?' asked Pod. 'He's got five.'

'That's why,' explained Homily. 'When you've got five, they're brought up rough. But never mind that now. . . . Who saw you?'

'A boy,' said Pod.

'A what?' exclaimed Homily, staring.

'A boy.' Pod sketched out a rough shape in the air with his hands. 'You know, a boy.'

'But there isn't—I mean, what sort of a boy?'

'I don't know what you mean "what sort of a boy." A boy in a night-shirt. A boy. You know what a boy is, don't you?'

'Yes,' said Homily, 'I know what a boy is. But there hasn't been a boy, not in this house, these twenty years.'

'Well,' said Pod, 'there's one here now.'

Homily stared at him in silence, and Pod met her eyes. 'Where did he see you?' asked Homily at last.

'In the schoolroom.'

'Oh,' said Homily, 'when you was getting the cup?'

'Yes,' said Pod.

'Haven't you got eyes?' asked Homily. 'Couldn't you have looked first?'

'There's never nobody in the schoolroom. And what's more,' he went on, 'there wasn't to-day.'

'Then where was he?'

'In bed. In the night-nursery or whatever it's called. That's where he was. Sitting up in bed. With the doors open.'

'Well, you could have looked in the nursery.'

'How could I—half-way up the curtain!'

'Is that where you was?'

'Yes.'

'With the cup?'

'Yes. I couldn't get up or down.'

'Oh, Pod,' wailed Homily, 'I should never have let you go. Not at your age!'

'Now, look here,' said Pod, 'don't mistake me. I got up all right. Got up like a bird, as you might say, bobbles or no bobbles. But'—he leaned towards her—'afterwards —with the cup in me hand, if you see what I mean. . . .' He picked it up off the table. 'You see, it's heavy like. You can hold it by the handle, like this . . . but it drops or droops, as you might say. You should take a cup like this in your two hands. A bit of cheese off a shelf, or an apple—well, I drop that . . . give it a push and it falls and I climbs down in me own time and picks it up. But with a cup—you see what I mean? And coming down, you got to watch your feet. And, as I say, some of the bobbles was missing. You didn't know what you could hold on to, not safely. . . .'

'Oh, Pod,' said Homily, her eyes full of tears, 'what did you do?'

'Well,' said Pod, sitting back again, 'he took the cup.'

'What do you mean?' exclaimed Homily, aghast.

Pod avoided her eyes. 'Well, he'd been sitting up in bed there watching me. I'd been on that curtain a good ten minutes, because the hall clock had just struck the quarter——'

'But how do you mean—"he took the cup"?'

'Well, he'd got out of bed and there he was standing, looking up. "I'll take the cup," he said.'

'Oh!' gasped Homily, her eyes staring, 'and you give it him?'

'He took it,' said Pod, 'ever so gentle. And then, when I was down, he give it me.' Homily put her face in her hands. 'Now don't take on,' said Pod uneasily.

'He might have caught you,' shuddered Homily in a stifled voice.

'Yes,' said Pod, 'but he just give me the cup. "Here you are," he said.'

Homily raised her face. 'What are we going to do?' she asked.

Pod sighed. 'Well, there isn't nothing we can do. Except——'

'Oh, no,' exclaimed Homily, 'not that. Not emigrate. Not that, Pod, now I've got the house so nice and a clock and all.'

'We could take the clock,' said Pod.

'And Arrietty? What about her? She's not like those cousins. She can *read*, Pod, and sew a treat——'

'He don't know where we live,' said Pod.

'But they look,' exclaimed Homily. 'Remember Hendreary! They got the cat and——'

'Now, now,' said Pod, 'don't bring up the past.'

'But you've got to think of it! They got the cat and——'

'Yes,' said Pod, 'but Eggletina was different.'

'How different? She was Arrietty's age.'

'Well, they hadn't told her, you see. That's where they went wrong. They tried to make her believe that there wasn't nothing but was under the floor. They never told her about Mrs. Driver or Crampfurl. Least of all about cats.'

'There wasn't any cat,' Homily pointed out, 'not till Hendreary was "seen."'

'Well, there was, then,' said Pod. 'You got to tell them, that's what I say, or they try to find out for themselves.'

'Pod,' said Homily solemnly, 'we haven't told Arrietty.'

'Oh, she knows,' said Pod; he moved uncomfortably. 'She's got her grating.'

'She doesn't know about Eggletina. She doesn't know about being "seen."'

'Well,' said Pod, 'we'll tell her. We always said we would. There's no hurry.'

Homily stood up. 'Pod,' she said, 'we're going to tell her now.'

CHAPTER FIVE

ARRIETTY had not been asleep. She had been lying under her knitted coverlet staring up at the ceiling. It was an interesting ceiling. Pod had built Arrietty's bedroom out of two cigar-boxes, and on the ceiling lovely painted ladies dressed in swirls of chiffon blew long trumpets against a background of blue sky; below there were feathery palm-trees and small white houses set about a square. It was a glamorous scene, above all by candle-light, but to-night Arrietty had stared without seeing. The wood of a cigar-box is thin and Arrietty, lying straight and still under the quilt, had heard the rise and fall of worried voices. She had heard her own name; she had heard Homily exclaim: 'Nuts and berries, that's what they eat!' and she had heard, after a while, the heart-felt cry of 'What shall we do?'

So when Homily appeared beside her bed, she wrapped herself obediently in her quilt and, padding in her bare feet along the dusty passage, she joined her parents in the warmth of the kitchen. Crouched on her little stool she sat clasping her knees, shivering a little, and looking from one face to another.

Homily came beside her and, kneeling on the floor, she placed an arm round Arrietty's skinny shoulders. 'Arrietty,' she said gravely, 'you know about upstairs?'

'What about it?' asked Arrietty.

'You know there are two giants?'

'Yes,' said Arrietty, 'Great Aunt Sophy and Mrs. Driver.'

'That's right,' said Homily, 'and Crampfurl in the garden.' She laid a roughened hand on Arrietty's clasped ones. 'You know about Uncle Hendreary?'

Arrietty thought awhile. 'He went abroad?' she said.

'Emigrated,' corrected Homily, 'to the other side of the world. With Aunt Lupy and all the children. To a badger's set—a hole in a bank under a hawthorn hedge Now why do you think he did this?'

'Oh,' said Arrietty, her face alight, 'to be out of doors ... to lie in the sun ... to run in the grass ... to swing on twigs like the birds do ... to suck honey ...'

'Nonsense, Arrietty,' exclaimed Homily sharply, 'that's a nasty habit! And your Uncle Hendreary's a rheumatic sort of man. He emigrated,' she went on, stressing the word, 'because he was "seen."'

'Oh,' said Arrietty.

'He was "seen" on the 23rd of April 1892, by Rosa Pickhatchet, on the drawing-room mantelpiece. Of all places ...' she added suddenly in a wondering aside.

'Oh,' said Arrietty.

'I have never heard nor no one has never seen fit to tell why he went on the drawing-room mantelpiece in the first place. There's nothing on it, your father assures me, which cannot be seen from the floor or by standing sideways on the handle of the bureau and steadying yourself on the key. That's what your father does if he ever goes into the drawing-room——'

'They said it was a liver pill,' put in Pod.

'How do you mean?' asked Homily, startled.

'A liver pill for Lupy.' Pod spoke wearily. 'Someone started a rumour,' he went on, 'that there were liver pills on the drawing-room mantelpiece. . . .'

'Oh,' said Homily and looked thoughtful, 'I never heard that. All the same,' she exclaimed, 'it was stupid and foolhardy. There's no way down except by the bell-pull. She dusted him, they say, with a feather duster, and he stood so still, alongside a cupid, that she might never have noticed him if he hadn't sneezed. She was new, you see, and didn't know the ornaments. We heard her screeching right here under the kitchen. And they could never get her to clean anything much after that that wasn't chairs or tables—least of all the tiger-skin rug.'

'I don't hardly never bother with the drawing-room,' said Pod. 'Everything's got its place like and they see what goes. There might be a little something left on a table or down the side of a chair, but not without there's been company, and there never is no company—not for the last ten or twelve year. Sitting here in this chair, I

can tell you by heart every blessed thing that's in that drawing-room, working round from the cabinet by the window to the——'

'There's a mint of things in that cabinet,' interrupted Homily, 'solid silver some of them. A solid silver violin, they got there, strings and all — just right for our Arrietty.'

'What's the good,' asked Pod, 'of things behind glass?'

'Couldn't you break it?' suggested Arrietty. 'Just a corner, just a little tap, just a . . .' Her voice faltered as she saw the shocked amazement on her father's face.

'Listen here, Arrietty,' began Homily angrily, and then she controlled herself and patted Arrietty's clasped hands. 'She don't know much about borrowing,' she explained to Pod. 'You can't blame her.' She turned again to Arrietty. 'Borrowing's a skilled job, an art like. Of all the families who've been in this house, there's only us left, and do you know for why? Because your father, Arrietty, is the best borrower that's been known in these parts since—well, before your grandad's time. Even your Aunt Lupy admitted that much. When he was younger I've seen your father walk the length of a laid dinner-table, after the gong was rung, taking a nut or sweet from every dish, and down by a fold in the table-cloth as the first people came in at the door. He'd do it just for fun, wouldn't you, Pod?'

Pod smiled wanly. 'There weren't no sense in it,' he said.

'Maybe,' said Homily, 'but you did it! Who else would dare?'

'I were younger then,' said Pod. He sighed and turned to Arrietty. 'You don't break things, lass. That's not the way to do it. That's not borrowing. . . .'

'We were rich then,' said Homily. 'Oh, we did have some lovely things! You were only a tot, Arrietty, and wouldn't remember. We had a whole suite of walnut furniture out of the doll's house and a set of wineglasses in green glass, and a musical snuff-box, and the cousins would come and we'd have parties. Do you remember, Pod? Not only the cousins. The Harpsichords came. Everybody came — except those Overmantels from the morning-room. And we'd dance and dance and the young people would sit out by the grating. Three tunes that snuff-box played—*Clementine, God Save the Queen,* and the *Post-Chaise Gallop*. We were the envy of everybody—even the Overmantels. . . .'

'Who were the Overmantels?'asked Arrietty.

'Oh, you must 've heard me talk of the Overman-tels,' exclaimed Homily, 'that stuck-up lot who lived in the wall high up—among the lath and plaster behind the man-telpiece in the morning-room. And a queer lot they were. The 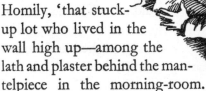 men smoked all the time because the tobacco jars were kept there; and they'd climb about and in and out the carvings of the overmantel, sliding down pillars and showing off. The women were a conceited lot too, always admiring themselves in all those bits of overmantel looking-glass. They never asked any one up there and I, for one, never wanted to go. I've no head for heights, and your father never liked the men. He's always lived steady, your father has, and not only the tobacco jars, but the whisky decanters too, were kept in the morning-room and they say those Overmantel men would suck up the dregs in the glasses through those quill pipe-cleaners they keep there on the mantelpiece. I don't know whether it's true but they do say that those Overmantel men used to have a party every Tuesday after the bailiff had been to talk business in the morning-room. Laid out, they'd be, dead drunk—or so the story goes—on the green plush table-cloth, all among the tin boxes and the account books——'

'Now, Homily,' protested Pod, who did not like gossip, 'I never see'd 'em.'

'But you wouldn't put it past them, Pod. You said yourself when I married you not to call on the Overmantels.'

'They lived so high,' said Pod, 'that's all.'

'Well, they were a lazy lot—that much you can't deny. They never had no kind of home life. Kept themselves warm in winter by the heat of the morning-room fire and ate nothing but breakfast food; breakfast, of course, was the only meal served in the morning-room.'

'What happened to them?' asked Arrietty.

'Well, when the Master died and She took to her bed, there was no more use for the morning-room. So the Overmantels had to go. What else could they do? No food, no fire. It's a bitter cold room in winter.'

'And the Harpsichords?' asked Arrietty.

Homily looked thoughtful. 'Well, they were different. I'm not saying they weren't stuck up too, because they were. Your Aunt Lupy, who married your Uncle Hendreary, was a Harpsichord by marriage and we all know the airs she gave herself.'

'Now, Homily——' began Pod.

'Well, she'd no right to.   She was only a Rain-Pipe from the stables before she married Harpsichord.'

'Didn't she marry Uncle Hendreary?' asked Arrietty.

'Yes, later.   She was a widow with two children and he was a widower with three.   It's no good looking at me like that, Pod.   You can't deny she took it out of poor Hendreary: she thought it was a come-down to marry a Clock.'

'Why?' asked Arrietty.

'Because we Clocks live under the kitchen, that's why. Because we don't talk fancy grammar and eat anchovy toast. But to live under the kitchen doesn't say we aren't educated. The Clocks are just as old a family as the Harpsichords. You remember that, Arrietty, and don't let any one tell you different.   Your grandfather could count and write down the numbers up to—what was it, Pod?'

'Fifty-seven,' said Pod.

'There,' said Homily, 'fifty-seven!   And your father can count, as you know, Arrietty; he can count and write down the numbers, on and on, as far as it goes.   How far does it go, Pod?'

'Close on a thousand,' said Pod.

'There!' exclaimed Homily, 'and he knows the alphabet because he taught you, Arrietty, didn't he?   And he would have been able to read—wouldn't you, Pod?—if he hadn't had to start borrowing so young.   Your Uncle Hendreary and your father had to go out borrowing at thirteen—your age, Arrietty, think of it!'

'But I should like——' began Arrietty.

'So he didn't have your advantages,' went on Homily

breathlessly, 'and just because the Harpsichords lived in the drawing-room—they moved in there, in 1837, to a hole in the wainscot just behind where the harpsichord used to stand, if ever there was one, which I doubt—and were really a family called Linen-Press or some such name and changed it to Harpsichord——'

'What did they live on,' asked Arrietty, 'in the drawing-room?'

'Afternoon tea,' said Homily, 'nothing but afternoon tea. No wonder the children grew up peaky.   Of course, in the old days it was better—muffins and crumpets and such, and good rich cake and jams and jellies.   And there was one old Harpsichord who could remember sillabub of an evening. But they had to do their borrowing in such a rush, poor things.   On wet days, when the human beings sat all afternoon in the drawing-room, the tea would be brought in and taken away again without a chance of the Harpsichords getting near it—and on fine days it might be taken out into the garden.   Lupy has told me that, sometimes, there were days and days when they lived on crumbs and on water out of the flower-vases.   So you can't be too hard on them; their only comfort, poor things, was to show off a bit and wear evening dress and talk like ladies and gentlemen. Did you ever hear your Aunt Lupy talk?'

'Yes.   No.   I can't remember.'

'Oh, you should have heard her say "Parquet"—that's the stuff the drawing-room floor's made of—"Parkay . . . Parr-r-kay," she'd say.   Oh, it was lovely.   Come to think of it, your Aunt Lupy was the most stuck up of them all. . . .'

Arrietty's shivering,' said Pod. 'We didn't get the little maid up to talk about Aunt Lupy.'

'Nor we did,' cried Homily, suddenly contrite, 'you should've stopped me, Pod. There, my lamb, tuck this quilt right round you and I'll get you a nice drop of piping hot soup!'

'And yet,' said Pod as Homily, fussing at the stove, ladled soup into the tea-cup, 'we did in a way.'

'Did what?' asked Homily.

'Get her here to talk about Aunt Lupy. Aunt Lupy, Uncle Hendreary, and'—he paused—'Eggletina.'

'Let her drink up her soup first,' said Homily.

'There's no call for her to stop drinking,' said Pod.

CHAPTER SIX

'YOUR mother and I got you up,' said Pod, 'to tell you about upstairs.'

Arrietty, holding the great cup in both hands, looked at him over the edge.

Pod coughed. 'You said a while back that the sky was dark brown with cracks in it. Well, it isn't.' He looked at her almost accusingly. 'It's blue.'

'I know,' said Arrietty.

'You know!' exclaimed Pod.

'Yes, of course I know. I've got the grating.'

'Can you see the sky through the grating?'

'Go on,' interrupted Homily, 'tell her about the gates.'

'Well,' said Pod ponderously, 'if you go outside this room, what do you see?'

'A dark passage,' said Arrietty.

'And what else?'

'Other rooms.'

'And if you go farther?'

'More passages.'

'And, if you go walking on and on, in all the passages under the floor, however they twist and turn, what do you find?'

'Gates,' said Arrietty.

'Strong gates,' said Pod, 'gates you can't open. What are they there for?'

'Against the mice?' said Arrietty.

'Yes,' agreed Pod uncertainly, as though he gave her half a mark, 'but mice never hurt no one.   What else?'

'Rats?' suggested Arrietty.

'We don't have rats,' said Pod.   'What about cats?'

'Cats?' echoed Arrietty, surprised.

'Or to keep you in?' suggested Pod.

'To keep me in?' repeated Arrietty, dismayed.

'Upstairs is a dangerous place,' said Pod. 'And you, Arrietty, you're all we've got, see? It isn't like Hendreary—he still has two of his own and three of hers. Once,' said Pod, 'Hendreary had three—three of his own.'

'Your father's thinking of Eggletina,' said Homily.

'Yes,' said Pod, 'Eggletina.   They never told her about upstairs.   And they hadn't got no grating.   They told her the sky was nailed up, like, with cracks in it——'

'A foolish way to bring up a child,' murmured Homily. She sniffed slightly and touched Arrietty's hair.

'But Eggletina was no fool,' said Pod; 'she didn't believe them.   So one day,' he went on, 'she went upstairs to see for herself.'

'How did she get out?' asked Arrietty, interested.

'Well, we didn't have so many gates then.   Just the one under the clock.   Hendreary must have left it unlocked or something.   Anyway, Eggletina went out . . .'

'In a blue dress,' said Homily, 'and a pair of button-boots your father made her, yellow kid with jet beads for buttons. Lovely they were.'

'Well,' said Pod, 'any other time it might have been all

right.   She'd have gone out, had a look around, had a bit of
a fright, maybe, and come back—none the worse and no one
the wiser . . . '

'But things had been happening,' said Homily.

'Yes,' said Pod, 'she didn't know, as they never told her,
that her father had been "seen" and that upstairs they had
got in the cat and——'

'They waited a week,' said Homily, 'and they waited a
month and they hoped for a year but no one ever saw Eggletina no more.'

'And that,' said Pod after a pause and eyeing Arrietty,
'is what happened to Eggletina.'

There was silence except for Pod's breathing and the faint bubble of the soup.

'It just broke up your Uncle Hendreary,' said Homily at last. 'He never went upstairs again—in case, he said, he found the button-boots. Their only future was to emigrate.'

Arrietty was silent a moment, then she raised her head. 'Why did you tell me?' she asked. 'Now? To-night?'

Homily got up. She moved restlessly towards the stove. 'We don't never talk of it,' she said, 'at least, not much, but, to-night, we felt——' She turned suddenly. 'Well, we'll just say it straight out: your father's been "seen," Arrietty!'

'Oh,' said Arrietty, 'who by?'

'Well, by a—something you've never heard of. But that's not the point: the point is——'

'You think they'll get a cat?'

'They may,' said Homily.

Arrietty set down the soup for a moment; she stared into the cup as it stood beside her almost knee high on the floor; there was a dreamy, secret something about her lowered face. 'Couldn't we emigrate?' she ventured at last, very softly.

Homily gasped and clasped her hands and swung away towards the wall. 'You don't know what you're talking about,' she cried, addressing a frying-pan which hung there. 'Worms and weazels and cold and damp and——'

'But supposing,' said Arrietty, 'that *I* went out, like Eggletina did, and the cat ate *me*. Then you and papa would emigrate. Wouldn't you?' she asked, and her voice faltered. 'Wouldn't you?'

Homily swung round again, this time towards Arrietty; her face looked very angry. 'I shall smack you, Arrietty Clock, if you don't behave yourself this minute!'

Arrietty's eyes filled with tears. 'I was only thinking,' she said, 'that I'd like to be there—to emigrate too. Uneaten,' she added softly and the tears fell.

'Now,' said Pod, 'this is enough! You get off to bed, Arrietty, uneaten and unbeaten both—and we'll talk about it in the morning.'

'It's not that I'm afraid,' cried Arrietty angrily; 'I like cats. I bet the cat didn't eat Eggletina. I bet she just ran away because she hated being cooped up . . . day after day . . . week after week . . . year after year. . . . Like I do!' she added on a sob.

'Cooped up!' repeated Homily, astounded.

Arrietty put her face into her hands. 'Gates . . .' she gasped, 'gates, gates, gates. . . .'

Pod and Homily stared at each other across Arrietty's bowed shoulders. 'You didn't ought to have brought it up,' he said unhappily, 'not so late at night . . .'

Arrietty raised her tear-streaked face. 'Late or early, what's the difference?' she cried. 'Oh, I know papa is a wonderful borrower. I know we've managed to stay when all the others have gone. But what has it done for us, in the end? I don't think it's so clever to live on alone, for ever and ever, in a great, big, half-empty house; under the floor, with no one to talk to, no one to play with, nothing to see but dust and passages, no light but candlelight and firelight and what comes through the cracks. Eggletina had brothers and Eggletina had half-brothers; Eggletina had a tame mouse;

Eggletina had yellow boots with jet buttons, and Eggletina did get out—just once!'

'Shush,' said Pod gently, 'not so loud.' Above their heads the floor creaked and heavy footfalls heaved deliberately to and fro. They heard Mrs. Driver's grumbling voice and the clatter of the fire-irons. 'Drat this stove,' they heard her say, 'wind's in the east again.' Then they heard her raise her voice and call, 'Crampfurl!'

Pod sat staring glumly at the floor; Arrietty shivered a little and hugged herself more tightly into the knitted quilt and Homily drew a long, slow breath. Suddenly she raised her head.

'The child is right,' she announced firmly.

Arrietty's eyes grew big. 'Oh, no——' she began. It shocked her to be right. Parents were right, not children. Children could say anything, Arrietty knew, and enjoy saying it—knowing always they were safe and wrong.

'You see, Pod,' went on Homily, 'it was different for you and me. There was other families, other children . . . the Sinks in the scullery, you remember? And those people who lived behind the knife machine—I forget their names now. And the Broom-Cupboard boys. And there was that underground passage from the stables—you know, that the Rain-Pipes used. We had more, as you might say, freedom.'

'Ah, yes,' said Pod, 'in a way. But where does freedom take you?' He looked up uncertainly. 'Where are they all now?'

'Some of them may have bettered themselves, I shouldn't wonder,' said Homily sharply. 'Times have changed in the whole house. Pickings aren't what they were. There were those that went, you remember, when they dug a trench for the gas-pipe. Over the fields, and through the wood, and all. A kind of tunnel it gave them, all the way to Leighton Buzzard.'

'And what did they find there?' said Pod unkindly. 'A mountain of coke!'

Homily turned away. 'Arrietty,' she said, in the same firm voice, 'supposing one day—we'd pick a special day when there was no one about, and providing they don't get a cat which I have my reasons for thinking they won't—supposing, one day, your father took you out borrowing, you'd be a good girl, wouldn't you? You'd do just what he said, quickly and quietly and no arguing?'

Arrietty turned quite pink; she clasped her hands together. 'Oh——' she began in an ecstatic voice, but Pod cut in quickly:

'Now, Homily, we got to think. You can't just say things like that without thinking it out proper. I been "seen" remember. This is no kind of time for taking a child upstairs.'

'There won't be no cat,' said Homily; 'there wasn't no screeching. It's not like that time with Rosa Pickhatchet.'

'All the same,' said Pod uncertainly, 'the risk's there. I never heard of no *girl* going borrowing before.'

'The way I look at it,' said Homily, 'and it's only now it's come to me: if you had a son, you'd take him borrowing, now wouldn't you? Well, you haven't got no son—only Arrietty. Suppose anything happened to you or me, where would Arrietty be—if she hadn't learned to borrow?'

Pod stared down at his knees. 'Yes,' he said after a moment, 'I see what you mean.'

'And it'll give her a bit of interest like and stop her hankering.'

'Hankering for what?'

'For blue sky and grass and suchlike.'   Arrietty caught her breath and Homily turned on her swiftly: 'It's no good, Arrietty, I'm not going to emigrate—not for you nor any one else!'

'Ah,' said Pod and began to laugh, 'so that's it!'

'Shush!' said Homily, annoyed, and glanced quickly at the ceiling. 'Not so loud! Now kiss your father, Arrietty,' she went on briskly, 'and pop off back to bed.'

As Arrietty snuggled down under the bed-clothes she felt, creeping up from her toes, a glow of happiness like a glow of warmth. She heard their voices rising and falling in the next room: Homily's went on and on, measured and confident—there was, Arrietty felt, a kind of conviction behind it; it was the winning voice.   Once she heard Pod get up and the scrape of a chair.   'I don't like it!' she heard him say.   And she heard Homily whisper 'Hush!' and there were tremulous footfalls on the floor above and the sudden clash of pans.

Arrietty, half dozing, gazed up at her painted ceiling. 'FLOR DE HAVANA,' proclaimed the banners proudly. 'Garantizados . . . Superiores . . . Non Plus Ultra . . . Esquisitos . . .' and the lovely gauzy ladies blew their trumpets, silently, triumphantly, on soundless notes of glee. . . .

CHAPTER SEVEN

FOR the next three weeks Arrietty was especially 'good': she helped her mother tidy the store-rooms; she swept and watered the passages and trod them down: she sorted and graded the beads (which they used as buttons) into the screw tops of aspirin bottles; she cut old kid gloves into squares for Pod's shoemaking; she filed fish-bone needles to a bee-sting sharpness; she hung up the washing to dry by the grating so that it blew in the soft air; and at last the day came—that dreadful, wonderful, never-to-be-forgotten day —when Homily, scrubbing the kitchen table, straightened her back and called 'Pod!'

He came in from his workroom, last in hand.

'Look at this brush!' cried Homily. It was a fibre brush with a plaited, fibre back.

'Aye,' said Pod, 'worn down.'

'Gets me knuckles now,' said Homily, 'every time I scrub.'

Pod looked worried. Since he had been 'seen,' they had stuck to kitchen borrowing, the bare essentials of fuel and food. There was an old mouse-hole under the kitchen stove upstairs which, at night when the fire was out or very low, Pod could use as a chute to save carrying. Since the window-curtain incident they had pushed a match-box chest of drawers below the mouse-hole, and had stood a wooden stool on the chest of drawers; and Pod, with much help and shoving from Homily, had learned to squeeze up the chute instead of down. In this way he need not venture into the great hall and passages; he could just nip out, from under the vast black stove in the kitchen, for a clove or a carrot or a tasty piece of ham. But it was not a satisfactory arrangement: even when the fire was out, often there was hot ash and cinders under the stove and once, as he emerged, a great brush came at him wielded by Mrs. Driver; and he slithered back, on top of Homily, singed, shaken, and coughing dust. Another time, for some reason, the fire had been in full blaze and Pod had arrived suddenly beneath a glowing inferno, dropping white-hot coals. But usually, at night, the fire was out, and Pod could pick his way through the cinders into the kitchen proper.

'Mrs. Driver's out,' Homily went on. 'It's her day off. And She'—they always spoke of Aunt Sophy as 'She'— 'is safe enough in bed.'

'It's not them that worries me,' said Pod.

'Why,' exclaimed Homily sharply, 'the boy's not still here?'

'I don't know,' said Pod; 'there's always a risk,' he added.

'And there always will be,' retorted Homily, 'like when you was in the coal-cellar and the coal-cart came.'

'But the other two,' said Pod, 'Mrs. Driver and Her, I always know where they are, like.'

'As for that,' exclaimed Homily, 'a boy's even better. You can hear a boy a mile off. Well,' she went on after a moment, 'please yourself. But it's not like you to talk of risks. . . .'

Pod sighed. 'All right,' he said and turned away to fetch his borrowing-bag.

'Take the child,' called Homily after him.

Pod turned. 'Now, Homily,' he began in an alarmed voice.

'Why not?' asked Homily sharply, 'it's just the day. You aren't going no farther than the front door. If you're nervous you can leave her by the clock, ready to nip underneath and down the hole. Let her just *see* at any rate. Arrietty!'

As Arrietty came running in Pod tried again. 'Now listen, Homily——' he protested.

Homily ignored him. 'Arrietty,' she said brightly, 'would you like to go along with your father and borrow me some brush fibre from the door-mat in the hall?'

Arrietty gave a little skip. 'Oh,' she cried, 'could I?'

'Well, take your apron off,' said Homily, 'and change your boots. You want light shoes for borrowing—better wear the red kid.' And then as Arrietty spun away Homily turned to Pod: 'She'll be all right,' she said; 'you'll see.'

As she followed her father down the passage Arrietty's heart began to beat faster. Now the moment had come at last she found it almost too much to bear. She felt light and trembly, and hollow with excitement.

They had three borrowing-bags between the two of them ('In case,' Pod had explained, 'we pick up something. A bad borrower loses many a chance for lack of an extra bag'), and Pod laid these down to open the first gate, which was latched by a safety-pin. It was a big pin, too strongly sprung for little hands to open, and Arrietty watched her

father swing his whole weight on the bar and his feet kick
loose off the ground.   Hanging from his hands, he shifted
his weight along the pin towards the curved sheath and, as
he moved, the pin sprang open and he, in the same instant,
jumped free.   'You couldn't do that,' he remarked, dusting
his hands; 'too light.   Nor could your mother.   Come
along now.   Quietly. . . .'

There were other gates; all of which Pod left open
('Never shut a gate on the way out,' he explained in a
whisper, 'you might need to get back quick') and, after a
while, Arrietty saw a faint light at the end of the passage.
She pulled her father's sleeve.   'Is that it?' she whispered.

Pod stood still.   'Quietly, now,' he warned her.   'Yes,
that's it: the hole under the clock!'   As he said these
words, Arrietty felt breathless but, outwardly, she made no
sign.   'There are three steps up to it,' Pod went on, 'steep
like, so mind how you go.   When you're under the clock
you just stay there; don't let your mind wander and keep
your eyes on me: if all's clear, I'll give you the sign.'

The steps were high and a little uneven but Arrietty took
them more lightly than Pod.   As she scrambled past the
jagged edges of the hole she had a sudden blinding glimpse
of molten gold: it was spring sunshine on the pale stones of
the hall floor.   Standing upright, she could no longer see
this; she could only see the cave-like shadows in the great
case above her and the dim outline of the hanging weights.
The hollow darkness around her vibrated with sound; it
was a safe sound—solid and regular; and, far above her
head, she saw the movement of the pendulum; it gleamed a
little in the half light, remote and cautious in its rhythmic

swing. Arrietty felt warm tears behind her eyelids and a
sudden swelling pride: so this, at last, was The Clock!
Their clock . . . after which her family was named! For
two hundred years it had stood here, deep-
voiced and patient, guarding their threshold,
and measuring their time.

But Pod, she saw, stood crouched
beneath the carved archway against
the light: 'Keep your eyes on
me,' he had said, so Arrietty
crouched too. She saw the
gleaming golden stone floor
of the hall stretching away
into distance; she saw
the edges of rugs, like
richly coloured islands
in a molten sea, and she
saw, in a glory of sun-
light—like a dreamed-of
gateway to fairyland—
the open front door.
Beyond she saw grass
and, against the clear,
bright sky, a waving
frond of green.

Pod's eyes slewed round.
'Wait,' he breathed, 'and
watch.' And then in a flash he
was gone.

Arrietty saw him scurry across the

sunlit floor. Swiftly he ran—as a mouse runs or a blown dry leaf—and suddenly she saw him as 'small.' 'But,' she told herself, 'he isn't small. He's half a head taller than mother. . . .' She watched him run round a chestnut-coloured island of door-mat into the shadows beside the door. There, it seemed, he became invisible.

Arrietty watched and waited. All was still except for a sudden whirr within the clock. A grinding whirr it was, up high in the hollow darkness above her head, then the sliding grate of slipped metal before the clock sang out its chime. Three notes were struck, deliberate and mellow: 'Take it or leave it,' they seemed to say, 'but that's the time——'

A sudden movement near the shadowed lintel of the front door and there was Pod again, bag in hand, beside the mat; it rose knee deep before him like a field of chestnut corn. Arrietty saw him glance towards the clock and then she saw him raise his hand.

Oh, the warmth of the stone flags as she ran across them . . . the glad-dening sunlight on her face and hands . . . the awful space above and around her! Pod caught her and held her at last, and patted her shoulder. 'There, there . . .' he said, 'get your breath—good girl!'

Panting a little, Arrietty gazed about her. She saw great chair legs rearing up into sunlight; she saw the shadowed under-sides of their seats spread

above her like canopies; she saw the nails and the strapping and odd tags of silk and string; she saw the terraced cliffs of the stairs, mounting up into the distance, up and up . . . she saw carved table legs and a cavern under the chest. And all the time, in the stillness, the clock spoke—measuring out the seconds, spreading its layers of calm.

And then, turning, Arrietty looked at the garden. She saw a gravelled path, full of coloured stones—the size of walnuts they were with, here and there, a blade of grass between them, transparent green against the light of the sun. Beyond the path she saw a grassy bank rising steeply to a tangled hedge; and beyond the hedge she saw fruit trees, bright with blossom.

'Here's a bag,' said Pod in a hoarse whisper; 'better get down to work.'

Obediently Arrietty started pulling fibre; stiff it was and full of dust. Pod worked swiftly and methodically, making small bundles, each of which he put immediately in the bag. 'If you have to run suddenly,' he explained, 'you don't want to leave nothing behind.'

'It hurts your hands,' said Arrietty, 'doesn't it?' and suddenly she sneezed.

'Not my hands it doesn't,' said Pod; 'they're hardened like,' and Arrietty sneezed again.

'Dusty, isn't it?' she said.

Pod straightened his back. 'No good pulling where it's knotted right in,' he said, watching her. 'No wonder it hurts your hands. See here,' he exclaimed after a moment, 'you leave it! It's your first time up like. You sit on the step there and take a peek out of doors.'

'Oh, no——' Arrietty began ('If I don't help,' she thought, 'he won't want me again'), but Pod insisted.

'I'm better on me own,' he said.   'I can choose me bits, if you see what I mean, seeing as it's me who's got to make the brush.'

CHAPTER EIGHT

THE step was warm but very steep. 'If I got down on to the path,' Arrietty thought, 'I might not get up again,' so for some moments she sat quietly. After a while she noticed the shoe-scraper.

'Arrietty,' called Pod softly, 'where have you got to?'

'I just climbed down the shoe-scraper,' she called back.

He came along and looked down at her from the top of the step. 'That's all right,' he said after a moment's stare, 'but never climb down anything that isn't fixed like. Supposing one of them came along and moved the shoe-scraper—where would you be then? How would you get up again?'

'It's heavy to move,' said Arrietty.

'Maybe,' said Pod,' but it's movable. See what I mean? There's rules, my lass, and you got to learn.'

'This path,' Arrietty said, 'goes round the house. And the bank does too.'

'Well,' said Pod, 'what of it?'

Arrietty rubbed one red kid shoe on a rounded stone. 'It's my grating,' she explained. 'I was thinking

64

that my grating must be just round the corner. My grating looks out on to this bank.'

'Your grating!' exclaimed Pod. 'Since when has it been your grating?'

'I was thinking,' Arrietty went on. 'Suppose I just went round the corner and called through the grating to mother?'

'No,' said Pod, 'we're not going to have none of that. Not going round corners.'

'Then,' went on Arrietty, 'she'd see I was all right like.'

'Well,' said Pod, and then he half smiled, 'go quickly then and call. I'll watch for you here. Not loud mind!'

Arrietty ran. The stones in the path were firmly bedded and her light, soft shoes hardly seemed to touch them. How glorious it was to run—you could never run under the floor: you walked, you stooped, you crawled—but you never ran. Arrietty nearly ran past the grating. She saw it just in time after she turned the corner. Yes, there it was quite close to the ground, embedded deeply in the old wall of the house; there was moss below it in a spreading, greenish stain.

Arrietty ran up to it. 'Mother!' she called, her nose against the iron grille. 'Mother!' She waited quietly and, after a moment, she called again.

At the third call Homily came. Her hair was coming down and she carried, as though it were heavy, the screw lid of a pickle jar, filled with soapy water. 'Oh,' she said in an annoyed voice, 'you didn't half give me a turn! What do you think you're up to? Where's your father?'

Arrietty jerked her head sideways. 'Just there—by the front door!' She was so full of happiness that, out of Homily's sight, her toes danced on the green moss. Here she was on the other side of the grating—here she was at last, on the outside—looking in!

'Yes,' said Homily, 'they open that door like that—the first day of spring. Well,' she went on briskly, 'you run back to your father. And tell him, if the morning-room door happens to be open that I wouldn't say no to a bit of red blotting-paper. Mind out of my way now—while I throw the water!'

'That's what grows the moss,' thought Arrietty as she sped back to her father, 'all the water we empty through the grating. . . .'

Pod looked relieved when he saw her but frowned at the message. 'How's she expect me to climb that desk without me pin? Blotting-paper's a curtain-and-chair job and she should know it. Come on now! Up with you!'

'Let me stay down,' pleaded Arrietty, 'just a bit longer. Just till you finish. They're all out. Except Her. Mother said so.'

'She'd say anything,' grumbled Pod, 'when she wants something quick. How does she know She won't take it into her head to get out of that bed of Hers and come downstairs with a stick? How does she know Mrs. Driver ain't stayed at home to-day—with a headache? How does she know that boy ain't still here?'

'What boy?' asked Arrietty.

Pod looked embarrassed. 'What boy?' he repeated vaguely and then went on: 'Or may be Crampfurl——'

'Crampfurl isn't a boy,' said Arrietty.

' No he isn't,' said Pod, 'not in a manner of speaking No,' he went on as though thinking this out, 'no, you wouldn't call Crampfurl a boy. Not, as you might say, a boy—exactly. Well,' he said, beginning to move away, 'stay down a bit if you like. But stay close!'

Arrietty watched him move away from the step and then she looked about her. Oh, glory! Oh, joy! Oh, freedom! The sunlight, the grasses, the soft, moving air and half-way up the bank, where it curved round the corner, a flowering cherry-tree! Below it on the path lay a stain of pinkish petals and, at the tree's foot, pale as butter, a nest of primroses.

Arrietty threw a cautious glance towards the front doorstep and then, light and dancey, in her soft red shoes, she ran towards the petals. They were curved like shells and rocked as she touched them. She gathered several up and laid them one inside the other . . . up and up . . . like a card castle. And then she spilled them. Pod came again to the top of the step and looked along the path. 'Don't you go far,' he said after a moment. Seeing his lips move, she smiled back at him: she was too far already to hear the words.

A greenish beetle, shining in the sunlight, came towards her across the stones. She laid her fingers lightly on its shell and it stood still, waiting and watchful, and when she moved her hand the beetle went swiftly on. An ant came hurrying in a busy zigzag. She danced in front of it to tease it and put out her foot. It stared at her, nonplussed, waving its antennae; then pettishly, as though put out, it swerved away.   Two birds came down, quarrelling shrilly, into the grass below the tree.   One flew away but Arrietty could see the other among the moving grass stems above her on the slope.   Cautiously she moved towards the bank and climbed a little nervously in amongst the green blades.   As she parted them gently with her bare hands, drops of water plopped on her skirt and she felt the red shoes become damp. But on she went, pulling herself up now and again by rooty stems into this jungle of moss and wood-violet and creeping leaves of clover.   The sharp-seeming grass blades, waist high, were tender to the touch and sprang back lightly behind her as she passed.   When at last she reached the foot of the tree, the bird took fright and flew away and she sat down suddenly on a gnarled leaf of primrose.   The air was filled with scent.   'But nothing will play with you,' she thought and saw the cracks and furrows of the primrose leaves held crystal beads of dew.   If she pressed the leaf these rolled like marbles.   The bank was warm, almost too warm here within the shelter of the tall grass, and the sandy earth smelled dry.   Standing up, she picked a primrose. The pink stalk felt tender and living in her hands and was covered with silvery hairs, and when she held the flower, like a parasol, between her eyes and the sky, she saw the sun's pale light through the veined petals.   On a piece of bark she found a wood-louse and she struck it lightly with her swaying flower.   It curled immediately and became a ball, bumping softly away downhill in amongst the grass roots.   But she knew about wood-lice.   There were plenty of them at home under the floor.   Homily always scolded her if she played with them because, she said, they smelled

of old knives.   She lay back among the stalks of the primroses and they made a coolness between her and the sun, and
then, sighing, she turned her head and looked sideways up
the bank among the grass stems.   Startled, she caught her
breath.   Something had moved above her on the bank.
Something had glittered.   Arrietty stared.

CHAPTER NINE

I<small>T</small> <small>WAS</small> an eye. Or it looked like an eye. Clear and bright like the colour of the sky. An eye like her own but enormous. A glaring eye. Breathless with fear, she sat up. And the eye blinked. A great fringe of lashes came curving down and flew up again out of sight. Cautiously, Arrietty moved her legs: she would slide noiselessly in among the grass stems and slither away down the bank.

'Don't move!' said a voice, and the voice, like the eye, was enormous but, somehow, hushed—and hoarse like a surge of wind through the grating on a stormy night in March.

Arrietty froze. 'So this is it,' she thought, 'the worst and most terrible thing of all: I have been "seen"! Whatever happened to Eggletina will now, almost certainly, happen to me!'

There was a pause and Arrietty, her heart pounding in her ears, heard the breath again drawn swiftly into the vast lungs. 'Or,' said the voice, whispering still, 'I shall hit you with my ash stick.'

Suddenly Arrietty became calm. 'Why?' she asked. How strange her own voice sounded! Crystal thin and harebell clear, it tinkled on the air.

'In case,' came the surprised whisper at last, 'you ran towards me, quickly, through the grass . . . in case,' it went on, trembling a little, 'you came and scrabbled at me with your nasty little hands.'

Arrietty stared at the eye; she held herself quite still. 'Why?' she asked again, and again the word tinkled—icy cold it sounded this time, and needle sharp.

'Things do,' said the voice. 'I've seen them. In India.'

Arrietty thought of her Gazetteer of the World. 'You're not in India now,' she pointed out.

'Did you come out of the house?'

'Yes,' said Arrietty.

'From whereabouts in the house?'

Arrietty stared at the eye. 'I'm not going to tell you,' she said at last bravely.

'Then I'll hit you with my ash stick!'

'All right,' said Arrietty, 'hit me!'

'I'll pick you up and break you in half!'

Arrietty stood up. 'All right,' she said and took two paces forward.

There was a sharp gasp and an earthquake in the grass: he spun away from her and sat up, a great mountain in a green jersey. He had fair, straight hair and golden eyelashes. 'Stay where you are!' he cried.

Arrietty stared up at him. So this was 'the boy'! Breathless, she felt, and light with fear. 'I guessed you were about nine,' she gasped after a moment.

He flushed. 'Well, you're wrong, I'm ten.' He looked down at her, breathing deeply. 'How old are you?'

'Fourteen,' said Arrietty. 'Next June,' she added, watching him.

There was silence while Arrietty waited, trembling a little. 'Can you read?' the boy said at last.

'Of course,' said Arrietty. 'Can't you?'

'No,' he stammered. 'I mean—yes. I mean I've just come from India.'

'What's that got to do with it?' asked Arrietty.

'Well, if you're born in India, you're bilingual. And if you're bilingual, you can't read. Not so well.'

Arrietty stared up at him: what a monster, she thought, dark against the sky.

'Do you grow out of it?' she asked.

He moved a little and she felt the cold flick of his shadow.

'Oh yes,' he said, 'it wears off. My sisters were bilingual; now they aren't a bit. They could read any of those books upstairs in the schoolroom.'

'So could I,' said Arrietty quickly, 'if someone could hold them, and turn the pages. I'm not a bit bilingual. I can read anything.'

'Could you read out loud?'

'Of course,' said Arrietty.

'Would you wait here while I run upstairs and get a book now?'

'Well,' said Arrietty; she was longing to show off; then a startled look came into her eyes. 'Oh——' she faltered.

'What's the matter?' The boy was standing up now. He towered above her.

'How many doors are there to this house?' She squinted up at him against the bright sunlight. He dropped on one knee.

'Doors?' he said. 'Outside doors?'

'Yes.'

'Well, there's the front door, the back door, the gun-room door, the kitchen door, the scullery door . . . and the french windows in the drawing-room.'

'Well, you see,' said Arrietty, 'my father's in the hall, by the front door, working. He . . . he wouldn't want to be disturbed.'

'Working?' said the boy. 'What at?'

'Getting material,' said Arrietty, 'for a scrubbing-brush.'

'Then I'll go in the side door'; he began to move away but turned suddenly and came back to her. He stood a moment, as though embarrassed, and then he said: 'Can you fly?'

'No,' said Arrietty, surprised; 'can you?'

His face became even redder. 'Of course not,' he said angrily; 'I'm not a fairy!'

'Well, nor am I,' said Arrietty, 'nor is anybody. I don't believe in them.'

He looked at her strangely. 'You don't believe in them?'

'No,' said Arrietty; 'do you?'

'Of course not!'

Really, she thought, he is a very angry kind of boy. 'My mother believes in them,' she said, trying to appease him. 'She thinks she saw one once. It was when she was a girl and lived with her parents behind the sand pile in the potting-shed.'

He squatted down on his heels and she felt his breath on her face: 'What was it like?' he asked.

'About the size of a glow-worm with wings like a butter-fly. And it had a tiny little face, she said, all alight and moving like sparks and tiny moving hands. Its face was

changing all the time, she said, smiling and short of shim-
mering. It seemed to be talking, she said, very quickly—
but you couldn't hear a word. . . .'

'Oh,' said the boy, interested. After a moment he asked:
'Where did it go?'

'It just went,' said Arrietty. 'When my mother saw it,
it seemed to be caught in a cobweb. It was dark at the
time. About five o'clock on a winter's evening. After
tea.'

'Oh,' he said again and picked up two petals of cherry-
blossom which he folded together like a sandwich and ate
slowly. 'Supposing,' he said, staring past her at the wall of
the house, 'you saw a little man, about as tall as a pencil,
with a blue patch in his trousers, half-way up a window
curtain, carrying a doll's tea-cup—would you say it was a
fairy?'

'No,' said Arrietty, 'I'd say it was my father.'

'Oh,' said the boy, thinking this out, 'does your father
have a blue patch on his trousers?'

'Not on his best trousers. He does on his borrowing
ones.'

'Oh,' said the boy again. He seemed to find it a safe
sound, as lawyers do. 'Are there many people like you?'

'No,' said Arrietty. 'None. We're all different.'

'I mean as small as you?'

Arrietty laughed. 'Oh, don't be silly!' she said. 'Surely
you don't think there are many people in the world your
size?'

'There are more my size than yours,' he retorted.

'Honestly——' began Arrietty helplessly and laughed

again. 'Do you really think—I mean, whatever sort of a world would it be? Those great chairs . . . I've seen them. Fancy if you had to make chairs that size for every one? And the stuff for their clothes . . . miles and miles of it . . . tents of it . . . and the sewing! And their great houses, reaching up so you can hardly see the ceilings . . . their great beds . . . the *food* they eat . . . great, smoking mountains of it, huge bogs of stew and soup and stuff.'

'Don't you eat soup?' asked the boy.

'Of course we do,' laughed Arrietty. 'My father had an uncle who had a little boat which he rowed round in the stock-pot picking up flotsam and jetsam. He did bottom-fishing too for bits of marrow until the cook got suspicious through finding bent pins in the soup. Once he was nearly shipwrecked on a chunk of submerged shin-bone. He lost his oars and the boat sprang a leak but he flung a line over the pot handle and pulled himself alongside the rim. But all that stock—fathoms of it! And the size of the stock-pot! I mean, there wouldn't be enough stuff in the world to go round after a bit! That's why my father says it's a good thing they're dying out . . . just a few, my father says, that's all we need—to keep us. Otherwise, he says, the whole thing gets'—Arrietty hesitated, trying to remember the word—'exaggerated, he says——'

'What do you mean,' asked the boy, '"to keep us"?'

CHAPTER TEN

So Arrietty told him about borrowing—how difficult it was and how dangerous. She told him about the store-rooms under the floor; about Pod's early exploits, the skill he had shown and the courage; she described those far-off days, before her birth, when Pod and Homily had been rich; she described the musical snuff-box, of gold filigree, and the little bird which flew out of it made of kingfisher feathers, how it flapped its wings and sang its song; she described the doll's wardrobe and the tiny green glasses; the little silver tea-pot out of the drawing-room case; the satin bedcovers and embroidered sheets . . . 'those we have still,' she told him, 'they're Her handkerchiefs. . . .' 'She,' the boy realized gradually was his Great Aunt Sophy up-stairs, bedridden since a hunting accident some twenty years before; he heard how Pod would borrow from Her room, picking his way—in the firelight—among the trinkets on Her dressing-table, even climbing Her bed-curtains and walking on Her quilt. And of how She would watch him and sometimes talk to him because, Arrietty explained, every day at six o'clock they brought Her a decanter of Fine Old Pale Madeira, and how before midnight She would drink the lot. Nobody blamed Her, not even Homily, because, as Homily would say, She had so few pleasures, poor soul, but, Arrietty explained, after the first three glasses Great Aunt Sophy never believed in anything she

saw. 'She thinks my father comes out of the decanter,'
said Arrietty, 'and one day when I'm older he's going to
take me there and She'll think I come out of the decanter

too. It'll please Her, my father thinks, as She's used to him
now. Once he took my mother, and She perked up like
anything and kept asking after her and why didn't she come
any more and saying they'd watered the Madeira because
once, She says, She saw a little man *and* a little woman and
now she only sees a little man. . . .'

'I wish she thought I came out of the decanter,' said the

boy. She gives me dictation and teaches me to write. I
only see her in the mornings when she's cross. She sends
for me and looks behind my ears and asks Mrs. D. if I've
learned my words.'

'What does Mrs. D. look like?' asked Arrietty. (How
delicious it was to say 'Mrs. D.' like that . . . how careless
and daring!)

'She's fat and has a moustache and gives me my bath and
hurts my bruise and my sore elbow and says she'll take a
slipper to me one of these days. . . .' The boy pulled up a
tuft of grass and stared at it angrily and Arrietty saw his lip
tremble. 'My mother's very nice,' he said. 'She lives in
India. Why did you lose all your worldly riches?'

'Well,' said Arrietty, 'the kitchen boiler burst and hot
water came pouring through the floor into our house and
everything was washed away and piled up in front of the
grating. My father worked night and day. First hot,
then cold. Trying to salvage things. And there's a
dreadful draught in March through that grating. He got
ill, you see, and couldn't go borrowing. So my Uncle
Hendreary had to do it and one or two others and my
mother gave them things, bit by bit, for all their trouble.
But the kingfisher bird was spoilt by the water; all its
feathers fell off and a great twirly spring came jumping out
of its side. My father used the spring to keep the door shut
against draughts from the grating and my mother put the
feathers in a little moleskin hat. After a while I got born
and my father went borrowing again. But he gets tired
now and doesn't like curtains, not when any of the bobbles
are off. . . .'

'I helped him a bit,' said the boy, 'with the tea-cup. He was shivering all over. I suppose he was frightened.'

'My father frightened!' exclaimed Arrietty angrily. 'Frightened of you!' she added.

'Perhaps he doesn't like heights,' said the boy.

'He loves heights,' said Arrietty. 'The thing he doesn't like is curtains. I've told you. Curtains make him tired.'

The boy sat thoughtfully on his haunches, chewing a blade of grass. 'Borrowing,' he said after a while. 'Is that what you call it?'

'What else could you call it?' asked Arrietty.

'I'd call it stealing.'

Arrietty laughed. She really laughed. 'But we *are* Borrowers,' she explained, 'like you're a—a Human Bean or whatever it's called. We're part of the house. You might as well say that the fire-grate steals the coal from the coal-scuttle.'

'Then what is stealing?'

Arrietty looked grave. 'Don't you know?' she asked. 'Stealing is—well, supposing my Uncle Hendreary borrowed an emerald watch from Her dressing-table and my father took it and hung it up on our wall. That's stealing.'

'An emerald watch!' exclaimed the boy.

'Well, I just said that because we have one on the wall at home, but my father borrowed it himself. It needn't be a watch. It could be anything. A lump of sugar even. But Borrowers don't steal.'

'Except from human beings,' said the boy.

Arrietty burst out laughing; she laughed so much that she had to hide her face in the primrose. 'Oh dear,' she gasped with tears in her eyes, 'you are funny!' She stared upwards at his puzzled face. 'Human beings are *for* Borrowers—like bread's for butter!'

The boy was silent awhile. A sigh of wind rustled the cherry-tree and shivered among the blossom.

'Well, I don't believe it,' he said at last, watching the falling petals. 'I don't believe that's what we're for at all and I don't believe we're dying out!'

'Oh, goodness!' exclaimed Arrietty impatiently, staring up at his chin. 'Just use your common sense: you're the only real human being I ever saw (although I do just know of three more—Crampfurl, Her, and Mrs. Driver). But I know lots and lots of Borrowers: the Overmantels and the Harpsichords and the Rain-Barrels and the Linen-Presses and the Boot-Racks and the Hon. John Studdingtons and——'

He looked down. 'John Studdington? But he was our grand-uncle——'

'Well, this family lived behind a picture,' went on Arrietty, hardly listening, 'and there were the Stove-Pipes and the Bell-Pulls and the——'

'Yes,' he interrupted, 'but did you see them?'

'I saw the Harpsichords. And my mother was a Bell-Pull. The others were before I was born. . . .'

He leaned closer. 'Then where are they now? Tell me that.'

'My Uncle Hendreary has a house in the country,' said Arrietty coldly, edging away from his great lowering face; it was misted over, she noticed, with hairs of palest gold. 'And five children, Harpsichords and Clocks.'

'But where are the others?'

'Oh,' said Arrietty, 'they're somewhere.' But where? she wondered. And she shivered slightly in the boy's cold shadow which lay about her, slant-wise, on the grass.

He drew back again, his fair head blocking out a great piece of sky. 'Well,' he said deliberately after a moment, and his eyes were cold, 'I've only seen two Borrowers but I've seen hundreds and hundreds and hundreds and hundreds and hundreds——'.

'Oh no——' whispered Arrietty.

'Of human beings.' And he sat back.

Arrietty stood very still. She did not look at him. After a while she said: 'I don't believe you.'

'All right,' he said, 'then I'll tell you——'

'I still won't believe you,' murmured Arrietty.

'Listen!' he said. And he told her about railway stations

and football matches and racecourses and royal processions and Albert Hall concerts. He told her about India and China and North America and the British Commonwealth. He told her about the July sales. 'Not hundreds,' he said, 'but thousands and millions and billions and trillions of great, big, enormous people. Now do you believe me?'

Arrietty stared up at him with frightened eyes: it gave her a crick in the neck. 'I don't know,' she whispered.

'As for you,' he went on, leaning closer again, 'I don't believe that there are any more Borrowers anywhere in the world. I believe you're the last three,' he said.

Arrietty dropped her face into the primrose. 'We're not. There's Aunt Lupy and Uncle Hendreary and all the cousins.'

'I bet they're dead,' said the boy. 'And what's more,' he went on, 'no one will ever believe I've seen *you*. And you'll be the very last because you're the youngest. One day,' he told her, smiling triumphantly, 'you'll be the only Borrower left in the world!'

He sat still, waiting, but she did not look up. 'Now you're crying,' he remarked after a moment.

'They're not dead,' said Arrietty in a muffled voice; she was feeling in her little pocket for a handkerchief. 'They live in a badger's set two fields away, beyond the spinney. We don't see them because it's too far. There are weasels and things and cows and foxes . . . and crows. . . .'

'Which spinney?' he asked.

'I don't KNOW!' Arrietty almost shouted. 'It's along by the gas-pipe—a field called Parkin's Beck.' She blew her nose. 'I'm going home,' she said.

'Don't go,' he said, 'not yet.'

'Yes, I'm going,' said Arrietty.

His face turned pink. 'Let me just get the book,' he pleaded.

'I'm not going to read to you now,' said Arrietty.

'Why not?'

She looked at him with angry eyes. 'Because——'

'Listen,' he said, 'I'll go to that field. I'll go and find Uncle Hendreary. And the cousins. And Aunt What-ever-she-is. And, if they're alive, I'll tell you. What about that? You could write them a letter and I'd put it down the hole——'

Arrietty gazed up at him: 'Would you?' she breathed.

'Yes, I would. Really I would. Now can I go and get the book? I'll go in by the side door.'

'All right,' said Arrietty absently. Her eyes were shining. 'When can I give you the letter?'

'Any time,' he said, standing above her. 'Where in the house do you live?'

'Well——' began Arrietty and stopped. Why once again did she feel this chill? Could it only be his shadow . . . towering above her, blotting out the sun? 'I'll put it some-where,' she said hurriedly, 'I'll put it under the hall mat.'

'Which one? The one by the front door?'

'Yes, that one.'

He was gone. And she stood there alone in the sunshine, shoulder deep in grass. What had happened seemed too big for thought; she felt unable to believe it really had happened: not only had she been 'seen' but she had been talked to; not only had she been talked to but she had——

'Arrietty!' said a voice.

She stood up startled and spun round: there was Pod, moon-faced, on the path looking up at her. 'Come on down!' he whispered.

She stared at him for a moment as though she did not recognize him; how round his face was, how kind, how familiar!

'Come on!' he said again, more urgently; and obediently because he sounded worried, she slithered quickly towards him off the bank, balancing her primrose. 'Put that thing down,' he said sharply, when she stood at last beside him on the path. 'You can't lug great flowers about—you got to carry a bag. What you want to go up there for?' he grumbled as they moved off across the stones. 'I might never have seen you. Hurry up now. Your mother'll have tea waiting!'

CHAPTER ELEVEN

HOMILY was there, at the last gate, to meet them. She had tidied her hair and smelled of coal-tar soap. She looked younger and somehow excited. 'Well——!' she kept saying. 'Well!' taking the bag from Arrietty and helping Pod to fasten the gate. 'Well, was it nice? Were you a good girl? Was the cherry-tree out? Did the clock strike?' She seemed, in the dim light, to be trying to read the expression on Arrietty's face. 'Come along now. Tea's all ready. Give me your hand. . . .'

Tea was indeed ready, laid on the round table in the sitting-room with a bright fire burning in the cog-wheel. How familiar the room seemed, and homely, but, suddenly, somehow strange: the firelight flickering on the wall-paper—the line which read: '. . . it would be so charming if——' If what? Arrietty always wondered. If our house were less dark, she thought, that would be charming. She looked at the home-made dips set in upturned drawing-pins which Homily had placed as candle-holders among the tea things; the old teapot, a hollow oak-apple, with its quill spout and wired-on handle—burnished it was now and hard with age; there were two roast sliced chestnuts which they would eat like toast with butter and a cold boiled chestnut which Pod would cut like bread; there was a plate of hot dried currants, well plumped before the fire; there were cinnamon breadcrumbs, crispy golden, and lightly dredged

with sugar, and in front of each place, oh, delight of delights, a single potted shrimp. Homily had put out the silver plates—the florin ones for herself and Arrietty and the half-crown one for Pod.

'Come along, Arrietty, if you've washed your hands,' exclaimed Homily, taking up the teapot, 'don't dream!'

Arrietty drew up a cotton-reel and sat down slowly. She watched her mother pulling on the spout of the teapot; this was always an interesting moment. The thicker end of the quill being inside the teapot, a slight pull just before pouring would draw it tightly into the hole and thus prevent a leak. If, as sometimes happened, a trace of dampness appeared about the join, it only meant a rather harder pull and a sudden gentle twist.

'Well?' said Homily, gingerly pouring. 'Tell us what you saw!'

'She didn't see so much,' said Pod, cutting himself a slice of boiled chestnut to eat with his shrimp.

'Didn't she see the overmantel?'

'No,' said Pod, 'we never went in the morning-room.'

'What about my blotting-paper?'

'I never got it,' said Pod.

'Now that's a nice thing——' began Homily.

'Maybe,' said Pod, munching steadily, 'but I had me feeling. I had it bad.'

'What's that?' asked Arrietty. 'His feeling?'

'Up the back of his head and in his fingers,' said Homily. 'It's a feeling your father gets when'—she dropped her voice—'there's someone about.'

'Oh,' said Arrietty and seemed to shrink.

'That's why I brought her along home,' said Pod.

'And was there any one?' asked Homily anxiously.

Pod took a mouthful of shrimp. 'Must have been,' he said, 'but I didn't see nothing.'

Homily leaned across the table. 'Did you have any feeling, Arrietty?'

Arrietty started. 'Oh,' she said, 'do we all have it?'

'Well, not in the same place,' said Homily. 'Mine starts at the back of me ankles and then me knees go. My mother—hers used to start just under her chin and run right round her neck——'

'And tied in a bow at the back,' said Pod, munching.

'No, Pod,' protested Homily, 'it's a fact. No need to be sarcastic. All the Bell-Pulls were like that. Like a collar, she said it was——'

'Pity it didn't choke her,' said Pod.

'Now, Pod, be fair; she had her points.'

'Points!' said Pod. 'She was all points!'

Arrietty moistened her lips; she glanced nervously from Pod to Homily. 'I didn't feel anything,' she said.

'Well,' said Homily, 'perhaps it was a false alarm.'

'Oh no,' began Arrietty, 'it wasn't——' and, as Homily glanced at her sharply, she faltered: 'I mean if papa felt something—I mean—— Perhaps,' she went on, 'I don't have it.'

'Well,' said Homily, 'you're young. It'll come, all in good time. You go and stand in our kitchen, just under the chute, when Mrs. Driver's raking out the stove upstairs. Stand right up on a stool or something—so's you're fairly near the ceiling. It'll come—with practice.'

After tea, when Pod had gone to his last and Homily was washing up, Arrietty rushed to her diary: 'I'll just open it,' she thought, trembling with haste, 'anywhere.' It fell open at the 9th and 10th of July: 'Talk of Camps but Stay at Home. Old Cameronian Colours in Glasgow Cathedral, 1885'—that's what it said for the 9th. And on the 10th the page was headed: 'Make Hay while the Sun Shines. Snowdon Peak sold for £5,750, 1889.' Arrietty tore out this last page. Turning it over she read on the reverse side: 'July 11th: Make Not a Toil of your Pleasure. Niagara passed by C. D. Graham in a cask, 1886.' No, she thought, I'll choose the 10th, 'Make Hay while the Sun Shines,'

and, crossing out her last entry ('Mother out of sorts'),
she wrote below it:

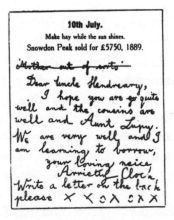

'What are you doing, Arrietty?' called Homily from the
kitchen.

'Writing in my diary.'

'Oh,' said Homily shortly.

'Anything you want?' asked Arrietty.

'It'll do later,' said Homily.

Arrietty folded the letter and placed it carefully between
the pages of Bryce's *Tom Thumb Gazetteer of the World* and,
in the diary, she wrote: 'Went borrowing. Wrote to H.
Talked to B.' After that Arrietty sat for a long time
staring into the fire, and thinking and thinking and
thinking. . . .

CHAPTER TWELVE

BUT it was one thing to write a letter and quite another to find some means of getting it under the mat. Pod, for several days, could not be persuaded to go borrowing: he was well away on his yearly turn-out of the store-rooms, mending partitions, and putting up new shelves. Arrietty usually enjoyed this spring sorting, when half-forgotten treasures came to light and new uses were discovered for old borrowings. She used to love turning over the scraps of silk or lace; the odd kid gloves; the pencil stubs; the rusty razor blades; the hairpins and the needles; the dried figs, the hazel-nuts, the powdery bits of chocolate, and the scarlet stubs of sealing-wax. Pod, one year, had made her a hairbrush from a toothbrush and Homily had made her a small pair of Turkish bloomers from two glove fingers for 'knocking about in the mornings.' There were reels and reels of coloured silks and cottons and small variegated balls of odd wool, pen-nibs which Homily used as flour scoops, and bottle-tops galore.

But this year Arrietty banged about impatiently and stole away whenever she dared, to stare through the grating, hoping to see the boy. She now kept the letter always with her, stuffed inside her jersey, and the edges became rubbed. Once he did run past the grating and she saw his woollen stockings; he was making a chugging noise in his throat like some kind of engine, and as he turned the corner he let out a piercing 'Ooooo—oo' (it was a train whistle, he told her afterwards) so he did not hear her call. One evening, after dark, she crept away and tried to open the first gate, but swing and tug as she might she could not budge the pin.

Homily, every time she swept the sitting-room, would grumble about the carpet. 'It may be a curtain-and-chair job,' she would say to Pod, 'but it wouldn't take you not a quarter of an hour, with your pin and name-tape, to fetch me a bit of blotting-paper from the desk in the morning-room . . . any one would think, looking at this floor, that we lived in a toad-hole. No one could call me house-proud,' said Homily. 'You couldn't be, not with my kind of family, but I do like,' she said, 'to keep "nice things nice."' And at last, on the fourth day, Pod gave in. He laid down his hammer (a small electric-bell clapper) and said to Arrietty: 'Come along. . . .'

Arrietty was glad to see the morning-room; the door luckily had been left ajar and it was fascinating to stand at last in the thick pile of the carpet gazing upwards at the shelves and pillars and towering gables of the famous over-mantel. So that's where they had lived, she thought, those pleasure-loving creatures, remote and gay and self-sufficient. She imagined the Overmantel women—a little 'tweedy,' Homily had described them, with wasp waists and piled Edwardian hair—swinging carelessly outwards on the pilasters, lissom and laughing; gazing at themselves in the inset looking-glass which reflected back the tobacco jars, the cut-glass decanters, the book-shelves, and the plush covered table. She imagined the Overmantel men—fair,

they were said to be, with long moustaches and nervous, slender hands—smoking and drinking and telling their witty tales. So they had never asked Homily up there! Poor Homily with her bony nose and never tidy hair.... They would have looked at her strangely, Arrietty thought, with their long, half-laughing eyes, and smile a little and, humming, turn away. And they had lived only on breakfast food—on toast and egg and tiny snips of mushroom; sausage they'd have had and crispy bacon and little sips of tea and coffee. Where were they now? Arrietty wondered. Where could such creatures go?

Pod had flung his pin so it stuck into the seat of the chair and was up the leg in a trice, leaning outwards on his tape; then, pulling out the pin, he flung it like a javelin, above his head, into a fold of curtain.

This is the moment, Arrietty thought, and felt for her precious letter. She slipped into the hall. It was darker, this time, with the front door closed, and she ran across it with a beating heart. The mat was heavy, but she lifted up the corner and slid the letter under by pushing with her foot. 'There!' she said, and looked about her ... shadows, shadows, and the ticking clock. She looked across

the great plain of floor to where, in the distance, the stairs mounted. 'Another world above,' she thought, 'world on world . . .' and shivered slightly.

'Arrietty,' called Pod softly from the morning-room, and she ran back in time to see him swing clear of the chair seat and pull himself upwards on the name-tape, level with the desk. Lightly he came down feet apart and she saw him, for safety's sake, twist the name-tape lightly round his wrist. 'I wanted you to see that,' he said, a little breath-less. The blotting-paper, when he pushed it, floated down quite softly, riding lightly on the air, and lay at last some feet beyond the desk, pink and fresh, on the carpet's dingy pile.

'You start rolling,' whispered Pod. 'I'll be down,' and Arrietty went on her knees and began to roll the blotting-paper until it grew too stiff for her to hold. Pod soon finished it off and lashed it with his name-tape, through which he ran his hat-pin, and together they carried the long cylinder, as two house-painters would carry a ladder, under the clock and down the hole.

Homily hardly thanked them when, panting a little, they dropped the bundle in the passage outside the sitting-room door. She looked alarmed. 'Oh, there you are,' she said. 'Thank goodness! That boy's about again. I've just heard Mrs. Driver talking to Crampfurl.'

'Oh!' cried Arrietty. 'What did she say?' and Homily glanced sharply at her and saw that she looked pale. Arrietty realized she should have said: 'What boy?' It was too late now.

'Nothing real bad,' Homily went on, as though to reassure her. 'It's just a boy they have upstairs. It's nothing at all, but I heard Mrs. Driver say that she'd take a slipper to him, see if she wouldn't, if he had the mats up once again in the hall.'

'The mats up in the hall!' echoed Arrietty.

'Yes. Three days running, she said to Crampfurl, he'd had the mats up in the hall. She could tell, she said, by the dust and the way he'd put them back. It was the hall part that worried me, seeing as you and your father—— What's the matter, Arrietty? There's no call for that sort of face! Come on now, help me move the furniture and we'll get down the carpet.'

'Oh dear, oh dear,' thought Arrietty miserably, as she helped her mother empty the match-box chest of drawers. 'Three days running he's looked and nothing there. He'll give up hope now . . . he'll never look again.'

That evening she stood for hours on a stool under the chute in their kitchen, pretending she was practising to get 'a feeling' when really she was listening to Mrs. Driver's

conversations with Crampfurl. All she learned was that
Mrs. Driver's feet were killing her, and that it was a pity
that she hadn't given in her notice last May, and would
Crampfurl have another drop, considering there was more
in the cellar than any one would drink in Her lifetime, and
if they thought she was going to clean the first-floor
windows single-handed they had better think again. But on
the third night, just as Arrietty had climbed down off the
stool before she overbalanced with weariness, she heard
Crampfurl say: 'If you ask me, I'd say he had a ferret.'
And quickly Arrietty climbed back again, holding her
breath.

'A ferret!' she heard Mrs. Driver exclaim shrilly.
'Whatever next? Where would he keep it?'

'That I wouldn't like to say,' said Crampfurl in his
rumbling earthy voice; 'all I know is he was up beyond
Parkin's Beck, going round all the banks and calling-like
down all the rabbit-holes.'

'Well, I never,' said Mrs. Driver. 'Where's your glass?'

'Just a drop,' said Crampfurl. 'That's enough. Goes
to your liver, this sweet stuff—not like beer, it isn't. Yes,'
he went on, 'when he saw me coming with a gun he pre-
tended to be cutting a stick like from the hedge. But I'd
see'd him all right and heard him. Calling away, his nose
down a rabbit-hole. It's my belief he's got a ferret.'
There was a gulp, as though Crampfurl was drinking.
'Yes,' he said at last, and Arrietty heard him set down the
glass, 'a ferret called Uncle something.'

Arrietty made a sharp movement, balanced for one
moment with arms waving, and fell off the stool. There

was a clatter as the stool slid sideways, banged against a chest of drawers and rolled over.

'What was that?' asked Crampfurl.

There was silence upstairs and Arrietty held her breath.

'I didn't hear nothing,' said Mrs. Driver.

'Yes,' said Crampfurl, 'it was under the floor like, there by the stove.'

'That's nothing,' said Mrs. Driver. 'It's the coals falling. Often sounds like that. Scares you sometimes when you're sitting here alone. . . . Here, pass your glass, there's only a drop left—might as well finish the bottle. . . .'

They're drinking Fine Old Madeira, thought Arrietty, and very carefully she set the stool upright and stood quietly beside it, looking up. She could see light through the crack, occasionally flicked with shadow as one person or another moved a hand or arm.

'Yes,' went on Crampfurl, returning to his story, 'and when I come up with m'gun he says, all innocent like—to put me off, I shouldn't wonder: "Any old badgers' sets round here?"'

'Artful,' said Mrs. Driver; 'the things they think of . . . badgers' sets . . .' and she gave her creaking laugh.

'As a matter of fact,' said Crampfurl, 'there did used to be one, but when I showed him where it was like he didn't take no notice of it. Just stood there, waiting for me to go.' Crampfurl laughed. 'Two can play at that game, I thought, so I just sits m'self down. And there we were the two of us.'

'And what happened?'

'Well, he had to go off in the end. Leaving his ferret.

I waited a bit, but it never came out. I poked around a bit and whistled. Pity I never heard properly what he called it. Uncle something it sounded like——' Arrietty heard the sudden scrape of a chair. 'Well,' said Crampfurl, 'I'd better get on now and shut up the chickens——'

The scullery door banged and there was a sudden clatter overhead as Mrs. Driver began to rake the stove. Arrietty replaced the stool and stole softly into the sitting-room, where she found her mother alone.

CHAPTER THIRTEEN

HOMILY was ironing, bending and banging and pushing the hair back out of her eyes. All round the room underclothes hung airing on safety-pins which Homily used like coat-hangers.

'What happened?' asked Homily. 'Did you fall over?'

'Yes,' said Arrietty, moving quietly into her place beside the fire.

'How's the feeling coming?'

'Oh, I don't know,' said Arrietty. She clasped her knees and laid her chin on them.

'Where's your knitting?' asked Homily. 'I don't know what's come over you lately. Always idle. You don't feel seedy, do you?'

'Oh,' exclaimed Arrietty, 'let me be!' And Homily for once was silent. 'It's the spring,' she told herself. 'Used to take me like that sometimes at her age.'

'I must see that boy,' Arrietty was thinking—staring blindly into the fire. 'I must hear what happened. I must hear if they're all right. I don't want us to die out. I don't want to be the last Borrower. I don't want'—and here Arrietty dropped her face on to her knees—'to live for ever and ever like this . . . in the dark . . . under the floor. . . .'

'No good getting supper,' said Homily, breaking the silence; 'your father's gone borrowing. To Her room. And you know what that means!'

Arrietty raised her head.   'No,' she said, hardly listening; 'what does it mean?'

'That he won't be back,' said Homily sharply, 'for a good hour and a half.   He likes it up there, gossiping with Her and poking about on the dressing-table.   And it's safe enough once that boy's in bed.   Not that there's anything we want special,' she went on.   'It's just these new shelves he's made.   They look kind of bare, he says, and he might, he says, just pick up a little something . . .'

Arrietty suddenly was sitting bolt upright: a thought had struck her, leaving her breathless and a little shaky at the knees.   'A good hour and a half,' her mother had said and the gates would be open!

'Where are you going?' asked Homily as Arrietty moved towards the door.

'Just along to the store-rooms,' said Arrietty, shading with one hand her candle-dip from the draught.   'I won't be long.'

'Now don't you untidy anything!' Homily called out after her.   'And be careful of that light!'

As Arrietty went down the passage she thought: 'It is true.   I am going to the store-rooms—to find another hat-pin.   And if I do find a hat-pin (and a piece of string— there won't be any name-tape) I still "won't be long" because I'll have to get back before papa.   And I'm doing it for their sakes,' she told herself doggedly, 'and one day they'll thank me.'   All the same she felt a little guilty. 'Artful'—that's what Mrs. Driver would say she was.

There was a hat-pin—one with a bar for a top—and she tied on a piece of string, very firmly, twisting it back and forth like a figure of eight and, as a crowning inspiration, she sealed it with sealing-wax.

The gates were open and she left the candle in the middle of the passage where it could come to no harm, just below the hole by the clock.

The great hall when she had climbed out into it was dim with shadows. A single gas jet, turned low, made a pool of light beside the locked front door and another faintly flickered on the landing half-way up the stairs. The ceiling sprang away into height and darkness and all around was space. The night-nursery, she knew, was at the end of the upstairs passage and the boy would be in bed—her mother had just said so.

Arrietty had watched her father use his pin on the chair and single stairs, in comparison, were easier. There was a kind of rhythm to it after a while: a throw, a pull, a scramble, and an upward swing. The stair rods glinted coldly, but the pile of the carpet seemed soft and warm and delicious to fall back on. On the half-landing she paused to get her breath. She did not mind the semi-darkness; she lived in darkness; she was at home in it and, at a time like this, it made her feel safe.

On the upper landing she saw an open door and a great square of golden light which like a barrier lay across the passage. 'I've got to pass through that,' Arrietty told herself, trying to be brave. Inside the lighted room a voice was talking, droning on. '. . . And this mare,' the voice said, 'was a five-year-old which really belonged to my brother in Ireland, not my elder brother but my younger brother, the one who owned Stale Mate and Oh My

Darling. He had entered her for several point-to-points . . .
but when I say "several" I mean three or at least two. . . .
Have you ever seen an Irish point-to-point?'

'No,' said another voice, rather absent-mindedly. 'That's
my father,' Arrietty realized with a start,' my father talking
to Great Aunt Sophy or rather Great Aunt Sophy talking
to my father.' She gripped her pin with its loops of string,
and ran into the light and through it to the passage beyond.
As she passed the open door she had a glimpse of firelight
and lamplight and gleaming furniture and dark-red silk
brocade.

Beyond the square of light the passage was dark again
and she could see, at the far end, a half-open door. 'That's
the day-nursery,' she thought, 'and beyond that is the
night-nursery.'

'There are certain differences,' Aunt Sophy's voice went
on, 'which would strike you at once. For instance . . .'
Arrietty liked the voice. It was comforting and steady,
like the sound of the clock in the hall, and as she moved off
the carpet on to the strip of polished floor beside the
skirting-board, she was interested to hear there were walls
in Ireland instead of hedges. Here by the skirting she
could run and she loved running. Carpets were heavy
going—thick and clinging, they held you up. The boards
were smooth and smelled of beeswax. She liked the
smell.

The schoolroom, when she reached it, was shrouded in
dust sheets and full of junk. Here too a gas jet burned,
turned low to a bluish flame. The floor was oilcloth,
rather worn, and the rugs were shabby. Under the table

was a great cavern of darkness.   She moved into it, feeling about, and bumped into a dusty hassock higher than her head.   Coming out again, into the half light, she looked up and saw the corner cupboard with the doll's tea-service, the painting above the fire-place, and the plush curtain where her father had been 'seen.'   Chair legs were every-where and chair seats obscured her view.   She found her way among them to the door of the night-nursery and there she saw, suddenly, on a shadowed plateau in the far corner, the boy in bed.   She saw his great face, turned towards her on the edge of the pillow; she saw the gaslight reflected in his open eyes; she saw his hand gripping the bed-clothes, holding them tightly pressed against his mouth.

She stopped moving and stood still.   After a while, when she saw his fingers relax, she said softly: 'Don't be frightened. . . .   It's me, Arrietty.'

He let the bed-clothes slide away from his mouth and said: 'Arri-*what*-y?'   He seemed annoyed.

'Etty,' she repeated gently.   'Did you take the letter?'

He stared at her for a moment without speaking, then he said: 'Why did you come creeping, creeping, into my room?'

'I didn't come creeping, creeping,' said Arrietty.   'I even ran.   Didn't you see?'

He was silent, staring at her with his great, wide-open eyes.

'When I brought the book,' he said at last, 'you'd gone.'

'I had to go.   Tea was ready.   My father fetched me.'

He understood this.   'Oh,' he said matter of factly, and did not reproach her.

'Did you take the letter?' she asked again.

'Yes,' he said, 'I had to go back twice. I shoved it down the badger's hole. . . .' Suddenly he threw back the bed-clothes and stood up in bed, enormous in his pale flannel night-shirt. It was Arrietty's turn to be afraid. She half turned, her eyes on his face, and began backing slowly towards the door. But he did not look at her; he was feeling behind a picture on the wall. 'Here it is,' he said, sitting down again, and the bed creaked loudly.

'But I don't want it back!' exclaimed Arrietty, coming forward again. 'You should have left it there! Why did you bring it back?'

He turned it over in his fingers. 'He's written on it,' he said.

'Oh, please,' cried Arrietty excitedly, 'show me!' She ran right up to the bed and tugged at the trailing sheet. 'Then they are alive! Did you see him?'

'No,' he

said, 'the letter was there, just down the hole where I'd put it.' He leaned towards her. 'But he's written on it. Look!'

She made a quick dart and almost snatched the letter out of his great fingers, but was careful to keep out of range of his hand. She ran with it to the door of the schoolroom where the light, though dim, was a little brighter. 'It's very faint,' she said, holding it close to her eyes. 'What's he written it with? I wonder. It's all in capitals——' She turned suddenly. 'Are you sure you didn't write it?' she asked.

'Of course not,' he began. 'I write small——' But she had seen by his face that he spoke the truth and began to spell out the letters. 'T—e—double l,' she said. 'Tell y—o—r—e.' She looked up. 'Yore?' she said.

'Yes,' said the boy, 'your.'

'Tell your a—n—t, ant?' said Arrietty. 'Ant? My ant?' The boy was silent, waiting. 'Ant L—u— Oh, Aunt Lupy!' she exclaimed. 'He says—listen, this is what he says: "Tell your Aunt Lupy to come home"!'

There was silence. 'Then tell her,' said the boy after a moment.

'But she isn't here!' exclaimed Arrietty. 'She's never been here! I don't even remember what she looked like!'

'Look,' said the boy, staring through the door, 'someone's coming!'

Arrietty whipped round. There was no time to hide: it was Pod, borrowing-bag in one hand and pin in the other. He stood in the doorway of the schoolroom. Quite still he stood, outlined against the light in the passage, his little shadow falling dimly in front of him.   He had seen her.

'I heard your voice,' he said, and there was a dreadful quietness about the way he spoke, 'just as I was coming out of Her room.'   Arrietty stared back at him, stuffing the letter up her jersey.   Could he see beyond her into the shadowed room.   Could he see the tousled shape in bed?

'Come on home,' said Pod, and turned away.

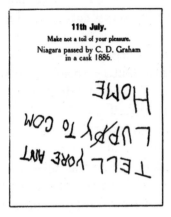

CHAPTER FOURTEEN

POD did not speak until they reached the sitting-room. Nor did he look at her. She had had to scramble after him as best she might. He had ignored her efforts to help him shut the gates, but once, when she tripped, he had waited until she had got up again, watching her, it seemed, almost without interest while she brushed the dust off her knees.

Supper was laid and the ironing put away and Homily came running in from the kitchen, surprised to see them together.

Pod threw down his borrowing-bag. He stared at his wife.

'What's the matter?' faltered Homily, looking from one to the other.

'She was in the night-nursery,' said Pod quietly, 'talking to that boy!'

Homily moved forward, her hands clasped tremblingly against her apron, her startled eyes flicking swiftly to and fro. 'Oh, no——' she breathed.

Pod sat down. He ran a tired hand over his eyes and forehead; his face looked heavy like a piece of dough. 'Now what?' he said.

Homily stood quite still; bowed she stood over her clasped hands and stared at Arrietty. 'Oh, you never——' she whispered.

'They are frightened,' Arrietty realized; 'they are not angry at all—they are very, very frightened.' She moved forward. 'It's all right——' she began.

Homily sat down suddenly on the cotton-reel; she had begun to tremble. 'Oh,' she said, 'whatever shall we do?' She began to rock herself, very slightly, to and fro.

'Oh, mother, don't!' pleaded Arrietty. 'It isn't so bad as that. It really isn't.' She felt up the front of her jersey; at first she could not find the letter—it had slid round her side to the back—but at last she drew it out, very crumpled. 'Look,' she said, 'here's a letter from Uncle Hendreary. I wrote to him and the boy took the letter——'

'You wrote to him!' cried Homily on a kind of suppressed shriek. 'Oh,' she moaned, and closed her eyes, 'whatever next! Whatever shall we do?' and she fanned herself limply with her bony hand.

'Get your mother a drink of water, Arrietty,' said Pod sharply. Arrietty brought it in a sawn-off hazel shell—it had been sawn off at the pointed end and was shaped like a brandy glass.

'But whatever made you do such a thing, Arrietty?' said Homily more calmly, setting the empty cup down on the table. 'Whatever came over you?'

So Arrietty told them about being 'seen'—that morning under the cherry-tree. And how she had kept it from them not to worry them. And what the boy said about 'dying out.' And how—more than important—how imperative it had seemed to make sure the Hendrearys were alive. 'Do understand,' pleaded Arrietty, 'please understand! I'm trying to save the race!'

'The expressions she uses!' said Homily to Pod under her breath, not without pride.

But Pod was not listening. 'Save the race!' he repeated grimly. 'It's people like you, my girl, who do things sudden like with no respect for tradition, who'll finish us Borrowers once for all. Don't you see what you've done?'

Arrietty met his accusing eyes. 'Yes,' she said falteringly, 'I've—I've got in touch with the only other ones still alive. So that,' she went on bravely, 'from now on we can all stick together. . . .'

'All stick together!' Pod repeated angrily. 'Do you think Hendreary's lot would ever come to live back here? Can you see your mother emigrating to a badger's set, two fields away, out in the open and no hot water laid on?'

'Never!' cried Homily in a full, rich voice which made them both turn and look at her.

'Or do you see your mother walking across two fields and a garden,' went on Pod, 'two fields full of crows and cows and horses and what-not, to take a cup of tea with your Aunt Lupy whom she never liked much anyway? But wait,' he said as Arrietty tried to speak, 'that's not the point—as far as all that goes we're just where we was—the point,' he went on, leaning forward and speaking with great solemnity, 'is this: that boy knows now where we live!'

'Oh no,' said Arrietty, 'I never told him that. I——'

'You told him,' interrupted Pod, 'about the kitchen pipe bursting; you told him how all our stuff got washed away to the grating.' He sat back again glaring at her. 'He's only got to think,' he pointed out. Arrietty was silent and Pod went on: 'That's a thing that has never happened before, never, in the whole long history of the Borrowers. Borrowers have been "seen"—yes; Borrowers have been caught—maybe: but no human being has ever known where any Borrower lived. We're in very grave danger, Arrietty, and you've put us there. And that's a fact.'

'Oh, Pod,' whimpered Homily, 'don't frighten the child.'

'Nay, Homily,' said Pod more gently, 'my poor old girl! I don't want to frighten no one, but this is serious. Suppose I said to you pack up to-night, all our bits and pieces, where would you go?'

'Not to Hendreary's,' cried Homily, 'not there, Pod! I couldn't never share a kitchen with Lupy——'

'No,' agreed Pod, 'not to Hendreary's. And don't you see for why? The boy knows about that too!'

'Oh!' cried Homily in real dismay.

'Yes,' said Pod, 'a couple of smart terriers or a well-trained ferret and that'd be the end of that lot.'

'Oh, Pod . . .' said Homily and began again to tremble. The thought of living in a badger's set had been bad enough, but the thought of not having even that to go to seemed almost worse. 'And I dare say I could have got it nice in the end,' she said, 'providing we lived quite separate——'

'Well, it's no good thinking of it now,' said Pod. He turned to Arrietty: 'What does your Uncle Hendreary say in his letter?'

'Yes,' exclaimed Homily, 'where's this letter?'

'It doesn't say much,' said Arrietty, passing over the paper; 'it just says "Tell your Aunt Lupy to come home."'

'What?' exclaimed Homily sharply, looking at the letter upside-down. 'Come home? What can he mean?'

'He means,' said Pod, 'that Lupy must have set off to come here and that she never arrived.'

'Set off to come here?' repeated Homily. 'But when?'

'How should I know?' said Pod.

'It doesn't say when,' said Arrietty.

'But,' exclaimed Homily, 'it might have been weeks ago!'

'It might,' said Pod. 'Long enough anyway for him to want her back.'

'Oh,' cried Homily, 'all those poor little children!'

'They're growing up now,' said Pod.

'But something must have happened to her!' exclaimed Homily.

'Yes,' said Pod. He turned to Arrietty. 'See what I mean, Arrietty, about those fields?'

'Oh, Pod,' said Homily, her eyes full of tears, 'I don't suppose none of us'll ever see poor Lupy again!'

'Well, we wouldn't have anyway,' said Pod.

'Pod,' said Homily soberly, 'I'm frightened. Everything seems to be happening at once. What are we going to do?'

'Well,' said Pod, 'there's nothing we can do to-night. That's certain. But have a bit of supper and a good night's rest.' He rose to his feet.

'Oh, Arrietty,' wailed Homily suddenly, 'you naughty wicked girl! How could you go and start all this? How could you go and talk to a human being? If only——'

'I was "seen,"' cried Arrietty. 'I couldn't help being "seen." Papa was "seen." I don't think it's all as awful as you're trying to make out. I don't think human beings are all that bad——'

'They're bad and they're good,' said Pod; 'they're honest and they're artful—it's just as it takes them at the moment. And animals, if they could talk, would say the same. Steer clear of them—that's what I've always been told. No matter what they promise you. No good never really came to no one from any human being.'

CHAPTER FIFTEEN

THAT night, while Arrietty lay straight and still under her
cigar-box cciling, Homily and Pod talked for hours.   They
talked in the sitting-room, they talked in the kitchen, and
later, much later, she heard them talk in their bedroom.
She heard drawers shutting and opening, doors creaking,
and boxes being pulled out from under beds.   'What are
they doing?' she wondered. 'What will happen next?' Very
still she lay in her soft little bed with her familiar belongings
about her: her postage stamp view of Rio harbour; her
silver pig off a charm bracelet; her turquoise ring whicn
sometimes, for fun, she would wear as a crown, and, dearest
of all, her floating ladies with the golden trumpets, tooting
above their peaceful town.   She did not want to lose these,
she realized suddenly, lying there straight and still in bed,
but to have all the other things as well, adventure and safety
mixed—that's what she wanted.   And that (the restless
bangings and whisperings told her) is just what you
couldn't do.

As it happened, Homily was only fidgeting: opening
drawers and shutting them, unable to be still.   And she
ended up, when Pod was already in bed, by deciding to
curl her hair.   'Now, Homily,' Pod protested wearily,
lying there in his night-shirt, 'there's really no call for that.
Who's going to see you?'

'That's just it,' exclaimed Homily, searching in a drawer for her curl-rags; 'in times like these one never knows. I'm not going to be caught out,' she said irritably, turning the drawer upside-down and picking over the spilled contents, 'with me hair like this!'

She came to bed at last, looking spiky, like a washed-out golliwog, and Pod with a sigh turned over at last and closed his eyes.

Homily lay for a long time staring at the oil-lamp; it was the silver cap of a scent-bottle with a tiny, floating wick. She felt unwilling, for some reason, to blow it out. There were movements upstairs in the kitchen above and it was late for movements—the household should be asleep—and the lumpy curlers pressed uncomfortably against her neck. She gazed—just as Arrietty had done—about the familiar room (too full, she realized, with little bags and boxes and make-shift cupboards) and thought: 'What now? Perhaps nothing will happen after all; the child perhaps is right, and we are making a good deal of fuss about nothing very much; this boy, when all's said and done, is only a guest; perhaps,' thought Homily, 'he'll go away again quite soon, and that,' she told herself drowsily, 'will be that.'

Later (as she realized afterwards) she must have dozed off because it seemed she was crossing Parkin's Beck; it was night and the wind was blowing and the field seemed very steep; she was scrambling up it, along the ridge by the gas-pipe, sliding and falling in the wet grass. The trees, it seemed to Homily, were threshing and clashing, their branches waving and sawing against the sky. Then (as she told them many weeks later) there was a sound of splintering wood. . . .

And Homily woke up.   She saw the room again and the oil-lamp flickering, but something, she knew at once, was different: there was a strange draught and her mouth felt dry and full of grit.   Then she looked up at the ceiling: 'Pod!' she shrieked, clutching his shoulder.

Pod rolled over and sat up.   They both stared at the ceiling: the whole surface was on a steep slant and one side of it had come right away from the wall—this was what had caused the draught—and down into the room, to within an inch of the foot of the bed, protruded a curious object: a huge bar of grey steel with a flattened, shining edge.

'It's a screwdriver,' said Pod.

They stared at it, fascinated, unable to move, and for a moment all was still.   Then slowly the huge object swayed upwards until the sharp edge lay against their ceiling and Homily heard a scrape on the floor above and a sudden human gasp.   'Oh, my knees,' cried Homily, 'oh, my feeling——' as, with a splintering wrench, their whole roof flew off and fell down with a clatter, somewhere out of sight.

Homily screamed then.   But this time it was a real scream, loud and shrill and hearty; she seemed almost to settle down in her scream, while her eyes stared up, half interested, into empty lighted space.   There was another ceiling, she realized, away up above them—higher, it seemed, than the sky; a ham hung from it and two strings of onions. Arrietty appeared in the doorway, scared and trembling, clutching her night-gown.   And Pod slapped Homily's back. 'Have done,' he said, 'that's enough,' and Homily, suddenly, was quiet.

A great face appeared then between them and that distant height. It wavered above them, smiling and terrible: there was silence and Homily sat bolt upright, her mouth open. 'Is that your mother?' asked a surprised voice after a moment, and Arrietty from the doorway whispered: 'Yes.'

It was the boy.

Pod got out of bed and stood beside it, shivering in his night-shirt. 'Come on,' he said to Homily, 'you can't stay there!'

But Homily could. She had her old night-dress on with the patch in the back and nothing was going to move her. A slow anger was rising up in Homily: she had been caught in her hair-curlers; Pod had raised his hand to her; and she remembered that, in the general turmoil and for once in her life, she had left the supper washing-up for morning, and there it would be, on the kitchen table, for all the world to see!

She glared at the boy—he was only a child after all. 'Put it back!' she said, 'put it back at once!' Her eyes flashed and her curlers seemed to quiver.

He knelt down then, but Homily did not flinch as the great face came slowly closer. She saw his under lip, pink and full—like an enormous exaggeration of Arriettys—and she saw it wobble slightly. 'But I've got something for you,' he said.

Homily's expression did not change and Arrietty called out from her place in the doorway: 'What is it?'

The boy reached behind him and very gingerly, careful to keep it upright, he held a wooden object above their heads. 'It's this,' he said, and very carefully, his tongue out and breathing heavily, he lowered the object slowly into their hole: it was a doll's dresser, complete with plates. It had two drawers in it and a cupboard below; he adjusted its position at the foot of Homily's bed. Arrietty ran round to see better.

'Oh,' she cried ecstatically. 'Mother, look!'

Homily threw the dresser a glance—it was dark oak and the plates were hand-painted—and then she looked quickly away again. 'Yes,' she said coldly, 'it's very nice.'

There was a short silence which no one knew how to break.

'The cupboard really opens,' said the boy at last, and the great hand came down all amongst them, smelling of bath soap. Arrietty flattened herself against the wall and Pod exclaimed, nervous: 'Now then!'

'Yes,' agreed Homily after a moment, 'I see it does.'

Pod drew a long breath—a sigh of relief as the hand went back.

'There, Homily,' he said placatingly, 'you've always wanted something like that!'

'Yes,' said Homily—she still sat bolt upright, her hands clasped in her lap. 'Thank you very much. And now,' she went on coldly, 'will you please put back the roof?'

'Wait a minute,' pleaded the boy. Again he reached behind him; again the hand came down; and there, beside the dresser, where there was barely room for it, was a very small doll's chair; it was a Victorian chair, upholstered in

red velvet. 'Oh!' Arrietty exclaimed again and Pod said
shyly: 'Just about fit me, that would.'

'Try it,' begged the boy, and Pod threw him a nervous
glance. 'Go on!' said Arrietty, and Pod sat down—in his
night-shirt, his bare feet showing. 'That's nice,' he said
after a moment.

'It would go by the fire in the sitting-room,' cried
Arrietty; 'it would look lovely on red blotting-paper!'

'Let's try it,' said the boy, and the hand came down
again. Pod sprang up just in time to steady the dresser
as the red velvet chair was whisked away above his head
and placed presumably in the next room but one. Arrietty
ran out of the door and along the passage to see. 'Oh,'
she called out to her parents, 'come and see. It's
lovely!'

But Pod and Homily did not move. The boy was leaning
over them, breathing hard, and they could see the middle

buttons of his night-shirt.   He seemed to be examining the
farther room.

'What do you keep in that mustard-pot?' he asked.

'Coal,' said Arrietty's voice.   'And I helped to borrow
this new carpet.   Here's the watch I told you about, and
the pictures. . . .'

'I could get you some better stamps than those,' the boy
said.   'I've got some jubilee ones with the Taj Mahal.'

'Look,' cried Arrietty's voice again, and Pod took
Homily's hand, 'these are my books——'

Homily clutched Pod as the great hand came down once
more in the direction of Arrietty.   'Quiet,' he whispered;
'sit still. . . .'   The boy, it seemed, was touching the books.

'What are they called?' he asked, and Arrietty reeled off
the names.

'Pod,' whispered Homily, 'I'm going to scream——'

'No,' whispered Pod.   'You mustn't.   Not again.'

'I feel it coming on,' said Homily.

Pod looked worried.   'Hold your breath,' he said, 'and
count ten.'

The boy was saying to Arrietty: 'Why couldn't you read
me those?'

'Well, I could,' said Arrietty, 'but I'd rather read something new.'

'But you never come,' complained the boy.

'I know,' said Arrietty, 'but I will.'

'Pod,' whispered Homily, 'did you hear that?   Did you
hear what she said?'

'Yes, yes,' Pod whispered; 'keep quiet——'

'Do you want to see the store-rooms?' Arrietty suggested

next and Homily clapped a hand to her mouth as though to stifle a cry.

Pod looked up at the boy. 'Hey,' he called, trying to attract his attention. The boy looked down. 'Put the roof back now,' Pod begged him, trying to sound matter of fact and reasonable; 'we're getting cold.'

'All right,' agreed the boy, but he seemed to hesitate: he reached across them for the piece of board which formed their roof. 'Shall I nail you down?' he asked, and they saw him pick up the hammer; it swayed above them, very dangerous looking.

'Of course nail us down,' said Pod irritably.

'I mean,' said the boy, 'I've got some more things upstairs——'

Pod looked uncertain and Homily nudged him. 'Ask him,' she whispered, 'what kind of things?'

'What kind of things?' asked Pod.

'Things from an old doll's house there is on the top shelf of the cupboard by the fire-place in the schoolroom.'

'I've never seen no doll's house,' said Pod.

'Well, it's in the cupboard,' said the boy, 'right up by the ceiling; you can't see it—you've got to climb on the lower shelves to get to it.'

'What sort of things *are* there in the doll's house?' asked Arrietty from the sitting-room.

'Oh, everything,' the boy told her; 'carpets and rugs and beds with mattresses, and there's a bird in a cage—not a real one—of course, and cooking pans and tables and five gilt chairs and a pot with a palm in it—a dish of plaster tarts and an imitation leg of mutton——'

Homily leaned across to Pod. 'Tell him to nail us down lightly,' she whispered. Pod stared at her and she nodded vigorously, clasping her hands.

Pod turned to the boy. 'All right,' he said, 'you nail us down. But lightly, if you see what I mean. Just a tap or two here and there. . . .'

CHAPTER SIXTEEN

Then began a curious phase in their lives: borrowings beyond all dreams of borrowing—a golden age. Every night the floor was opened and treasures would appear: a real carpet for the sitting-room, a tiny coal-scuttle, a stiff little sofa with damask cushions, a double bed with a round bolster, a single ditto with a striped mattress, framed pictures instead of stamps, a kitchen stove which didn't work but which looked 'lovely' in the kitchen; there were oval tables and square tables and a little desk with one drawer; there were two maple wardrobes (one with a looking-glass) and a bureau with curved legs. Homily grew not only accustomed to the roof coming off but even went so far as to suggest to Pod that he put the board on hinges. 'It's just the hammering I don't care for,' she explained; 'it brings down the dirt.'

When the boy brought them

121

a grand piano Homily begged Pod to build a drawing-room. 'Next to the sitting-room,' she said, 'and we could move the store-rooms farther down.   Then we could have those gilt chairs he talks about and the palm in a pot. . . .'   Pod, however, was a little tired of furniture removing; he was looking forward to the quiet evenings when he could doze at last beside the fire in his new red velvet chair.   No sooner had he put a chest of drawers in one place when Homily, coming in and out at the door—'to get the effect'—made him 'try' it somewhere else.   And every evening, at about his usual bedtime, the roof would fly up and more stuff would arrive.   But Homily was tireless; bright-eyed and pink-cheeked, after a long day's pushing and pulling, she still would leave nothing until morning.   'Let's just *try* it,' she would beg, lifting up one end of a large doll's sideboard, so that Pod would have to lift the other; 'it won't take a minute!'   But as Pod well knew, in actual fact it would be several hours before, dishevelled and aching, they finally dropped into bed.   Even then Homily would sometimes hop out 'to have one last look.'

In the meantime, in payment for these riches, Arrietty would read to the boy—every afternoon in the long grass beyond the cherry-tree.   He would lie on his back and she would stand beside his shoulder and tell him when to turn the page.   They were happy days to look back on afterwards, with the blue sky beyond the cherry boughs, the grasses softly stirring,

and the boy's great ear listening beside her.   She grew to
know that ear quite well, with its curves and shadows
and sunlit pinks and golds.   Sometimes, as she grew
bolder, she would lean against his shoulder.   He was
very still while she read to him and always grateful.
What worlds they would explore together—strange worlds
to Arrietty.   She learned a lot and some of the things she
learned were hard to accept.   She was made to realize once
and for all that this earth on which they lived turning
about in space did not revolve, as she had believed, for
the sake of little people.   'Nor for big people either,' she
reminded the boy when she saw his secret smile.

In the cool of the evening Pod would come for her—a
rather weary Pod, dishevelled and dusty—to take her back
for tea.   And at home there would be an excited Homily
and fresh delights to discover.   'Shut your eyes!' Homily
would cry.   'Now open them!' and Arrietty, in a dream of
joy, would see her home transformed.   All kinds of sur-
prises there were—even, one day, lace curtains at the grating,
looped up with pink string.

Their only sadness was that there was no one there to
see: no visitors, no casual droppers-in, no admiring cries
and envious glances!   What would Homily have not given
for an Overmantel or a Harpsichord?   Even a Rain-Barrel
would have been better than no one at all.   'You write to
your Uncle Hendreary,' Homily suggested, 'and tell *him*.
A nice long letter, mind, and don't leave anything out!'
Arrietty began the letter on the back of one of the discarded
pieces of blotting-paper, but it became as she wrote it just
a dull list, far too long, like a sale catalogue or the inventory

of a house to let; she would have to keep jumping up to count spoons or to look up words in the dictionary, and after a while she laid it aside: there was so much else to do, so many new books to read, and so much, now, that she could talk of with the boy.

'He's been ill,' she told her mother and father; 'he's been here for the quiet and the country air. But soon he'll go back to India. Did you know,' she asked the amazed Homily, 'that the Arctic night lasts six months, and that the distance between the two poles is less than that between the two extremities of a diameter drawn through the equator?'

Yes, they were happy days and all would have been well, as Pod said afterwards, if they had stuck to borrowing from the doll's house. No one in the human household seemed to remember it was there and, consequently nothing was missed. The drawing-room, however, could not help but be a temptation: it was so seldom used nowadays; there were so many knick-knack tables which had been out of Pod's reach, and the boy, of course, could turn the key in the glass doors of the cabinet.

The silver violin he brought them first and then the silver harp; it stood no higher than Pod's shoulder and Pod restrung it with horse-hair from the sofa in the morning-room. 'A musical conversazione, that's what we could have!' cried the exulting Homily as Arrietty struck a tiny, tuneless note on a horse-hair string. 'If only,' she went on fervently, clasping her hands, 'your father would start on the drawing-room!' (She curled her hair nearly every evening nowadays and, since the house was more or

less straight, she would occasionally change for dinner into
a satin dress; it hung like a sack, but Homily called it
'Grecian.') 'We could use your painted ceiling,' she
explained to Arrietty, 'and there are quite enough of those
toy builders' bricks to make a parquet floor.' ('Parkay,'
she would say. 'Par-r-r-kay . . .,' just like a Harpsichord.)

Even Great Aunt Sophy, right away upstairs in the
littered grandeur of her bedroom, seemed distantly affected
by a spirit of endeavour which seemed to flow, in gleeful
whorls and eddies, about the staid old house. Several
times lately Pod, when he went to her room, had found
her out of bed. He went there nowadays not to borrow,
but to rest: the room, one might almost say, had become
his club; a place to which he could go 'to get away from
things.' Pod was a little irked by his riches; he had never
visualized, not in his wildest dreams, borrowing such as
this. Homily, he felt, should call a halt; surely, now, their
home was grand enough; these jewelled snuff-boxes and
diamond-encrusted miniatures, these filigree vanity-cases
and Dresden figurines—all, as he knew, from the drawing-
room cabinet—were not really necessary: what was the good
of a shepherdess nearly as tall as Arrietty or an outsize
candle-snuffer? Sitting just inside the fender, where he
could warm his hands at the fire, he watched Aunt Sophy
hobble slowly round the room on her two sticks. 'She'll
be downstairs soon, I shouldn't wonder,' he thought
glumly, hardly listening to her oft-told tale about a royal
luncheon aboard a Russian yacht, 'then she'll miss these
things. . . .'

It was not Aunt Sophy, however, who missed them first.

It was Mrs. Driver. Mrs. Driver had never forgotten the trouble over Rosa Pickhatchet. It had not been, at the time, easy to pin-point the guilt. Even Crampfurl had felt under suspicion. 'From now on,' Mrs. Driver had said, 'I'll manage on me own. No more strange maids in *this* house—not if I'm to stay on meself!' A drop of Madeira here, a pair of old stockings there, a handkerchief or so, an odd vest, or an occasional pair of gloves—these, Mrs. Driver felt, were different; these were within her rights. But trinkets out of the drawing-room cabinet— that, she told herself grimly, staring at the depleted shelves, was a different story altogether!

She felt tricked. Standing there, on that fateful day, in the spring sunshine, feather duster in hand, her little black eyes had become slits of anger and cunning. It was, she calculated, as though someone, suspecting her dishonesty, were trying to catch her out. But who could it be? Crampfurl? That boy? The man who came to wind the clocks? These things had disappeared gradually, one by one: it was someone, of that she felt sure, who knew the house—and someone who wished her ill. Could it, she wondered suddenly, be the old lady herself? The old girl had been out of bed lately and walking about her room. Might she not have come downstairs in the night, poking about with her stick, snooping and spying (Mrs. Driver remembered suddenly the empty Madeira bottle and the two glasses which, so often, were left on the kitchen table.) Ah, thought Mrs. Driver, was not this just the sort of thing she might do—the sort of thing she would cackle over, back upstairs again among her pillows, watching and waiting for Mrs. Driver to report the loss? 'Everything all right downstairs, Driver?'—that's what she'd always say and she would look at Mrs. Driver sideways out of those wicked old eyes of hers. 'I wouldn't put it past her!' Mrs. Driver exclaimed aloud, gripping her feather duster as though it were a club. 'And a nice merry-andrew she'd look if I caught her at it—creeping about the downstairs rooms in the middle of the night. All right, my lady,' muttered Mrs. Driver grimly, 'pry and potter all you want —two can play at that game!'

CHAPTER SEVENTEEN

MRS. DRIVER was short with Crampfurl that evening; she would not sit down and drink with him as usual, but stumped about the kitchen, looking at him sideways every now and again out of the corners of her eyes. He seemed uneasy—as indeed he was: there was a kind of menace in her silence, a hidden something which no one could ignore. Even Aunt Sophy had felt it when Mrs. Driver brought up her wine; she heard it in the clink of the decanter against the glass as Mrs. Driver set down the tray and in the rattle of the wooden rings as Mrs. Driver drew the curtains; it was in the tremble of the floor-boards as Mrs. Driver crossed the room and in the click of the latch as Mrs. Driver closed the door. 'What's the matter with her now?' Aunt Sophy wondered vaguely as delicately, ungreedily, she poured the first glass.

The boy had felt it too. From the way Mrs. Driver had stared at him as he sat hunched in the bath; from the way she soaped the loofah and the way she said: 'And now!' She had scrubbed him slowly, with a careful, angry steadiness, and all through the bathing time she did not say a word. When he was in bed she had gone through all his things, peering into cupboards and opening his drawers. She had pulled his suit-case out from under the wardrobe and found his dear dead mole and his hoard of sugar-lumps and her best potato knife. But even then she had not spoken. She had thrown the mole into the waste-paper basket and had made angry noises with her tongue; she pocketed the potato knife and all the sugar-lumps. She had stared at him a moment before she turned the gas low —a strange stare it had been, more puzzled than accusing.

Mrs. Driver slept above the scullery. She had her own back-stairs. That night she did not undress. She set the alarm clock for midnight and put it, where the tick would not disturb her, outside her door; she unbuttoned her tight shoes and crawled, grunting a little, under the eiderdown. She had 'barely closed her eyes' (as she told Crampfurl afterwards) when the clock shrilled off—chattering and rattling on its four thin legs on the bare boards of the passage-way. Mrs. Driver tumbled herself out of bed and fumbled her way to the door. 'Shush,' she said to the clock as she felt for the catch, 'Shush!' and clasped it to her bosom. She stood there, in her stockinged feet, at the head of the scullery stairs: something, it seemed, had flickered below—a hint of light. Mrs. Driver peered down the dark curve of the narrow stairway. Yes, there it was again—a moth-wing flutter! Candlelight—that's what it was! A moving candle—beyond the stairs, beyond the scullery, somewhere within the kitchen.

Clock in hand, Mrs. Driver creaked down the stairs in her stockinged feet, panting a little in her eagerness. There seemed a sigh in the darkness, an echo of movement. And it seemed to Mrs. Driver, standing there on the cold stone flags of the scullery, that this sound that was barely a sound could only mean one thing: the soft swing-to of the green baize door—that door which led out of the kitchen into the main hall beyond. Hurriedly Mrs. Driver felt her way into the kitchen and fumbled for matches along the ledge above the stove; she knocked off a pepper-pot and a paper bag of cloves, and glancing quickly downwards saw a filament of light; she saw it in the second before she struck a match—a thread of light, it looked like, on the floor beside her feet; it ran in an oblong shape, outlining a rough square. Mrs. Driver gasped and lit the gas and the room leapt up around her: she glanced quickly at the baize door; there seemed to her startled eye a quiver of movement in it, as though it had just swung to; she ran to it and pushed it open, but the passage beyond was still and dark—no flicker of shadow nor sound of distant footfall. She let the door fall to again and watched it as it swung back, slowly, regretfully, held by its heavy spring. Yes, that was the sound she had heard from the scullery—that sighing whisper—like an indrawn breath.

Cautiously, clutching back her skirts, Mrs. Driver moved towards the stove. An object lay there, something pinkish, on the floor beside the jutting board. Ah, she realized, that board—that was where the light had come from! Mrs. Driver hesitated and glanced about the kitchen: everything else looked normal and just as she had left it—the plates on the dresser, the saucepans on the wall, and the row of tea-towels hanging symmetrically on their string above the stove. The pinkish object, she saw now, was a heart-shaped cachou-box—one that she knew well—from the glassed-in tray-table beside the fire-place in the drawing-room. She picked it up; it was enamel and gold and set with tiny brilliants.

'Well, I'm——' she began, and stooping swiftly with a sudden angry movement, she wrenched back the piece of floor.

And then she shrieked, loud and long. She saw movement: a running, a scrambling, a fluttering! She heard a squeaking, a jabbering, and a gasping. Little people, they looked like, with hands and feet ... and mouths opening. That's what they looked like ... but they couldn't *be* that, of course! Running here, there, and everywhere. 'Oh! oh! oh!' she shrieked and felt behind her for a chair. She clambered on to it and it wobbled beneath her and she climbed, still shrieking, from the chair to the table. . . .

And there she stood, marooned, crying and gasping, and calling out for help, until, after hours it seemed, there was a rattling at the scullery door. Crampfurl it was, roused at last by the light and the noise. 'What is it?' he called. 'Let me in!' But Mrs. Driver would not leave the table. 'A nest! A nest!' she shouted. 'Alive and squeaking!'

Crampfurl threw his weight against the door and burst open the lock. He staggered, slightly dazed, into the kitchen, his corduroy trousers pulled on over his night-shirt. 'Where?' he cried, his eyes wide beneath his tousled hair. 'What sort of a nest?'

Mrs. Driver, sobbing still with fright, pointed at the floor. Crampfurl walked over in his slow, deliberate way and stared down. He saw a hole in the floor, lined and cluttered with small objects—children's toys, they looked like, bits of rubbish—that was all. 'It's nothing,' he said after a moment; 'it's that boy, that's what it is.' He stirred the contents with his foot and all the partitions fell down. 'There ain't nothing alive in there.'

'But I saw them, I tell you,' gasped Mrs. Driver, 'little people like with hands—or mice dressed up. . . .'

Crampfurl stared into the hole. 'Mice dressed up?' he repeated uncertainly.

'Hundreds of them,' went on Mrs. Driver, 'running and squeaking. I saw them, I tell you!'

'Well, there ain't nothing there now,' said Crampfurl, and he gave a final stir round with his boot.

'Then they've run away,' she cried, 'under the floor . . . up inside the walls . . . the place is alive with them.'

'Well,' said Crampfurl stolidly, 'maybe. But if you ask me, I think it's that boy—where he hides things.' His eye brightened and he went down on one knee. 'Where he's got the ferret, I shouldn't wonder.'

'Listen,' cried Mrs. Driver, and there was a despairing note in her voice, 'you've got to listen. This wasn't no boy and it wasn't no ferret.' She reached for the back of

the chair and lowered herself clumsily on to the floor; she
came beside him to the edge of the hole. 'They had hands
and faces, I tell you. Look,' she said, pointing, 'see that?
It's a bed. And now I come to think of it one of 'em
was in it.'

'Now you come to think of it,' said Crampfurl.

'Yes,' went on Mrs. Driver firmly, 'and there's something else I come to think of. Remember that girl, Rosa
Pickhatchet?'

'The one that was simple?'

'Well, simple or not, she saw one—on the drawing-room
mantelpiece, with a beard.'

'One what?' asked Crampfurl.

Mrs. Driver glared at him. 'What I've been telling you
about—one of these—these——'

'Mice dressed up?' said Crampfurl.

'Not mice!' Mrs. Driver almost shouted. 'Mice don't
have beards.'

'But you said——' began Crampfurl.

'Yes, I know I said it. Not that these had beards. But
what would you call them? What could they be but mice?'

'Not so loud!' whispered Crampfurl. 'You'll wake the
house up.'

'They can't hear,' said Mrs. Driver, 'not through the
baize door.' She went to the stove and picked up the
fire-tongs. 'And what if they do? We ain't done nothing.
Move over,' she went on, 'and let me get at the hole.'

One by one Mrs. Driver picked things out—with many
shocked gasps, cries of amazement, and did-you-evers. She
made two piles on the floor—one of valuables and one of

what she called 'rubbish.' Curious objects dangled from the tongs: 'Would you believe it—her best lace handkerchiefs! Look, here's another . . . and another! And my big mattress needle—I knew I had one—my silver thimble, if you please, and one of hers! And look, oh my, at the wools . . . the cottons! No wonder you can never find a reel of white cotton if you want one. Potatoes . . . nuts . . . look at this, a pot of caviar—CAVIAR! No, it's too much, it really is. Doll's chairs . . . tables . . . and look at all this blotting-paper—so that's where it goes! Oh, my goodness gracious!' she cried suddenly, her eyes staring. 'What's this?' Mrs. Driver laid down the tongs and leaned over the hole—tentatively and fearfully as though afraid of being stung. 'It's a watch—an emerald watch—her watch! And she's never missed it!' Her voice rose. 'And it's going! Look, you can see by the kitchen clock! Twenty-five past twelve!' Mrs. Driver sat down suddenly on a hard chair; her eyes were staring and her face looked white and flabby, as though deflated. 'You know what this means?' she said to Crampfurl.

'No?' he said.

'The police,' said Mrs. Driver, 'that's what this means —a case for the police.'

CHAPTER EIGHTEEN

THE boy lay, trembling a little, beneath the bed-clothes. The screwdriver was under his mattress. He had heard the alarm clock; he had heard Mrs. Driver exclaim on the stairs and he had run. The candle on the table beside his bed still smelt a little and the wax must still be warm. He lay there waiting, but they did not come upstairs. After hours, it seemed, he heard the hall clock strike one. All seemed quiet below, and at last he slipped out of bed and crept along the passage to the head of the stairway. There he sat for a while, shivering a little, and gazing downwards into the darkened hall. There was no sound but the steady tick of the clock and occasionally that shuffle or whisper which might be wind, but which, as he knew, was the sound of the house itself—the sigh of the tired floors and the ache of knotted wood. So quiet it was that at last he found courage to move and to tiptoe down the staircase and along the kitchen passage. He listened awhile outside the baize door, and at length, very gently, he pushed it open. The kitchen was silent and filled with greyish darkness. He felt, as Mrs. Driver had done, along the shelf for the matches and he struck a light. He saw the gaping hole in the floor and the objects piled beside it and, in the same flash, he saw a candle on the shelf. He lit it clumsily, with trembling hands. Yes, there they lay—the contents of the little home —higgledy-piggledy on the boards and the tongs lay beside

them.   Mrs. Driver had carried away all she considered
valuable and had left the 'rubbish.'   And rubbish it looked
thrown   down   like   this—balls   of   wool,   old   potatoes,
odd pieces of doll's furniture, match-boxes, cotton reels,
crumpled squares of blotting-paper. . . .

He knelt down.   The 'house' itself was a shambles—
partitions fallen, earth floors revealed (where Pod had dug
down to give greater height to the rooms), match-sticks, an
old cog-wheel, onion skins, scattered bottle-tops. . . .   The
boy stared, blinking his eyelids and tilting the candle so that
the grease ran hot on his hand.   Then he got up from his
knees and, crossing the kitchen on tiptoe, he closed the
scullery door.   He came back to the hole and, leaning
down, he called softly: 'Arrietty . . . Arrietty!'   After a
while he called again.   Something else fell hot on his hand:
it was a tear from his eye.   Angrily he brushed it away,
and, leaning farther into the hole, he called once more.
'Pod,' he whispered.   'Homily!'

They appeared so quietly that at first, in the wavering
light of the candle, he did not see them.
Silent they stood, looking up at him
with scared white faces from what
had been the passage outside
the store-rooms.

'Where have you been?'
asked the boy.

Pod cleared his throat.
'Up at the end of the
passage.   Under the
clock.'

'I've got to get you out,' said the boy.

'Where to?' asked Pod.

'I don't know.   What about the attic?'

'That ain't no good,' said Pod.   'I heard them talking. They're going to get the police and a cat and the sanitary inspector and the rat-catcher from the town hall at Leighton Buzzard.'

They were all silent.   Little eyes stared at big eyes. 'There won't be nowhere in the house that's safe,' Pod said at last.   And no one moved.

'What about the doll's house on the top shelf in the schoolroom?' suggested the boy.   'Even a cat can't get there.'

Homily gave a little moan of assent.   'Yes,' she said, 'the doll's house. . . .'

'No,' said Pod in the same expressionless voice, 'you can't live on a shelf.   Maybe the cat can't get up, but no more can't you get down.   You're stuck.   You got to have water.'

'I'd bring you water,' said the boy; he touched the pile of 'rubbish.'   'And there are beds and things here.'

'No,' said Pod, 'a shelf ain't no good.   Besides, you'll be going soon, or so they say.'

'Oh, Pod,' pleaded Homily in a husky whisper, 'there's stairs in the doll's house, and two bedrooms, and a diningroom, and a kitchen.   And a bathroom,' she said.

'But it's up by the ceiling,' Pod explained wearily.   'You got to eat, haven't you,' he asked, 'and drink?'

'Yes, Pod, I know.   But——'

'There ain't no buts,' said Pod.   He drew a long breath. We got to emigrate,' he said.

'Oh,' moaned Homily softly and Arrietty began to cry.

'Now don't take on,' said Pod in a tired voice.

Arrietty had covered her face with her hands and her tears ran through her fingers; the boy, watching, saw them glisten in the candlelight. 'I'm not taking on,' she gasped, 'I'm so happy . . . happy.'

'You mean,' said the boy to Pod, but with one eye on Arrietty, 'you'll go to the badger's set?' He too felt a mounting excitement.

'Where else?' asked Pod.

'Oh, my goodness gracious!' moaned Homily, and sat down on the broken match-box chest of drawers.

'But you've got to go somewhere to-night,' said the boy. 'You've got to go somewhere before to-morrow morning.'

'Oh, my goodness gracious!' moaned Homily again.

'He's right at that,' said Pod. 'Can't cross them fields in the dark. Bad enough getting across them in daylight.'

'I know,' cried Arrietty. Her wet face glistened in the candlelight; it was alight and tremulous and she raised her arms a little as though about to fly, and she swayed as she balanced on her toe-tips. 'Let's go to the doll's house just for to-night and to-morrow'—she closed her eyes against the brightness of the vision—'to-morrow the boy will take us—take us——' and she could not say to where.

'Take us?' cried Homily in a strange hollow voice. 'How?'

'In his pockets,' chanted Arrietty; 'won't you?' Again she swayed, with lighted upturned face.

'Yes,' he said, 'and bring the luggage up afterwards—in a fish basket.'

'Oh, my goodness!' moaned Homily.

'I'll pick all the furniture out of this pile here. Or most of it. They'll hardly notice. And anything else you want.'

'Tea,' murmured Homily. 'Enough for our lifetimes.'

'All right,' said the boy. 'I'll get a pound of tea. And coffee too if you like. And cooking pots. And matches. You'll be all right,' he said.

'But what do they eat?' wailed Homily. 'Caterpillars?'

'Now, Homily,' said Pod, 'don't be foolish. Lupy was always a good manager.'

'But Lupy isn't there,' said Homily. 'Berries. Do they eat berries? How do they cook? Out of doors?'

'Now, Homily,' said Pod, 'we'll see all that when we get there.'

'I couldn't light a fire of sticks,' said Homily, 'not in the wind. What if it rains?' she asked. 'How do they cook in the rain?'

'Now, Homily——' began Pod—he was beginning to lose patience—but Homily rushed on.

'Could you get us a couple of tins of sardines to take?' she asked the boy. 'And some salt? And some candles? And matches? And could you bring us the carpets from the doll's house?'

'Yes,' said the boy, 'I could. Of course I could. Anything you want.'

'All right,' said Homily. She still looked wild, partly because some of her hair had rolled out of the curlers, but she seemed appeased. 'How are you going to get us upstairs? Up to the schoolroom?'

The boy looked down at his pocketless night-shirt. 'I'll carry you,' he said.

'How?' asked Homily. 'In your hands?'

'Yes,' said the boy.

'I'd rather die,' said Homily. 'I'd rather stay right here and be eaten by the rat-catcher from the town hall at Leighton Buzzard.'

The boy looked round the kitchen; he seemed bewildered. 'Shall I carry you in the peg-bag?' he asked at last, seeing it hanging in its usual place on the handle of the scullery door.

'All right,' said Homily. 'Take out the pegs first.'

But she walked into it bravely enough when he laid it out on the floor. It was soft and floppy and made of woven raffia. When he picked it up Homily shrieked and clung to Pod and Arrietty. 'Oh,' she gasped as the bag swayed a little, 'oh, I can't! Stop it! Put me out! Oh! Oh!' And, clutching and slipping, they fell into a tangle at the bottom.

'Be quiet, Homily, can't you!' exclaimed Pod angrily, and held her tightly by the ankle. It was not easy to control her as he was lying on his back with his face pushed forward on his chest and one leg, held upright by the side of the bag, somewhere above his head. Arrietty climbed up, away from them, clinging to the knots of raffia, and looked out over the edge.

'Oh, I can't! I can't!' cried Homily. 'Stop it, Pod. I'm dying. Tell him to put us down.'

'Put us down,' said Pod in his patient way, 'just for a moment. That's right. On the floor,' and, as once again the bag was placed beside the hole, they all ran out.

'Look here,' said the boy unhappily to Homily, 'you've got to try.'

'She'll try all right,' said Pod. 'Give her a breather, and take it slower, if you see what I mean.'

'All right,' agreed the boy, 'but there isn't much time. Come on,' he said nervously, 'hop in.'

'Listen!' cried Pod sharply, and froze.

The boy, looking down, saw their three upturned faces catching the light—like pebbles they looked, still and stony, against the darkness within the hole. And then in a flash they were gone—the boards were empty and the hole was bare. He leaned into it. 'Pod!' he called in a frantic whisper. 'Homily! Come back!' And then he too became frozen, stooped and rigid above the hole. The scullery door creaked open behind him.

It was Mrs. Driver. She stood there silent, this time in her night-dress. Turning, the boy stared up at her. 'Hallo,' he said, uncertainly, after a moment.

She did not smile, but something lightened in her eyes —a malicious gleam, a look of triumph. She carried a candle which shone upwards on her face, streaking it strangely with light and shadow. 'What are you doing down here?' she asked.

He stared at her, but he did not speak.

'Answer me,' she said. 'And what are you doing with the peg-bag?'

Still he stared at her, almost stupidly. 'The peg-bag?'

he repeated and looked down as though surprised to see it in his hand. 'Nothing,' he said.

'Was it you who put the watch in the hole?'

'No,' he said, staring up at her again, 'it was there already.'

'Ah,' she said and smiled, 'so you knew it was there?'

'No,' he said; 'I mean yes.'

'Do you know what you are?' asked Mrs. Driver, watching him closely. 'You are a sneaking, thieving, noxious little dribbet of no-good!'

His face quivered. 'Why?' he said.

'You know why. You're a wicked, black-hearted, fribbling little pickpocket. That's what you are. And so are they. They're nasty little crafty, scampy, scurvy, squeaking little——'

'No they're not,' he put in quickly.

'And you're in league with them!' She came across to him and, taking him by the upper arm, she jerked him to his feet. 'You know what they do with thieves?' she asked.

'No,' he said.

'They lock them up. That's what they do with thieves. And that's what's going to happen to you!'

'I'm not a thief,' cried the boy, his lips trembling, 'I'm a borrower.'

'A what?' She swung him round by tightening the grip on his arm.

'A borrower,' he repeated; there were tears on his eyelids; he hoped they would not fall.

'So that's what you call it!' she exclaimed (as he

had done—so long ago, it seemed now—that day with Arrietty).

'That's their name,' he said. 'The kind of people they are—they're Borrowers.'

'Borrowers, eh?' repeated Mrs. Driver wonderingly. She laughed. 'Well, they've done all the borrowing they're ever going to do in this house!' She began to drag him towards the door.

The tears spilled over his eyelids and ran down his cheeks. 'Don't hurt them,' he begged. 'I'll move them. I promise. I know how.'

Mrs. Driver laughed again and pushed him roughly through the green baize door. 'They'll be moved all right,' she said. 'Don't worry. The rat-catcher will know how. Crampfurl's old cat will know how. So will the sanitary inspector. And the fire-brigade, if need be. The police'll know how, I shouldn't wonder. No need to worry about moving them. Once you've found the nest,' she went on, dropping her voice to a vicious whisper as they passed Aunt Sophy's door, 'the rest is easy!'

She pushed him into the schoolroom and locked the door and he heard the boards of the passage creak beneath her tread as, satisfied, she moved away. He crept into bed then, because he was cold, and cried his heart out under the blankets.

CHAPTER NINETEEN

'AND that,' said Mrs. May, laying down her crochet hook, 'is really the end.'

Kate stared at her. 'Oh, it can't be,' she gasped, 'oh, please . . . *please*. . . .'

'The last square,' said Mrs. May, smoothing it out on her knee, 'the hundred and fiftieth. Now we can sew them together——'

'Oh,' said Kate, breathing again, 'the quilt! I thought you meant the story.'

'It's the end of the story too,' said Mrs. May absently, 'in a way. He never saw them again,' and she began to sort out the squares.

'But,' stammered Kate, 'you can't—I mean——' and she looked, quite suddenly, everything they had said she was—wild, self-willed, and all the rest of it. 'It's not fair,' she cried, 'it's cheating. It's——' Tears sprang to her eyes; she threw her work down on the table and her crochet hook after it, and she kicked the bag of wools which lay beside her on the carpet.

'Why, Kate, why?' Mrs. May looked genuinely surprised.

'Something more must have happened,' cried Kate angrily. 'What about the rat-catcher? And the policeman? And the——'

'But something more did happen,' said Mrs. May, 'a lot more happened. I'm going to tell you.'

'Then why did you say it was the end?'

'Because,' said Mrs. May (she still looked surprised), 'he never saw them again.'

'Then how can there be more?'

'Because,' said Mrs. May, 'there is more.'

Kate glared at her. 'All right,' she said, 'go on.'

Mrs. May looked back at her. 'Kate,' she said after a moment, 'stories never really end. They can go on and on and on. It's just that sometimes, at a certain point, one stops telling them.'

'But not at this kind of point,' said Kate.

'Well, thread your needle,' said Mrs. May, 'with grey wool, this time. And we'll sew these squares together. I'll start at the top and you can start at the bottom. First a grey square, then an emerald, then a pink, and so on——'

'Then you didn't really mean it,' said Kate irritably, trying to push the folded wool through the narrow eye of the needle, 'when you said he never saw them again?'

'But I did mean it,' said Mrs. May. 'I'm telling you just what happened. He had to leave suddenly—at the end of the week—because there was a boat for India and a family who could take him. And for the three days before he left they kept him locked up in those two rooms.'

'For three days!' exclaimed Kate.

'Yes. Mrs. Driver, it seemed, told Aunt Sophy that he had a cold. She was determined, you see, to keep him out of the way until she'd got rid of the Borrowers.'

'And did she?' asked Kate. 'I mean—did they all come? The policeman? And the rat-catcher? And the——'

'The sanitary inspector didn't come. At least, not while my brother was there. And they didn't have the rat-catcher from the town hall, but they had the local man. The policeman came——' Mrs. May laughed. 'During those three days Mrs. Driver used to give my brother a running commentary on what was going on below. She loved to grumble, and my brother, rendered harmless and shut away upstairs, became a kind of neutral. She used to bring his meals up, and, on that first morning, she brought all the doll's furniture up on the breakfast tray and made my brother climb the shelves and put it back in the doll's house. It was then she told him about the policeman. Furious he said she was.'

'Why?' asked Kate.

'Because the policeman turned out to be Nellie Runacre's son Ernie, a boy Mrs. Driver had chased many a time for stealing russet apples from the tree by the gate—"A nasty, thieving, good-for-nothing dribbet of no-good," she told my brother. "Sitting down there he is now, in the kitchen, large as life with his note-book out, laughing fit to bust . . . twenty-one, he says he is now, and as cheeky as you make 'em. . . ."'

'And was he,' asked Kate, round-eyed, 'a dribbet of no-good?'

'Of course not. Any more than my brother was. Ernie Runacre was a fine, upstanding young man and a credit to the police force. And he did not actually laugh at Mrs,

Driver when she told him her story, but he gave her what Crampfurl spoke of afterwards as "an old-fashioned look" when she described Homily in bed—"Take more water with it," it seemed to say.'

'More water with what?' asked Kate.

'The Fine Old Pale Madeira, I suppose,' said Mrs. May. 'And Great Aunt Sophy had the same suspicion: she was furious when she heard that Mrs. Driver had seen several little people when she herself on a full decanter had only risen to one or, at most, two. Crampfurl had to bring all the Madeira up from the cellar and stack the cases against the wall in a corner of Aunt Sophy's bedroom where, as she said, she could keep an eye on it.'

'Did they get a cat?' asked Kate.

'Yes, they did. But that wasn't much of a success either. It was Crampfurl's cat, a large yellow tom with white streaks in it. According to Mrs. Driver, it had only two ideas in its head—to get out of the house or into the larder. "Talk of borrowers," Mrs. Driver would say as she slammed down the fish-pie for my brother's luncheon, "that cat's a borrower, if ever there was one; borrowed the fish, that cat did, and a good half-bowl of egg sauce!' But the cat wasn't there long. The first thing the rat-catcher's terriers did was to chase it out of the house. There was a dreadful set-to, my brother said. They chased it everywhere—upstairs and downstairs, in and out all the rooms, barking their heads off. The last glimpse my brother had of the cat was streaking away through the spinney and across the fields with the terriers after it.'

'Did they catch it?'

'No,' Mrs. May laughed. 'It was still there when I went, a year later. A little morose, but as fit as a fiddle.'

'Tell about when *you* went.'

'Oh, I wasn't there long,' said Mrs. May rather hastily, 'and after that the house was sold. My brother never went back.'

Kate stared at her suspiciously, pressing her needle against the centre of her lower lip. 'So they never caught the little people?' she said at last.

Mrs. May's eyes flicked away. 'No, they never actually caught them, but'—she hesitated—'as far as my poor brother was concerned, what they did do seemed even worse.'

'What did they do?'

Mrs. May laid down her work and stared for a moment, thoughtfully, at her idle hands. 'I hated the rat-catcher,' she said suddenly.

'Why, did you know him?'

'Everybody knew him. He had a wall eye and his name was Rich William. He was also the pig-killer, and, well —he did other things as well—he had a gun, a hatchet, a spade, a pick-axe, and a contraption with bellows for smoking things out. I don't know what the smoke was exactly—poison fumes of some kind which he made himself from herbs and chemicals. I only remember the smell of it; it clung round the barns or wherever he'd been. You can imagine what my brother felt on that third day, the day he was leaving, when suddenly he smelled that smell. . . .

'He was all dressed and ready to go. The bags were

packed and down in the hall. Mrs. Driver came and unlocked the door and took him down the passage to Aunt Sophy. He stood there, stiff and pale, in gloves and overcoat beside the curtained bed. "Seasick already?" Aunt Sophy mocked him, peering down at him over the edge of the great mattress.

'"No," he said, "it's that smell."

'Aunt Sophy lifted her nose. She sniffed. "What smell is it, Driver?"

'"It's the rat-catcher, my lady," explained Mrs. Driver, reddening, "down in the kitchen."

'"What!" exclaimed Aunt Sophy, "are you smoking them out?" and she began to laugh. "Oh dear . . . oh dear!" she gasped, "but if you don't like them, Driver, the remedy's simple."

'"What is that, my lady?" asked Mrs. Driver coldly, but even her chins were red.

'Helpless with mirth Aunt Sophy waved a ringed hand towards her, her eyes were screwed up and her shoulders shaking: "Keep the bottle corked," she managed at last and motioned them weakly away. They heard her laughing still as they went on down the stairs.

'"She don't believe in them," muttered Mrs. Driver, and she tightened her grip on my brother's arm. "More fool her! She'll change her tune, like enough, when I take them up afterwards, laid out in sizes, on a clean piece of newspaper . . ." and she dragged him roughly across the hall.

'The clock had been moved, exposing the wainscot, and, as my brother saw at once, the hole had been blocked and sealed. The front door was open as usual and the sunshine streamed in. The bags stood there beside the fibre mat, cooking a little in the golden warmth. The fruit trees beyond the bank had shed their petals and were lit with tender green, transparent in the sunlight. "Plenty of time," said Mrs. Driver, glancing up at the clock, "the cab's not due 'til three-thirty——'

'"The clock's stopped," said my brother.

'Mrs. Driver turned. She was wearing her hat and her best black coat, ready to take him to the station. She looked strange and tight and chapel-going—not a bit like "Driver." "So it has," she said; her jaw dropped and her cheeks became heavy and pendulous. "It's moving it," she decided after a moment. "It'll be all right," she went on, "once we get it back. Mr. Frith comes on Monday," and she dragged again at his arm above the elbow.

'"Where are we going?" he asked, holding back.

'"Along to the kitchen. We've got a good ten minutes. Don't you want to see them caught?"

'"No," he said, "no!" and pulled away from her.

'Mrs. Driver stared at him, smiling a little; there was a strange expression on her face, both cruel and curious. "I do," she said; "I'd like to see 'em close. He puffs this stuff in and they come running out. At least, that's how it works with rats. But first, he says, you block up all the exits . . ." and her eyes followed his to the hole below the wainscot.

'"How did they find it?" the boy asked (puttied it looked, and with a square of brown paper pasted on crooked).

'"Rich William found it. That's his job."

'"They could unstick that," said the boy after a moment.

'Mrs. Driver laughed. "Oh no they couldn't! Cemented, that is. A great block of it, right inside, with a sheet of iron across from the front of that old stove in the outhouse. He and Crampfurl had to have the morning-room floor up to get at it. All Tuesday they was working, up till tea-time. We aren't going to have no more capers of that kind. Not under the clock. Once you get that clock back, it can't be moved again in a hurry. Not if you want it to keep time, it can't. See where it's stood—where the floor's washed away like?" It was then my brother saw, for the first and last time, that raised platform of unscrubbed stone. "Come on now," said Mrs. Driver and took him by the arm. "We'll hear the cab from the kitchen."

'But the kitchen, as she dragged him past the baize door, seemed a babel of sound. No approaching cab could be heard here—what with yelps and barks and stampings and excited voices. "Steady, steady, steady, steady, steady . . . " Crampfurl was saying, on one loud note, as he held back the rat-catcher's terriers which shrilled and panted on the leash. The policeman was there, Nellie Runacre's son Ernie. He had come out of interest and stood back from the others a little, in view of his calling, with a cup of tea in his hand and his helmet pushed off his forehead. But his face was pink with boyish excitement and he stirred the teaspoon round and round. "Seeing's believing!" he said cheerfully to Mrs. Driver when he saw her come in at the door. A boy from the village was there with a ferret. It kept sort of pouring out of his pocket, my brother said, and the boy kept pushing it back. Rich William himself was crouched on the floor by the hole. He had lighted something beneath a piece of sacking and the stench of its smouldering eddied about the room. He was working the bellows now, with infinite care, stooping over them—rapt and tense.

'My brother stood there as though in a dream ("Perhaps it was a dream," he said to me later—much later, after we were all grown up). He gazed round the kitchen. He saw the sunlit fruit trees through the window and a bough of the cherry-tree which stood upon the bank; he saw the empty tea-cups on the table, with spoons stuck in them and one without a saucer; he saw, propped against the wall close beside the baize door, the rat-catcher's belongings— a frayed coat, patched with leather; a bundle of rabbit snares; two sacks; a spade, a gun, and a pick-axe. . . .

'"Stand by now,"' Rich William was saying; there was a rising note of excitement in his voice, but he did not turn his head. "Stand by. Ready now to slip the dogs."

'Mrs. Driver let go my brother's arm and moved towards the hole. "Keep back," said the rat-catcher, without turning. "Give us room——" and Mrs. Driver backed nervously towards the table. She put a chair beside it and half raised one knee, but lowered it again when she caught Ernie Runacre's mocking glance. "All right, ma," he said, cocking one eyebrow, "we'll give you a leg up when the time comes," and Mrs. Driver threw him a furious look; she snatched up the three cups from the table and stumped away with them, angrily, into the scullery. "Good-for-nothing seemingless smutch of something-or-other . . ." my brother heard her mutter as she brushed

past him.   And at those words, suddenly, my brother came
to life. . . .

'He threw a quick glance about the kitchen: the men
were absorbed; all eyes were on the rat-catcher—except
those of the village boy who was getting out his ferret.
Stealthily my brother drew off his gloves and began to
move   backwards . . . slowly . . . slowly . . . towards   the
green baize door; as he moved, gently stuffing his gloves
into his pocket, he kept his eyes on the group around the
hole.   He paused a moment beside the rat-catcher's tools,
and stretched out a wary, groping hand; his fingers closed
at last on a wooden handle—smooth it was and worn with
wear; he glanced down quickly to make sure—yes, it was,
as he hoped, the pick-axe.   He leaned back a little and
pushed—almost imperceptibly—against the door with his
shoulders: it opened sweetly, in its silent way.   Not one
of the men had looked up.   "Steady now," the rat-
catcher was saying, stooping closely over the bellows, "it
takes a moment like to go right through . . . there ain't
much ventilation, not under a floor. . . ."

'My brother slid through the barely opened door and it
sighed to behind him, closing out the noise.   He took a
few steps on tiptoe down the dark kitchen passage and
then he ran.

There was the hall again, steeped in sunshine, with his
bags beside the door.   He bumped against the clock and
it struck a note, a trembling note—urgent and deep.   He
raised the pick-axe to the height of his shoulder and aimed
a sideways blow at the hole below the wainscot.   The paper
tore, a few crumbs of plaster fell out, and the pick-axe

rebounded sharply, jarring his hands. There was indeed iron behind the cement—something immovable. Again he struck. And again and again. The wainscot above the hole became split and scratched, and the paper hung down in strips, but still the pick-axe bounced. It was no good; his hands, wet with sweat, were sliding and slipping on the

wood. He paused for breath and, looking out, he saw the cab. He saw it on the road, beyond the hedge on the far side of the orchard; soon it would reach the russet apple-tree beside the gate; soon it would turn into the drive. He glanced up at the clock. It was ticking steadily

—the result, perhaps, of his knock. The sound gave him comfort and steadied his thumping heart; time, that's what he needed, a little more time. "It takes a moment like," the rat-catcher had said, "to go right through . . . there ain't much ventilation, not under a floor. . . ."

"'Ventilation"—that was the word, the saving word. Pick-axe in hand my brother ran out of the door. He stumbled once on the gravel path and nearly fell; the pick-axe handle came up and struck him a sharp blow on the temple. Already, when he reached it, a thin filament of smoke was eddying out of the grating and he thought, as he ran towards it, that there was a flicker of movement against the darkness between the bars. And that was where they would be, of course, to get the air. But he did not stop to make sure. Already he heard behind him the crunch of wheels on the gravel and the sound of the horse's hoofs. He was not, as I have told you, a very strong little boy, and he was only nine (not ten, as he had boasted to Arrietty) but, with two great blows on the brickwork, he dislodged one end of the grating. It fell down sideways, slightly on a slant, hanging—it seemed—by one nail. Then he clambered up the bank and threw the pick-axe with all his might into the long grass beyond the cherry-tree. He remembered thinking as he stumbled back, sweaty and breathless, towards the cab, how that too—the loss of the pick-axe—would cause its own kind of trouble later.'

CHAPTER TWENTY

'But,' exclaimed Kate, 'didn't he see them come out?'

'No. Mrs. Driver came along then, in a flurry of annoyance, because they were late for the train. She bustled him into the cab because she wanted to get back again, she said, as fast as she could to be "in at the death."'

Kate was silent a moment, looking down. 'So that *is* the end,' she said at last.

'Yes,' said Mrs. May, 'it could be.'

'But'—Kate raised a worried face—'perhaps they didn't escape through the grating? Perhaps they were killed after all?'

'Oh, they escaped all right,' said Mrs. May lightly.

'But how do you know?'

'I just know,' said Mrs. May.

'But how did they get across those fields? With the cows and things? And the crows?'

'They walked, I suppose. The Hendrearys did it. People can do anything when they have a mind to.'

'But poor Homily! She'd be so upset.'

'Yes, she was upset,' said Mrs. May.

'And how would they know the way?'

'By the gas-pipe,' said Mrs. May. 'There's a kind of ridge all along, through the spinney and across the fields. You see, when men dig a trench and put a pipe in it all the earth they've dug out doesn't quite fit when they've put it back. The ground looks different.'

'But poor Homily—she didn't have her tea or her furniture or her carpets or anything. Do you suppose they took anything?'

'Oh, people always grab something,' said Mrs. May shortly, 'the oddest things sometimes—if you've read about shipwrecks.' She spoke hurriedly, as though she were tired of the subject. 'Do be careful, child—not grey next to pink. You'll have to unpick it.'

'But,' went on Kate in a despairing voice as she picked up the scissors, 'Homily would hate to arrive there all poor and dessitute in front of Lupy.'

'Destitute,' said Mrs. May patiently, 'and Lupy wasn't there remember. Lupy never came back. And Homily would tie on her apron and think at once: "These poor motherless boys!"'

'Were they all boys?'

'Yes, Harpsichords and Clocks. And they'd spoil Arrietty dreadfully.'

'What did they eat? Did they eat caterpillars, do you think?'

'Oh, goodness, child, of course they didn't. They could live very well. Badgers' sets are almost like villages—full of passages and chambers and storehouses. They could gather hazel-nuts and beech-nuts and chestnuts; they could gather corn—which they could store and grind into flour, just as humans do—it was all there for them: they didn't even have to plant it. They had honey. They could make elderflower tea and lime tea. They had hips and haws and blackberries and sloes and wild strawberries. The boys could fish in the stream and a minnow to them would be as big as a mackerel is to you. They had birds' eggs—any amount of them—for custards and cakes and omelettes. You see, they would know where to look for things. And they had greens and salads, of course. Think of a salad made of those tender shoots of young hawthorn—bread and cheese we used to call it—with sorrel and dandelion and a sprinkling of thyme and wild garlic. Homily was a good cook remember. It wasn't for nothing that the Clocks had lived under the kitchen.'

'But the danger,' cried Kate; 'the weasels and the crows and the stoats and all those things?'

'Yes,' agreed Mrs. May, 'of course there was danger. There's danger everywhere, but no more for them than for many human beings. At least, they didn't have *wars*. And what about the early settlers in America? And those people who farm in the middle of the big game country in

Africa and on the edge of the jungles in India? They get
to know the habits of the animals. Few animals kill for
the sake of killing. Even rabbits know when a fox isn't
hunting; they will run quite near him when he's full fed
and lazing in the sun. These were boys remember; they
would learn to hunt for the pot and how to protect themselves. I don't suppose Arrietty and Homily would wander
far afield.'

'Arrietty would,' said Kate.

'Yes,' agreed Mrs. May, laughing, 'I suppose Arrietty
might.'

'So they'd have meat?' said Kate.

'Yes, sometimes. But Borrowers are Borrowers; not
killers. I think,' said Mrs. May, 'that if a stoat, say, killed
a partridge they would borrow a leg!'

'And if a fox killed a rabbit they'd use the fur?'

'Yes, for rugs and things.'

'Supposing,' said Kate, 'when they had a little roast, they
skinned haws and baked them, would they taste like
browned potatoes?'

'Perhaps,' said Mrs. May.

'But they couldn't cook in the badger's set. I suppose
they cooked out of doors. How would they keep warm
then in winter?'

'Do you know what I think?' said Mrs. May; she laid
down her work and leaned forward a little. 'I think that
they didn't live in the badger's set at all. I think they used
it, with all its passages and store-rooms, as a great honey-
comb of an entrance hall. None but they would know the
secret way through the tunnels which led at last to their

home. Borrowers love passages and they love gates; and they love to live a long way from their own front doors.'

'Where *would* they live then?'

'I was wondering,' said Mrs. May, 'about the gas-pipe——'

'Oh yes,' cried Kate, 'I see what you mean!'

'The soil's all soft and sandy up there. I think they'd go right through the badger's set and dig out a circular chamber, level with the gas-pipe. And off this chamber, all around it, there'd be little rooms, like cabins. And I think,' said Mrs. May, 'that they'd bore three little pin-holes in the gas-pipe. One would be so tiny that you could hardly see it and that one would be always alight. The other two would have stoppers in them which, when they wanted to light the gas, they would pull out. They would light the bigger ones from the small burner. That's where they'd cook and that would give them light.'

'But would they be so clever?'

'But they are clever,' Mrs. May assured her, 'very clever. Much too clever to live near a gas-pipe and not use it. They're Borrowers remember.'

'But they'd want a little air-hole?'

'Oh,' said Mrs. May quickly, 'they did have one.'

'How do you know?' asked Kate.

'Because once when I was up there I smelled hot-pot.'

'Oh,' cried Kate excitedly; she twisted round and knelt up on the hassock, 'so you did go up there? So that's how you know! You saw them too!'

'No, no,' said Mrs. May, drawing back a little in her chair, 'I never saw them. Never.'

'But you went up there?   You know something!   I can see you know!'

'Yes, I went up there.'   Mrs. May stared back into Kate's eager face; hesitant, she seemed, almost a little guilty. 'Well,' she conceded at last, 'I'll tell you.   For what it's worth.   When I went to stay in that house it was just before Aunt Sophy went into the nursing home.   I knew the place was going to be sold, so I'—again Mrs. May hesitated, almost shyly—'well, I took all the furniture out of the doll's house and put it in a pillow-case and took it up there.   I bought things too out of my pocket money—tea and coffee beans and salt and pepper and cloves and a great packet of lump sugar.   And I took a whole lot of little pieces of silk which were over from making a patchwork quilt.   And I took them some fish-bones for needles.   I took the tiny thimble I had got in a Christmas pudding and a whole collection of scraps and cracker things I'd had in a chocolate box——'

'But you never saw them!'

'No.   I never saw them.   I sat for hours against the bank below the hawthorn hedge.   It was a lovely bank, twined with twisted hawthorn roots and riddled with sandy holes and there were wood-violets and primroses and early campion.   From the top of the bank you could see for miles across the fields: you could see the woods and the valleys and the twisting lanes; you could see the chimneys of the house.'

'Perhaps it was the wrong place.'

'I don't think so.   Sitting there in the grass, half dreaming and watching beetles and ants, I found an oak-apple; it was smooth and polished and dry and there was a hole bored in one side of it and a slice off the top——'

'The teapot!' exclaimed Kate.

'I think so. I looked everywhere, but I couldn't find the quill spout. I called then, down all the holes—as my brother had done. But no one answered. Next day, when I went up there, the pillow-case had gone.'

'And everything in it?'

'Yes, everything. I searched the ground for yards around, in case there might be a scrap of silk or a coffee bean. But there was nothing. Of course, somebody passing might just have picked it up and carried it away. That was the day,' said Mrs. May, smiling, 'that I smelled hot-pot.'

'And which was the day,' asked Kate, 'that you found Arrietty's diary?'

Mrs. May laid down her work. 'Kate,' she began in a startled voice, and then, uncertainly, she smiled, 'what makes you say that?' Her cheeks had become quite pink.

'I guessed,' said Kate. 'I knew there was something— something you wouldn't tell me. Like—like reading somebody else's diary.'

'It wasn't the diary,' said Mrs. May hastily, but her cheeks had become even pinker. 'It was the book called "Memoranda," the book with blank pages. That's where she'd written it. And it wasn't on that day I found it, but three weeks later—the day before I left.'

Kate sat silent, staring at Mrs. May. After a while she drew a long breath. 'Then that proves it,' she said finally, 'underground chamber and all.'

'Not quite,' said Mrs. May.

'Why not?' asked Kate.

'Arrietty used to make her "e's" like little half-moons with a stroke in the middle——'

'Well?' said Kate.

Mrs. May laughed and took up her work again. 'My brother did too,' she said.

THE BORROWERS AFIELD

for
CHARLOTTE AND VICTORIA

CHAPTER ONE

'WHAT HAS BEEN, MAY BE'
First recorded eclipse of the moon, 721 B.C.
[*Extract from Arrietty's Diary and Proverb Book, March 19th.*]

IT WAS Kate who, long after she was grown up, completed the story of the borrowers. She wrote it all out, many years later, for her four children, and compiled it as you compile a case-history or a biographical novel from all kinds of evidence—things she remembered, things she had been told, and one or two things—we had better confess it—at which she just guessed. The most remarkable piece of evidence was a miniature Victorian note-book with gilt-edged pages, discovered by Kate in a gamekeeper's cottage on the Studdington estate near Leighton Buzzard, Bedfordshire.

Old Tom Goodenough, the gamekeeper, had never wanted the story put in writing, but as he had been dead now for so many years and as Kate's children were so very much alive, she thought perhaps that wherever he might be (and with a name like Goodenough it was bound to be heaven) he would have overcome this kind of prejudice and would by now perhaps forgive her and understand. Anyway, Kate, after some thought, decided to take the risk.

When Kate had been a child herself and was living with her parents in London, an old lady shared their home (she was, I think, some kind of relation): her name was Mrs May. And it was Mrs May, on those long winter evenings beside the fire when she was teaching Kate to crochet, who had first told Kate about the borrowers.

At the time, Kate never doubted their existence—a race of tiny creatures, as like to humans as makes no matter, who live their secret lives under the floors and behind the wainscots of certain quiet old houses. It was only later that she began to wonder (and how wrong she was you will very soon be told. There were stranger happenings to come—developments more unlooked for and extraordinary than any Mrs May had dreamed of).

The original story had smacked a little of hearsay: Mrs May admitted—in fact, had been at some pains to convince Kate—that she, Mrs May, had never actually seen a borrower herself; any knowledge of such beings she had gained at second hand from her younger brother, who she admitted was a little boy with not only a vivid imagination but well known to be a tease. So there you were, Kate decided—thinking it over afterwards—you could take it or leave it.

And, truth to tell, in the year or so which followed Kate tended rather to leave it: the story of the borrowers became pushed away in the back of her mind with other childish fantasies. During this year she changed her school, made new friends, acquired a dog, took up skating, and learned to ride a bicycle. And there was no thought of 'borrowers' in Kate's mind (nor did she notice the undercurrent of excitement in Mrs May's usually calm voice) when, one morning at breakfast in early spring, Mrs May passed a letter across the table, saying: 'This will interest you, Kate, I think.'

It didn't interest Kate a bit (she was about eleven years

old at the time): she read it through twice in a bewildered kind of way but could make neither head nor tail of it.   It was a lawyer's letter from a firm called Jobson, Thring, Beguid & Beguid; not only was it full of long words like 'beneficiary' and 'disentailment' but even the medium-sized words were arranged in such a manner that, to Kate, they made no sense at all (what, for instance, could 'vacant possession' mean?   However much you thought about it, it could only describe a state of affairs which was manifestly quite impossible).   Names there were in plenty—Studdington, Goodenough, Amberforce, Pocklinton—and quite a family of people who spelled their name 'deceased' with a small 'd.'

'Thank you very much,' Kate had said politely, passing it back.

'I thought, perhaps,' said Mrs May (and her cheeks, Kate noticed, looked slightly flushed as though with shyness), 'you might like to go down with me.'

'Go down where?' asked Kate, in her vaguest manner.

'My dear Kate,' exclaimed Mrs May, 'what was the point of showing you the letter? To Leighton Buzzard, of course.'

Leighton Buzzard?   Years afterwards, when Kate described this scene to her children, she would tell them how, at these words, her heart began to bump long before her mind took in their meaning: Leighton Buzzard . . . she knew the name, of course: the name of an English country town . . . somewhere in Bedfordshire, wasn't it?

'Where Great-aunt Sophy's house was,' said Mrs May, prompting her.   'Where my brother used to say he saw the borrowers.' And before Kate could get back her breath she went on, in a matter-of-fact voice: 'I have been left a little cottage, part of the Studdington estate, and,' her colour deepened as though what she was about to say now might sound slightly incredible, 'three hundred and fifty-five pounds. Enough,' she added, in happy wonderment, 'to do it up.'

Kate was silent. She stared at Mrs May, her clasped hands pressed against her middle as though to still the beating of her heart.

'Could we see the house?' she said at last, a kind of croak in her voice.

'Of course, that's why we're going.'

'I mean the big house, Aunt Sophy's house?'

'Oh, that house? Firbank Hall, it was called.' Mrs May seemed a little taken aback. 'I don't know. We could ask, perhaps; it depends of course on whoever is living there now.'

'I mean,' Kate went on, with controlled eagerness, 'even if we couldn't get inside, you could show me the grating, and Arrietty's bank; and even if they opened the front door only ever so little, you could show me where the clock was. You could kind of point with your finger, quickly . . .' and, as Mrs May still seemed to hesitate, Kate added suddenly on a note of anguish: 'You did believe in them, didn't you? Or was it'—her voice faltered—'only a story?'

'And what if it were only a story,' said Mrs May quickly, 'so long as it was a good story? Keep your sense of wonder, child, and don't be so literal. And anything we haven't experienced for ourselves sounds like a story. All we can ever do about such things is'—she hesitated, smiling at Kate's expression—'keep an open mind and try to sift the evidence.'

Sift the evidence? There was, Kate realized, calming down a little, a fair amount of that: even before Mrs May had spoken of such creatures, Kate had suspected their existence. How else to explain the steady, but inexplicable, disappearance of certain small objects about the house?

Not only safety-pins, needles, pencils, blotting-paper, match-boxes, and those sort of things, but, even in Kate's short life, she had noticed that if you did not open a drawer for any length of time you never found it quite as you left it: something was always missing—your best handkerchief, your only bodkin, your carnelian heart, your lucky six-pence. . . . 'But I *know* I put it in this drawer'—how often had she said these words herself, and how often had she heard them said? As for attics—'I am absolutely certain,' Kate's mother had wailed only last week, on her knees before an open trunk searching vainly for a pair of shoe buckles, 'that I put them in this box with the ostrich-fan. They were wrapped in a piece of black wadding and I slipped them here, just below the handle. . . .' And the same thing with writing-desks, sewing-baskets, button-boxes: there was never as much tea next day as you had seen in the caddy the evening before. Nor rice for that matter, nor lump sugar. Yes, Kate decided, evidence there was in plenty, if only one knew how to sift it.

'I suppose,' she remarked thoughtfully, as she began to fold up her napkin, 'some houses are more apt to have them than others.'

'Some houses,' said Mrs May, 'do not have them at all. And according to my brother,' she went on, 'it's the tidier houses, oddly enough, which attract them most. Borrowers, he used to say, are nervous people; they must know where things are kept and what each human being is likely to be doing at any hour of the day. In untidy, noisy, badly run houses, oddly enough, you can leave your belongings about with impunity—as far as borrowers are concerned, I mean.' And she gave a short laugh.

'Could borrowers live out of doors?' asked Kate suddenly.

'Not easily, no,' said Mrs May. 'They need human beings; they live by the same things human beings live by.'

'I was thinking,' went on Kate, 'about Pod and Homily, and little Arrietty. I mean—when they were smoked out from under the floor, how do you think they managed?'

'I often wonder,' said Mrs May.

'Do you think,' asked Kate, 'that Arrietty did become the last living borrower? Like your brother said she would?'

'Yes, he said that, didn't he—the last of her race? I sincerely hope not. It was unkind of him,' Mrs May added reflectively.

'I wonder, though, how they got across those fields? Do you think they ever did find the badgers' set?'

'We can't tell. I told you about the pillow-case incident —when I took all the doll's house furniture up there in a pillow-case?'

'And you smelled something cooking? But that doesn't say our family ever got there—Pod and Homily and

Arrietty. The cousins lived in the badgers' set too, didn't they—the Hendrearys? It might have been their cooking.'

'It might, of course,' said Mrs May.

Kate was silent for a while, lost in reflection; suddenly her whole face lit up and she swivelled round in her chair.

'If we do go,' she cried (and there was an awed look in her eyes as though vouchsafed by some glorious vision), 'where shall we stay? In an *inn*?'

CHAPTER TWO

'WITHOUT PAINS, NO GAINS'
British Residency at Manipur attacked 1891
[*Extract from Arrietty's Diary and Proverb Book, March 24th.*]

BUT NOTHING turns out in fact as you have pictured it; the 'inn' was a case in point—and so, alas, was Great-aunt Sophy's house. Neither of these, to Kate, were at all as they should be:

An inn, of course, was a place you came to at night, not at three o'clock in the afternoon, preferably a rainy night— wind, too, if it could be managed; and it should, of course, be situated on a moor ('bleak,' Kate knew, was the adjective here). And there should be scullions; mine host should be gravy-stained and broad in the beam with a tousled apron pulled across his stomach; and there should be a tall, dark stranger—the one who speaks to nobody—warming thin hands before the fire. And the fire should *be* a fire— crackling and blazing, laid with an impossible size log and roaring its great heart out up the chimney. And there should be some sort of cauldron, Kate felt, somewhere about—and a couple of mastiffs, perhaps, thrown in for good measure.

But, here, were none of these things: there was a quiet-voiced young woman in a white blouse who signed them in at the desk; there was a waitress called Maureen (blonde) and one called Margaret (mousy, with pebble glasses) and an elderly waiter, the back part of whose hair did not at all match the front; the fire was not made out of logs but of bored-looking coals tirelessly licked by an abject electric flicker; and (worst of all) standing in front of it, instead of a tall dark stranger, was Mr Beguid, the lawyer (pronounced 'Be good')—plump, pink, but curiously cool-looking, with his silvery hair and steel-grey eye.

But outside Kate saw the bright spring sunshine and she liked her bedroom with its view over the market-place, its tall mahogany wardrobe, and its constant H. and C.   And she knew that to-morrow they would see the house—this legendary, mysterious house which now so surprisingly had become real, built no longer of airy fantasy but, she gathered, of solid bricks and mortar, standing firmly in its own grounds two miles along the road.   Close enough, Kate realized, if only Mrs May would not talk so much with Mr Beguid, for them to have walked there after tea.

But when, next morning, they did walk there (Mrs May in her long, slightly deer-stalker-looking coat and with her rubber-tipped walking-stick made of cherry wood), Kate was disappointed; the house looked nothing at all like she had imagined it: a barrack of red brick, it appeared to her, with rows of shining windows staring blankly through her, as though they were blind.

'They've taken the creeper down,' said Mrs May (she too sounded a little surprised), but after a moment, as they stood there at the head of the drive, she rallied slightly and added on a brisker note: 'And quite right too—there's nothing like creeper for damaging brickwork,' and, as they began to walk on down the driveway, she went on to explain to Kate that this house had always been considered a particularly pure example of early Georgian architecture.

'Was it really *here*?' Kate kept asking in an incredulous voice as though Mrs May might have forgotten.

'Of course, my dear, don't be so silly.   This is where the apple-tree was, the russet apple by the gate . . . and the third window on the left, the one with bars across, used to

be my bedroom the last few times I slept here.   The night-nursery, of course, looks out over the back.   And there's the kitchen garden.   We used to jump off that wall, my brother and I, and on to the compost heap.   Ten feet high, it's supposed to be—I remember one day Crampfurl scolding us and measuring it with his besom.'

(Crampfurl?   So there had been such a person. . . .)

The front door stood open (as it must have stood, Kate realized suddenly, years ago on that never-to-be-forgotten day for Arrietty when she first saw the 'great out-doors'), and the early spring sunshine poured across the newly whitened step into the high dark hall beyond; it made a curtain of light through which it was hard to see. Beside the step, Kate noticed, was an iron shoe-scraper. Was this the one down which Arrietty had climbed? Her heart began to beat a little faster. 'Where's the grating?' she whispered, as Mrs May pulled the bell (they heard it jangle far off in the dim distance, miles away it seemed).

'The grating?' said Mrs May, stepping backwards on the gravel path and looking along the house front. 'There,' she said, with a slight nod—keeping her voice low. 'It's been repaired,' she whispered, 'but it's the same one.'

Kate wandered towards it: yes, there it was, the actual grating through which they had escaped—Pod, Homily, and little Arrietty; there was the greenish stain and a few bricks which looked newer than the others. It stood higher than she had imagined; they must have had a bit of a jump to get down. Going up to it, she stooped, trying to see inside; dank darkness, that was all. So this had been their home. . . .

'Kate!' called Mrs May softly, from beside the door-step (as Pod must have called that day to Arrietty when she ran off down the path), and Kate, turning, saw suddenly a sight she recognized, something which at last was like she had imagined it—the primrose bank. Tender, blue-green blades among the faded winter grasses—sown, spattered, almost drenched they seemed—with palest gold. And the azalea bush, Kate saw, had become a tree.

After a moment Mrs May called again and Kate came back to the front door. 'We'd better ring again,' she said, and once more they heard the ghostly jangle. 'It rings near the kitchen,' explained Mrs May, in a whisper, 'just beyond the green baize door.'

('The Green Baize Door' . . . she seemed, Kate thought, to speak these words in capitals.)

At last they saw a figure through the sunbeams; it was a slatternly girl in a wet, sack-cloth apron, her bare feet in run-down sandals.

'Yes?' she said, staring at them and frowning against the sun.

Mrs May stiffened. 'I wonder,' she said, 'if I could see the owner of the house?'

'You mean Mr Dawsett-Poole?' said the girl, 'or the headmaster?' She raised her forearm, shading her eyes, a wet floor-cloth, dripping slightly, clasped in her grimy hand.

'Oh!' exclaimed Mrs May. 'Is it a school?' Kate caught her breath—that, then, explained the barracky appearance.

'Well, it always has been, hasn't it?' said the girl.

'No,' replied Mrs May, 'not always. When I was a child I used to stay here. Perhaps, then, I might speak to who-ever is in charge?'

'There's only my mum,' said the girl; 'she's the care-taker. They're all away over Easter—the masters and that.'

'Well, in that case,' began Mrs May uncertainly, 'I mustn't trouble you——' and was preparing to turn away when Kate, standing her ground, addressed the girl: 'Can't we just see inside the hall?'

'Help yourself,' said the girl, looking mildly surprised, and she retreated slightly into the shadows as though to make way. 'It's okay by me.'

They stepped through the veil of sunlight into a dimmer

coolness.   Kate looked about her: it was wide and high and panelled and there were the stairs 'going up and up, world upon world, as Arrietty had described them'—all the same, it was nothing like she had imagined it.   The floor was covered with burnished, dark green linoleum; there was a sourish smell of soapy water and the clean smell of wax.

'There's a beautiful stone floor under this,' said Mrs May, tapping the linoleum with her rubber-tipped walking-stick.

The girl stared at them curiously for a moment and then, as though bored, she turned away and disappeared into the shadowy passage beyond the staircase, scuffling a little in her downtrodden shoes.

Kate, about to comment, felt a touch on her arm. 'Listen,' hissed Mrs May sharply; and Kate, holding her breath to complete the silence, heard a curious sound, a cross between a sigh and moan.   Mrs May nodded.   'That's it,' she whispered, 'the sound of the green baize door.'

'And where was the clock?' asked Kate.

Mrs May indicated a piece of wall, now studded with a row of coat pegs.   'There; Pod's hole must have been just behind where that radiator is now.   A radiator, they'd have liked that. . . .'   She pointed to a door across the hall, now labelled, in neat white lettering, 'Headmaster's Study.' 'And that was the morning-room,' she said.

'Where the Overmantels lived?   And Pod got the blotting-paper?'   Kate stared a moment and then, before Mrs May could stop her, ran across and tried the handle.

'No, Kate, you mustn't.   Come back.'

'It's locked,' said Kate, turning back.   'Could we just peep upstairs?' she went on.   'I'd love to see the night nursery. I could go terribly quietly. . . .'

'No, Kate, come along: we must go now.   We've no business to be here at all,' and Mrs May walked firmly towards the door.

'Couldn't I just peep in the kitchen window?' begged Kate at last, when they stood once again in the sunshine.

'No, Kate,' said Mrs May.

'Just to see where they lived?   Where that hole was under the stove which Pod used as a chute—*please*.'

'Quickly, then,' said Mrs May; she threw a nervous glance in each direction as Kate sped off down the path.

This too was a disappointment.   Kate knew where the kitchen was because of the grating, and making blinkers of her cupped hands against the reflected sunshine, she pushed her face up close against the glass. Dimly the room came into view, but it was nothing like a kitchen: shelves of bottles, gleaming retorts, heavy bench-like tables, rows of Bunsen burners: the kitchen was now a lab.

And that was that. On the way home Kate picked a very small bunch of dog-violets; there was veal and ham pie for luncheon, with salad, with the choice of plums and junket or baked jam roll; and, after luncheon, Mr Beguid arrived with car and chauffeur to take them to see the cottage.

At first Kate did not want to go: she had a secret plan of walking up to the field called Perkin's Beck and mooching about by herself, looking for badgers' sets, but when Mrs May explained to her that the field was just behind the cottage, and by the time Mr Beguid had stared long enough and pointedly enough out of the window with a bored, dry, if-this-were-my-child kind of expression on his face, Kate decided to go in the car after all, just to spite him. And it was a good thing (as she so often told her own children years afterwards) that she did: otherwise, she might never have talked to or (which was more important) made friends with—Thomas Goodenough.

CHAPTER THREE

'WINK AT SMALL FAULTS'
Anna Seward died 1809
[*Extract from Arrietty's Diary and Proverb Book, March 25th.*]

'AND ABOUT vacant possession,' Mrs May asked in the car, 'he really is going, this old man? I've forgotten his name——'

'Old Tom Goodenough? Yes, he's going all right; we've got him an almshouse. Not,' Mr Beguid added, with a short laugh, 'that he deserves it.'

'Why not?' asked Kate in her blunt way.

Mr Beguid glanced at her—a little put out, he seemed, as though the dog had spoken. 'Because,' he said, ignoring Kate and addressing Mrs May, 'he's a tiresome old humbug, that's why.' He laughed again, his complacent, short laugh. 'And the biggest liar in five counties, as they put it down in the village.'

The stone cottage stood in a field; it stood high, its back to the woods; it had a derelict look, Kate thought, as they toiled up the slope towards it, but the thatch seemed good. Beside the front door stood a water-butt leaking a little at seams and green with moss; there was slime on the brick path and a thin trickle of moisture which lost itself among the dock and thistles. Against the far end was a wooden outhouse on the walls of which Kate saw the skins of several small mammals nailed up to dry in the sun.

'I didn't realize it was quite so remote,' panted Mrs May,

as Mr Beguid knocked sharply on the blistered paint of the front door. She waved her rubber-tipped stick towards the sunken lane below the sloping field of meadow grass. 'We'll have to make some kind of path up to here.'

Kate heard a shuffling movement within and Mr Beguid, rapping again, called out impatiently: 'Come on, old Tom. Open up.'

There were footsteps and, as the door creaked open, Kate saw an old man—tall, thin, but curiously heavy about the shoulders. He carried his head sunk a little on to his chest, and inclined sideways; and when he smiled (as he did at once) this gave him a sly look: he had bright, dark, strangely luminous eyes which he fixed immediately on Kate.

'Well, Tom,' said Mr Beguid briskly, 'how are you keeping? Better, I hope. Here is Mrs May, the lady who owns your cottage. May we come in?'

'There's naught to hide,' said the old man, backing slightly to let them pass, but smiling only at Kate; it was, Kate thought, as though he could not see Mr Beguid.

They filed past him into the principal room; it was bareish but neat enough, except for a pile of wood shavings on the

stone floor and a stack of something Kate took to be kindling beside the window embrasure. A small fire smouldered in a blackened grate which seemed to be half oven.

'You've tidied up a bit, I see,' said Mr Beguid, looking about him. 'Not that it matters much,' he added, speaking aside to Mrs May, but barely lowering his voice; 'before the builders come in, if I were you I'd get the whole place washed through and thoroughly fumigated.'

'I think it looks lovely,' cried Kate warmly, shocked by this want of manners, and Mrs May hastened to agree with her, addressing a friendly look towards the old man.

But old Tom gave no sign of having noticed: quietly he stood, looking down at Kate, smiling his secret smile.

'The stairs are through here,' said Mr Beguid, leading the way to a farther door; 'and here,' they heard him say, 'is the scullery.' Mrs May, about to follow, hesitated on the threshold. 'Don't you want to come, Kate, and see round the cottage?'

Kate stood stolidly where she was; she threw a quick glance at the old man, and back again to Mrs May. 'No thanks,' she said shortly. And as Mrs May, a little surprised, followed Mr Beguid into the scullery, Kate moved towards the pile of peeled sticks. There was a short silence. 'What are you making?' Kate asked at last, a little shyly. The old man came back from his dream. 'Them?' he said in his soft voice. 'Them's sprays—for thatching.' He picked up a knife, tested the blade on his horny thumb, and pulling up a lowish stool, he sat down. 'Come you here,' he said, 'by me, and I'll show 'ee.'

Kate drew up a chair beside him and watched him in silence as he cut several small lengths of the hazel sapling which at first she had taken for kindling. After a moment he said softly without looking up: 'You don't want to take no notice of him.'

'Mr Beguid?' said Kate. 'I don't. Be good! It's a silly kind of name. Compared to yours, I mean,' she added warmly; 'whatever you did wouldn't matter really with a name like Good Enough.'

The old man half turned his head in a warning gesture towards the scullery; he listened a moment and then he said: 'They're going upstairs,' and Kate, listening too, heard clumping footsteps on wooden treads. 'You know how long I bin in this cottage?' the old man asked, his head still cocked as though listening while the footsteps crossed and

recrossed what must have been his bedroom. 'Nigh on eighty years,' he added after a moment. He took up a peeled sapling, grasping it firmly at either end.

'And now you've got to go?' said Kate, watching his hands as he took a firmer grip on the wood.

The old man laughed as though she had made a joke: he laughed quite silently, Kate noticed, shaking his head. 'So they make out,' he said in an amused voice, and with a twist of his two wrists he wrung the tough sapling as you wring out a wet cloth, and in the same movement doubled it back on itself. 'But I bain't going,' he added, and he threw the bent stick on the pile.

'But they wouldn't want to turn you out,' said Kate, 'not if you don't want to go, at least,' she added cautiously. 'I don't think Mrs May would.'

'Her–r–r?' he said, rolling the 'r's' and looking up at the ceiling; 'she's hand and glove with him.'

'She used to come and stay here,' Kate told him, 'when she was a child, did you know? Down at the big house. Firbank, isn't it?'

'Ay,' he said.

'Did you know her?' asked Kate curiously. 'She was called Miss Ada?'

'I knew Miss Ada all right,' said the old man, 'and her aunty. *And* her brother.' He laughed again. 'I knew the whole lot of 'em, come to that.'

As he spoke, Kate had a strange feeling; it was as though she had heard these words before, spoken by just such an old man as this and, she seemed to remember, it was in some such similar place—the sunlit window of a darkish cottage on a bright but cold spring day. She looked round wonderingly at the whitewashed walls—flaking a little they were, in a pattern she seemed to recognize; even the hollows and cracks of the worn brick floor also seemed curiously familiar—strange, because (of this she was certain) she had never been here before. She looked back at the old man, getting up courage to go a step farther. 'Did you know Crampfurl?' she asked after a moment, and before he spoke she knew what would be his answer.

'I knew Crampfurl all right,' said the old man, and he laughed again, nodding his head, enjoying some secret joke.

'And Mrs Driver, the cook?'

Here the joke became almost too much for old Tom. 'Ay,' he said, wheezing with silent laughter, 'Mrs Driver!' and he wiped the corner of his eye with his sleeve.

'Did you know Rosa Pickhatchet?' went on Kate, 'that housemaid, the one who screamed?'

'Nay,' said old Tom, nodding and laughing. 'But I heard tell of her—screamed the house down, so they say.'

'But do you know why?' cried Kate excitedly.

He shook his head. 'No reason at all, as I can see.'

'But didn't they tell you that she saw a little man, on the drawing-room mantel-shelf, about the size of the china cupid; that she thought he was an ornament and tried to dust him with a feather duster—and suddenly he sneezed? Anyone would scream,' Kate concluded breathlessly.

'For why?' said old Tom, deftly sliding the bark from the wood as though it were a glove finger. 'They don't hurt you, borrowers don't. And they don't make no mess neither. Not like field-mice. Beats me, always has, the fuss folk'll make about a borrower, screeching and screaming and all that caper.' He ran an appreciative finger along the peeled surface. 'Smoking 'em out and them kind of games. No need for it, not with borrowers. They go quiet enough, give 'em time, once they know they've been seen. Now take field-mice——' The old man broke off to twist his stick, catching his breath with the effort.

'Don't let's,' cried Kate, 'please! I mean, tell me some more about borrowers.'

'There's naught to tell,' said the old man, tossing his stick on the pile and selecting a fresh one. 'Borrowers is as like to humans as makes no matter, and what's to tell about humans? Now you take field-mice—once one of them critturs finds a way indoors, you're done and strung up as you might say: you can't leave the place not for a couple of hours but you don't get the whole lot right down on you like a flock of starlings. Mess! And it ain't a question of getting 'em out: they've come and they've gone, if you see what I mean. Plague o' locusts ain't in it. Yes,' he went on, 'no doubt about it—in a house like this, you're apt to get more trouble from field-mice than ever you get from any borrower; in a house like this,' he repeated, 'set away like at the edge of the woods, borrowers can be company like as not.' He glanced up at the ceiling, which creaked slightly as footsteps passed and repassed in the room above. 'What you reckon they're up to?' he said.

'Measuring,' Kate said. 'Mrs May brought a yardstick. They'll be down soon,' she went on hurriedly, 'and I want to ask you something—something important. If they send me for a walk to-morrow—by myself, I mean, while they talk business, could I come up and be with you?'

'I don't see no reason why not,' said the old man, at work on his next stick. 'If you brings along a sharp knife, I'll learn you to make sprays.'

'You know,' said Kate impressively, with a glance at the ceiling, dropping her voice. 'Her brother, Mrs May's brother—or Miss Ada's or whatever you like to call her— he *saw* those borrowers down at the big house!' She paused for effect, watching his face.

'What of it?' said the old man impassively. 'You only got to keep your eyes skinned. I seen stranger things in my time than them sort of critturs—take badgers—now you come up here to-morrow and I'll tell you summat about badgers you wouldn't credit, but that I seen it with me own two eyes——'

'But have you ever seen a *borrower*?' cried Kate impatiently. 'Did you ever see any of these ones down at the big house?'

'Them as they had in the stables?'

'No, the ones who lived under the kitchen?'

'Oh, them,' he said, 'smoked out, they were. But it ain't true——' he began, raising his face suddenly, and Kate saw that it was a sad face when it was not smiling.

'What isn't true?'

'What they say: that I set the ferret on 'em. I wouldn't. Not once I knew they was borrowers.'

'Oh!' exclaimed Kate, kneeling up on her chair with excitement, 'you were the boy with the ferret?'

Old Tom looked back at her—his sideways look. 'I were a boy,' he admitted guardedly, 'and I did have a ferret.'

'But they did escape, didn't they?' Kate persisted anxiously. 'Mrs May says they escaped by the grating.'

'That's right,' said old Tom, 'made off across the gravel and up the bank.'

'But you don't know for certain,' said Kate; 'you didn't see them go. Or *could* you see them from the window?'

'I know for certain, all right,' said old Tom. 'True enough I saw 'em from the window, but that ain't how——' he hesitated, looking at Kate; amused he seemed but still wary.

'Please tell me. Please——' begged Kate.

The old man glanced upwards at the ceiling. 'You know what he is?' he said, inclining his head.

'Mr Beguid? A lawyer.'

The old man nodded. 'That's right. And you don't want nothing put down in writing.'

'I don't understand,' said Kate.

The old man sighed and took up his whittling knife. 'What I tells *you*, you tells *her*, and *he* puts it all down in writing.'

'Mrs May wouldn't tell,' said Kate, 'she's——'

'She's hand in glove with him, that's what I maintain. And it's no good telling me no different. Seemingly now, you can't die no more where you reckons to die. And you know for why?' he said, glaring at Kate. 'Because of what's put down in writing.' And with a curiously vicious twist he doubled back his stick. Kate stared at him non-plussed. 'If I promised not to tell?' she said at last, in a timid voice.

'Promises!' exclaimed the old man; staring at Kate, he jerked a thumb towards the ceiling. 'Her–r–r great-uncle, old Sir Montague that was, *promised* me this cottage —"It's for your lifetime, Tom" he says. Promises!' he repeated angrily, and he almost spat the word. 'Promises is pie-crust.'

Kate's eyes filled with tears. 'All right,' she snapped, 'I don't care—then don't tell me!'

Tom's expression changed too, almost as violently. 'Now don't 'ee cry, little maid,' he begged, surprised and distressed.

But Kate, to her shame, could not stop; the tears ran down her cheeks and she felt the familiar hot feeling at the tip of her nose as though it were swelling. 'I was only wondering,' she gasped, fumbling for a handkerchief, 'if they were all right—and how they managed—and whether they found the badgers' set——'

'They found the badgers' set all right,' said old Tom. 'Now, don't 'ee cry, my maiden, not no more.'

'I'll stop in a minute,' Kate assured him in a stifled voice, blowing her nose.

'Now look 'ee here,' the old man went on—very upset he sounded, 'you dry your eyes and stop your weeping and old Tom'll show you summat.' Awkwardly he got up off his stool and hovered over her, drooping his shoulders like some great protective bird. 'Something you'd like. How's that, eh?'

'It's all right,' Kate said, giving a final scrub. She stuffed away her handkerchief and smiled up at him. 'I've stopped.'

Old Tom put his hand in his pocket and then, throwing a cautious glance towards the ceiling, he seemed to change his mind: for a moment it had sounded as though the footsteps had been moving towards the stairs. 'It's all right,' whispered Kate, after listening, as he searched again and drew out a battered tin box, the kind in which pipe-smokers keep tobacco, and with his knotted fingers fumbled awkwardly with the lid; at last it

was open and, breathing heavily, he turned it over and slid some object out. 'Here . . .' he said, and there on his calloused palm Kate saw the tiny book.

'Oh . . .' she breathed, staring incredulously.

'Take it up,' said old Tom, 'it won't bite you.' And, as gingerly Kate put out her hand, he added smiling: ''Tis Arrietty's diary.'

But Kate knew this, even before she saw the faded gilt lettering—'Diary and Proverb Book,' and in spite of the fact that it was weather-stained and time-worn, that when she opened it the bulk of its pages slipped out from between the covers, and the ink or pencil or sap—or whatever Arrietty had used to write with—had faded to various shades of brown and sepia and a curious sickly yellow. It had opened at August the 31st, and the proverb, Kate saw, was 'Earth is the Best Shelter,' and below this the bald statement, 'Disastrous Earthquake at Charleston, U.S., 1866,' and on the page itself, in Arrietty's scratchy handwriting were three entries for the three successive years:

'Spiders in store-room.'

'Mrs D. dropped pan.   Soup-leak in ceiling.'

'Talked to Spiller.'

Who was Spiller? Kate wondered.   August 31st?   That was after they left the big house: Spiller, she realized, must be part of the new life, the life out of doors.   At random, she turned back a few pages:

'Mother bilious.'

'Threaded green beads.'

'Climbed hedge.   Eggs bad.'

Climbed hedge?   Arrietty must have gone birds'-nesting

—and the eggs would be bad in (Kate glanced at the date)
. . . yes, it was still August, and the motto for that day was
'Grasp all, lose all.'

'Where did you get this book?' Kate asked aloud in a
stunned voice.

'I found it,' said old Tom.

'But where?' cried Kate.

'Here,' said Old Tom, and Kate saw his eyes stray in the
direction of the fire-place.

'In this house,' she exclaimed in an unbelieving voice
and, staring up at his mysterious old face, Mr Beguid's
unkind words came back to her suddenly, 'the biggest liar
in five counties.'   But here, in her hand, was the actual
book; she stared down at it trying to sort out her thoughts.

'You want I should show you summat else?' he asked
her, suddenly and a little pathetically, as though aware of
her secret doubts.   'Come you here,' and getting up slowly
from her chair, Kate followed like a sleep-walker as he went
towards the fire-place.

The old man stooped down, and panting a little with the
effort, he dragged and tugged at the heavy wood-box; as he
shifted it aside a board fell forward with a slight clatter and
the old man, alarmed, glanced up at the ceiling; but Kate,
leaning forward, saw the board had covered a sizable rat-
hole gouged out of the skirting and Gothic in shape, like an
opened church door.

'See?' said old Tom, after listening a moment—a little
breathless from tugging, 'goes right through to the scullery: they'd got fire this side and water t'other.   Years,
they lived here.'

Kate knelt down, staring into the hole. 'Here? In your house?' Her voice became more and more scared and unbelieving. 'You mean ... Pod? And Homily? ... And little Arrietty?'

'Them, too,' said old Tom, 'in the end, as it were.'

'But didn't they live out of doors? That's what Arrietty was longing to do——'

'They lived out of doors all right.' He gave a short laugh. 'If you call it living. Or come to that, if you can call it out-doors! But you take a look at this,' he went on softly, with a note in his voice of thinly disguised pride, 'goes right up inside the wall, stairs they got and all betwixt the lath and the plaster. Proper tenement, they got here—six floors—and water on every floor. See that?' he asked, laying his hand on a rusty pipe; 'comes down from the cistern in the roof, that does, and goes on through to the scullery. Tapped it, they did, in six different places—and never a drop or a leak!'

He was silent a moment, lost in thought, before he propped back the board again and shoved the wood-box back into place. 'Years they lived here,' he said affection-ately, and he sighed a little as he straightened up, dusting his hands together.

'But *who* lived here?' Kate whispered hurriedly (the foot-steps above had crossed the landing and were now heard approaching the head of the stairs). 'You don't mean my ones? You said they found the badgers' set?'

'They found the badgers' set all right,' said old Tom, and gave his short laugh.

'But how do you know? Who told you?' Twittering

with anxiety she followed behind him as he limped towards his stool.

Old Tom sat down, selected a stick, and with maddening deliberation tested the edge of his knife. 'She told me,' he said at last, and he cut the stick in three lengths.

'You mean you talked to Arrietty!'

He made a warning sign at her raised voice, lifting his eyebrows and jerking his head: the footsteps, Kate heard, were clumping now down the wooden treads of the stairs. 'You don't talk to that one,' he whispered, 'not while she's got a tongue to wag.'

Kate went on staring; if he had hit her on the head with a log from the log-box, she could not have appeared more stunned. 'Then she must have told you everything!' she gasped.

'Hush!' said the old man, his eye on the door.

Mrs May and Mr Beguid, it seemed, had reached the bottom of the stairs, and from the sound of their voices had turned again into the scullery for a last look round. 'Two fitted basins, at least,' Mrs May was heard saying, in a matter-of-fact tone.

'Pretty nigh on everything, I reckon,' whispered old Tom. 'She'd creep out most evenings, pretty regular.' He smiled as he spoke, glancing towards the hearth. And Kate, watching his face, suddenly saw the picture: the firelit cottage, the lonely boy at his whittling, and almost invisible in the shadows this tiny creature, seated maybe on a match-box; the fluty, monotonous voice going on and on and on . . . after a while, Kate thought, he would hardly hear it: it would merge and become part of the room's living stillness, like the simmer of the kettle or the ticking of the clock. Night after night; week after week; month after month; year, perhaps, after year . . . yes, indeed, Kate realized (staring at old Tom in the same stunned way even though, at this minute, Mrs May and Mr Beguid came back to the room talking so loudly about washbasins), Arrietty must have told Tom everything!

CHAPTER FOUR

'NO TALE LOSES IN THE TELLING'
Longfellow, American poet, died 1882; also Walt Whitman, 1891
[*Extract from Arrietty's Diary and Proverb Book, March 26th.*]

AND ALL THAT was needed now, she thought (as she lay that night in bed, listening to the constant gurgle in the pipes of the constant H. and C.), was for old Tom to tell *her* everything in fullest detail—as Arrietty must have told it to him. And, having gone so far, he might do this, she felt—in spite of his fear of things put down in writing. And she wouldn't tell either, she resolved staunchly—at any rate, not during his lifetime (although why he should mind so much she couldn't understand, seeing that he was known already as 'the biggest liar in five counties'). But what seemed still more hopeful was that, having shown her the little book, he had not asked for it back: she had it now in bed with her stuffed beneath her pillow and this, at any rate, was full of 'things in writing.' Not that she could understand them quite: the entries were too short, little headings, they seemed like, jotted down by Arrietty to remind herself of dates. But some of them sounded extraordinarily weird and mysterious . . . yes, she decided—suddenly inspired—that was the way to work it: she would ask old Tom to explain the headings—'What could Arrietty have meant,' she would ask, 'by "Black men. Mother saved"?'

And this, more or less, was what did happen. While

Mrs May talked business each day with Messrs Jobson, Thring, Beguid & Beguid, or argued with builders and plumbers and plumbers' mates, Kate would wander off alone across the fields and find her own way to the cottage, seeking out old Tom.

On some days (as Kate, in later years, would explain to her children) he would seem a bit 'cagey' and disinterested, but on other days a particular heading in the diary would seem to inspire him and his imagination would take wings and sail away on such swirls and eddies of miraculous memory that Kate, spellbound, could hardly believe that he had not at some time (in some other life, perhaps) been a borrower himself. And Mrs May, Kate remembered, had once said just this of her younger brother: this brother who, although three years his junior, had been known to old Tom (old Tom himself had admitted this much). Had they been friends? Great friends, perhaps? They certainly seemed birds of a feather—one famous for telling tall stories because 'he was such a tease'; the other more simply described as 'the biggest liar in five counties.' And it was this thought which, long after she was grown up, decided Kate to tell the world what was said to have happened to Pod and Homily and little Arrietty after that dreadful day when, smoked out of their house under the kitchen, they sought for refuge in the wild outdoors.

Here is her story—all 'put down in writing.' We can sift the evidence ourselves.

CHAPTER FIVE

'STEP BY STEP CLIMBS THE HILL'
Victoria Tubular Bridge, Montreal, opened 1866
[*Extract from Arrietty's Diary and Proverb Book, August 25th.*]

WELL, AT FIRST, it seems they just ran, but they ran in the right direction—up the azalea bank, where (so many months ago now) Arrietty had first met the boy, and through the long grass at the top; how they got through that, Homily used to say afterwards, she never knew—nothing but stalks, close set. And insects: Homily had never dreamed there could be so many different kinds of insect—slow ones, hanging on things; fast, scuttling ones, and ones (these were the worst) which stared at you and did not move at once and then backed slowly, still staring; it was as though, Homily said, they had made up their mind to bite you and then (still malicious) changed it out of caution. 'Wicked,' she said, 'that's what they were; oh, wicked, wicked, wicked. . . .'

As they shoved their way through the long grass, they were choked with pollen loosened in clouds from above;

there were sharp-edged leaves, deceptively sappy and swaying, which cut their hands, gliding across the skin like the softly drawn bow of a violin but leaving blood behind; there were straw-dry, knotted stems, which caught them round the shins and ankles and which made them stumble and trip forward; often they would land on that cushiony plant with silvery, hairlike spines—spines which pricked and stung.   Long grass . . . long grass . . . for ever afterwards it was Homily's nightmare.

Then, to get to the orchard, came a scramble through the privet hedge: dead leaves, below the blackened boughs of privet . . . dead leaves and rotting, desiccated berries which rose waist high as they swam their way through them, and, below the leaves, a rustling dampness.   And here again were insects: things which turned over on their backs or hopped suddenly, or slyly slid away.

Across the orchard—easier going this, because the hens had fed there achieving their usual 'blasted heath' effect— a flattened surface of lava-coloured earth; and the visibility was excellent.   But, if they could see, they could also be seen: the fruit trees were widely spaced, giving little cover; anyone glancing from a first-floor window in the house might well exclaim curiously: 'What's that, do you think, moving across the orchard?   There by the second tree on the right—like leaves blowing.   But there isn't a wind. More like something being drawn along on a thread—too steady to be birds. . . .'   This was the thought in Pod's mind as he urged Homily onwards.   'Oh, I can't,' she would cry. 'I must sit down!   Just a moment, Pod—please!'

But he was adamant.   'You can sit down,' he'd say,

gripping her below the elbow, and spinning her forward across the rubble, 'once we get to the wood. You take her other arm, Arrietty, but keep her moving!'

Once within the wood, they sank down on the side of the well-worn path, too exhausted to seek further cover. 'Oh dear . . . oh dear . . . oh dear . . .' Homily kept saying (mechanically, because she always said it), but behind her bright dark eyes in her smudged face they could see her brain was busy: and she was not hysterical, they could see that too; they could see, in other words, that Homily was 'trying.' 'There's no call for all this running,' she announced after a moment, when she could get her breath, 'nobody didn't see us go: fer all they know we're still there, trapped-like—under the floor.'

'I wouldn't be so sure,' said Arrietty, 'there was a face at the kitchen window. I saw it as we were going up the bank. A boy it looked like, with a cat or something.'

'If anyone'd seen us,' remarked Homily, 'they'd have been after us, that's what I say.'

'That's a fact,' said Pod.

'Well, which way do we go from here?' asked Homily, gazing about among the tree-trunks. There was a long scratch across her cheek and her hair hung down in wisps.

'Well, we'd better be getting these loads sorted out first,' said Pod. 'Let's see what we've brought. What have you got in that borrowing-bag, Arrietty?'

Arrietty opened the bag she had packed so hurriedly two days before against just this emergency; she laid out the contents on the hardened mud of the path and they looked an odd collection. There were three tin lids of varying sizes of pill bottles which fitted neatly one inside the other; a sizable piece of candle and seven wax-vestas; a change of underclothes and an extra jersey knitted by Homily on blunted darning-needles from a much washed, unravelled sock, and last, but most treasured, her pencil from a dance programme and her Diary and Proverb Book.

'Now why did you want to cart that along?' grumbled Pod, glancing sideways at this massive tome as he laid out his own belongings. For the same reason, Arrietty thought to herself as she glanced at Pod's unpacking, that you brought along your shoemaker's needle, your hammer made from an electric bell-clapper, and a stout ball of twine: each to his hobby and the tools of the craft he loves (and hers she felt to be literature).

Besides his shoemaking equipment, Pod had brought the half nail-scissor, a thin sliver of razor-blade, ditto of child's fret-saw, an aspirin bottle with screw lid filled with water, a small twist of fuse wire, and two steel hat-pins, the shorter of which he gave to Homily. 'It'll help you up the hill,' he told her; 'we may have a bit of a climb.'

Homily had brought her knitting-needles, the rest of the unravelled sock, three pieces of lump sugar, the finger of a lady's kid glove filled with salt and pepper mixed, tied up at the neck with cotton, some broken pieces of digestive biscuit, a small tin box made for phonograph needles which now contained dry tea, a chip of soap, and her hair curlers.

Pod gazed glumly at the curious collection. 'Like as not we brought the wrong things,' he said, 'but it can't be helped now. Better pack 'em up again,' he went on, suiting the action to the word, 'and let's get going. Good idea of yours, Arrietty, the way you fitted together them tin lids. Not sure, though, we couldn't have done with a couple more——'

'We've only got to get to the badgers' set,' Arrietty excused herself. 'I mean Aunt Lupy will have most things, won't she—like cooking utensils and such?'

'I don't know anyone as couldn't do with more,' remarked Homily, stuffing in the remains of the sock and lashing up the neck of her bag with a length of blue embroidery silk, 'especially when they live in a badgers' set. And who's to say your Aunt Lupy's there at all?' She went on. 'I thought she got lost or something, crossing them fields out walking.'

'Well, she may be found again by now,' said Pod. 'Over a year ago, wasn't it, when she set out walking?'

'And anyway,' Arrietty pointed out, 'she wouldn't go walking with the cooking-pots.'

'I never could see,' said Homily, standing up and trying out the weight of her bag, 'nor never will, no matter what nobody tells me, what your Uncle Hendreary saw fit to marry in a stuck-up thing like that Lupy.'

'That's enough,' said Pod, 'we don't want none of that now.'

He stood up and slung his borrowing-bag on his steel hat-pin, swinging it over his shoulder. 'Now,' he asked, looking them up and down, 'sure you're both all right?'

'Not that, when put to it,' went on Homily, 'that she isn't good-hearted. It's the kind of way she does it.'

'What about your boots?' asked Pod. 'They quite comfortable?'

'Yes,' said Homily, 'for the moment,' she added.

'What about you, Arrietty?'

'I'm all right,' said Arrietty.

'Because,' said Pod, 'it's going to be a long pull. We're going to take it steady. No need to rush. But we don't want no stopping. Nor no grumbling. Understand?'

'Yes,' said Arrietty.

'And keep your eyes skinned,' Pod went on, as they all moved off along the path. 'If you see anything, do as I do —and sharp, mind. We don't want no running every which way. We don't want no screaming.'

'I know,' said Arrietty irritably, adjusting her pack. She moved ahead as though trying to get out of earshot.

'You *think* you know,' called Pod after her. 'But you don't know nothing really; you don't know nothing about cover; nor does your mother: cover's a trained job, an art-like——'

'I know,' repeated Arrietty; 'you told me.' She glanced sideways into the shadowy depths of the brambles beside the path; she saw a great spider, hanging in space, his web was invisible: he seemed to be staring at her—she saw his eyes. Defiantly, Arrietty stared back.

'You can't tell no one in five minutes,' persisted Pod, 'things you got to learn from experience. What I told you, my girl, that day I took you out borrowing, wasn't even the A B C. I tried my best, because your mother asked me. And see where it's got us!'

'Now, Pod,' panted Homily (they were walking too fast for her), 'no need to bring up the past.'

'That's what I mean,' said Pod, 'the past *is* experience:

that's all you got to learn from. You see, when it comes to borrowing——'

'But you had a lifetime of it, Pod: you was in training—Arrietty'd only been out that once——'

'That's what I *mean*,' cried Pod, and, in stubborn desperation, he stopped in his tracks for Homily to catch up, 'about cover, if only she'd known the A B C——'

'Look out!' sang Arrietty shrilly, now some way ahead.

There was a rushing clatter and a dropped shadow and a hoarse, harsh cry; and, suddenly, there was Pod—alone on the path—face to face with a large, black crow.

The bird stared, wickedly, but a little distrustfully, his cramped toes turned in slightly, his great beak just open. Frozen to stillness Pod stared back—something growing in the path, that's what he looked like—a rather peculiar kind of chunky toadstool. The great bird, very curious, turned his head sideways and tried Pod with his other eye. Pod, motionless, stared back. The crow made a murmur in its throat—a tiny bleat—and, puzzled, it moved forward. Pod let it come, a couple of sideways steps, and then—out of a still face—he spoke: 'Get back to where you was,' he said evenly, almost conversationally, and the bird seemed to hesitate. 'We don't want no nonsense from you,' Pod went on steadily; 'pigeon-toed, that's what you are! Crows is pigeon-toed, first time it struck me. Staring away like that, with one eye, and your head turned sideways . . . think it pretty, no doubt'—Pod spoke quite pleasantly—'but it ain't, not with *that* kind of beak. . . .'

The bird became still, its expression no longer curious: there was stark amazement in every line of its rigid body and, in its eye, a kind of ghastly disbelief. 'Go on! Get off with you!' shouted Pod suddenly, moving towards it. 'Shoo . . .!' And, with a distraught glance and panic-stricken croak, the great bird flapped away. Pod wiped his brow with his sleeve as Homily, white faced and still trembling, crawled out from under a foxglove leaf. 'Oh, Pod,' she gasped, 'you were brave—you were wonderful!'

'It's nothing,' said Pod, 'it's a question of keeping your nerve.'

'But the size of it!' said Homily. 'You'd never think seeing them flying they was that size!'

'Size is nothing,' said Pod, 'it's the talk that gets them.' He watched Arrietty climb out from a hollow stump and begin to brush herself down. When she looked up, he looked away. 'Well,' he said, after a moment, 'we'd better keep moving.'

Arrietty smiled; she hesitated a moment then ran across to him.

'What's that for?' asked Pod weakly, as she flung her arms round his neck. 'Oh,' cried Arrietty, hugging him, 'you deserve a medal—the way you faced up to it, I mean.'

'No, lass,' said Pod, 'you don't mean that: the way I was caught out, that's what you mean—caught out, good and proper, talking of cover.' He patted her hand. 'And, what's more, you're right: we'll face up to that one, too. You and your mother was trigger quick and I'm proud of you.' He let go her hand and swung his pack up on to his shoulders. 'But another time, remember,' he added, turning suddenly, 'not stumps. Hollow they may be but not always empty, see what I mean, and you're out of the frying-pan into the fire. . . .'

On and on they went, following the path which the workmen had made when they dug out the trench for the gas-pipe.   It led them through two fields of pasture land, on a gradually rising slope alongside; they could walk with perfect ease under the lowest rungs of any five-barred gate, picking a careful way across the clusters of sun-dried cattle tracks; these were crater-like but crumbling, and Homily, staggering a little beneath her load, slipped once and grazed her knee.

On the third field the gas-pipe branched away obliquely to the left, and Pod, looking ahead to where against the skyline he could just make out a stile, decided that they could safely now forsake the gas-pipe and stick to the path beside the hedge.   'Won't be so long now,' he explained comfortingly when Homily begged to rest, 'but we got to keep going.   See that stile?   That's what we're aiming for and we got to make it afore sunset.'

So on they plodded and, to Homily, this last lap seemed the worst: her tired legs moved mechanically like scissors; stooping under her load, she was amazed each time she saw a foot come forward—it no longer seemed to be her foot; she wondered how it got there.

Arrietty wished they could not see the stile: their tiny steps seemed to bring it no nearer; it worked better she found to keep her eyes on the ground and then every now and again if she looked up she could see they had made progress.

But at last they reached the crest of the hill; towards the right, on the far side of the cornfield beyond the hazel hedge, lay the woods, and ahead of them, after a slight dip, rose a vast sloping field, crossed with shadow from where the sun was setting behind the trees.

On the edge of this field they stood and stared, awed by its vastness, its tilted angle against the rosy sky; on this endless sea of lengthening shadows and dreaming grassland floated an island of trees dimmed already by its long-thrown trail of dusk.

'This is it,' said Pod, after a long moment, 'Perkin's Beck.' They stood, all three of them, underneath the stile, loath to lose its shelter.

'Perkin's what?' asked Homily uneasily.

'Perkin's Beck. You know—the name of the field. This is where they live, the Hendrearies.'

'You mean,' said Homily, after a pause, 'where the badgers' set is?'

'That's right,' said Pod, staring ahead.

Homily's tired face looked yellow in the golden light; her jaw hung loose. 'But where?' she asked.

Pod waved his arm. 'Somewhere; it's in this field anyway.'

'In this field . . .' repeated Homily dully, her eyes fixed on the dim boundaries, the distant group of shadowy trees.

'Well, we got to look,' explained Pod uneasily. 'You didn't think we'd go straight to it, did you?'

'I thought you knew where it was,' said Homily. Her voice sounded husky. Arrietty, between them, stood strangely silent.

'Well, I've brought you this far. Haven't I?' said Pod. 'If the worst comes to the worst, we can camp for the night, and look round in the morning.'

'Where's the stream?' asked Arrietty. 'There's supposed to be a stream.'

'Well, there is,' said Pod, 'it flows down there, along that distant hedge, and then comes in like—do you see?—across that far corner. That thicker green there—can't you see?—them's rushes.'

Arrietty screwed up her eyes. 'Yes,' she said uncertainly, and added: 'I'm thirsty.'

'And so am I,' said Homily; she sat down suddenly as though deflated. 'All the way up that hill, step after step, hour after hour, I bin saying to meself "Never mind, the first thing we'll do as soon as we get to that badgers' set is sit down and have a nice cup o' tea"—it kept me going.'

'Well, we will have one,' said Pod. 'Arrietty's got the candle.'

'And I'll tell you another thing,' went on Homily, staring ahead, 'I couldn't walk across that there field, not if you offered me a monkey in a cage: we'll have to go round by the edges.'

'Well, that's just what we're going to do,' said Pod, 'you don't find no badgers' sets in the middle of a field. We'll work round, systematic-like, bit by bit, starting out in the morning. But we got to sleep rough to-night, that's one thing certain. No good poking about to-night: it'll be dark soon; the sun's near off that hill already.'

'And there are clouds coming up,' said Arrietty, gazing at the sunset, 'and moving fast.'

'Rain?' cried Homily, in a stricken voice.

'Well, we'll move fast,' said Pod, slinging his pack up. 'Here, give me yours, Homily, you'll travel lighter. . . .'

'Which way are we going?' asked Arrietty.

'We'll keep along by this lower hedge,' said Pod, setting off. 'And make towards the water. If we can't make it before the rain comes, we'll just take any shelter.'

'What sort of shelter?' asked Homily, stumbling after him through the tussocky grass. 'Look out, Pod, them's nettles!'

'I can see them,' said Pod (they were walking in a shallow ditch). 'A hole or something,' he went on. 'There's a hole there, for instance. See? Under that root.'

Homily peered at it as she came abreast. 'Oh, I couldn't go in there,' she said, 'there might be something in it.'

'Or we could go right into the hedge,' Pod called back.

'There's not much shelter in the hedge,' said Arrietty. She walked alone, on the higher ground where the grass was shorter. 'I can see from here: it's all stems and branches.'

She shivered a little in a light wind which set the leaves of the hedge plants suddenly a-tremble, clashing the drying teazles as they swung and locked together. 'It's clouding right over,' she called.

'Yes, it'll be dark soon,' said Pod, 'you'd better come down here with us; you don't want to get lost.'

'I won't get lost; I can see better from here. Look!' she called out suddenly, 'there's an old boot. Wouldn't that do?'

'An old what?' asked Homily incredulously.

'Might do,' said Pod, looking about him.   'Where is it?'

'To your left.   There.   In the long grass . . .'

'An old boot!' cried Homily, as she saw him set down the borrowing-bags.   'What's the matter with you, Pod—have you gone out of your mind?'   Even as she spoke, it began

to rain, great summer drops which bounced among the grasses.

'Take the borrowing-bags and get under that dock-leaf—both of you—while I look.'

'An old boot . . .' repeated Homily incredulously, as she and Arrietty crouched under the dock-leaf; she had to raise her voice—the rain, on the swaying leaf, seemed to clatter rather than patter.   'Hark at it!' complained Homily. 'Come in closer, Arrietty, you'll catch your death.   Oh, my goodness me—it's running down my back!'

'Look—he's calling to us,' said Arrietty, 'come on!'

Homily bent her neck and peered out from under the swaying leaf: there stood Pod, some yards away, barely visible among the steaming grasses, dimmed by the curtain of rain. 'A tropical scene,' Arrietty thought, remembering her *Gazetteer of the World*. She thought of man against the elements, jungle swamps, steaming forests, and Mr Livingstone she presumed. . . . 'What's he want?' she heard her mother complaining. 'We can't go out in this—look at it!'

'It's coming in under-foot now,' Arrietty told her, 'can't you see? This is a ditch. Come on, we must run for it; he wants us.'

They ran, half-crouching, stunned by the pounding water. Pod pulled them up into the longer grass, snatching their borrowing-bags, gasping instructions, as they slid and slithered after him through—what Arrietty thought of as 'the bush.'

'Here it is,' said Pod. 'Get in here.'

The boot lay on its side; they had to crouch to enter. 'Oh, my goodness,' Homily kept saying. 'Oh, my goodness me . . .' and would glance fearfully about the darkness inside. 'I wonder whoever wore it.'

'Go on,' said Pod, 'get further down; it's all right.'

'No, no,' said Homily, 'I'm not going in no further: there might be something in the toe.'

'It's all right,' said Pod, 'I've looked: there's nothing but a hole in the toe.' He stacked the borrowing-bags against the inner side. 'Something to lean against,' he said.

'I wish I knew who'd wore this boot,' Homily went on,

peering about uncomfortably, wiping her wet face on her wetter apron.

'What good would that do you?' Pod said, untying the strings of the largest bag.

'Whether he was clean or dirty or what,' said Homily, 'and what he died of. Suppose he died of something infectious?'

'Why suppose he died?' said Pod. 'Why shouldn't he be hale and hearty, and just had a nice wash and be sitting down to a good tea this very minute.'

'Tea?' said Homily, her face brightening. 'Where's the candle, Pod?'

'It's here,' said Pod. 'Give me a wax-vesta, Arrietty, and a medium-sized aspirin lid. We got to go careful with the tea, you know; we got to go careful with everything.'

Homily put out a finger and touched the worn leather. 'I'll give this boot a good clean out in the morning,' she said.

'It's not bad,' said Pod, taking out the half nail-scissor. 'If you ask me, we been lucky to find a boot like this. There ain't nothing to worry about: it's disinfected, all right—what with the sun and the wind and the rain, year after year of it.' He stuck the blade of the nail-scissor through an eyelet hole and lashed it firm with a bit of old bootlace.

'What are you doing that for, Papa?' asked Arrietty.

'To stand the lid on, of course,' said Pod, 'a kind of bracket over the candle; we haven't got no tripod. Now you go and fill it with water, there's a good girl—there's plenty outside . . .'

There was plenty outside: it was coming down in torrents; but the mouth of the boot faced out of the wind and there was a little dry patch before it. Arrietty filled the tin lid quite easily by tipping a large pointed fox-glove leaf towards it so the rain ran off and down the point. All about her was the steady sound of rain, and the lighted candle within the boot made the dusk seem darker: there was a smell of wildness, of space, of leaves and grasses and, as she turned away with the filled tin-lid, another smell— winy, fragrant, spicy. Arrietty took note of it to remember it for morning—it was the smell of wild strawberries.

After they had drunk their hot tea and eaten a good half of sweet, crumbly digestive biscuit, they took off their wet outer clothes and hung them out along the handle of the nail-scissor above the candle. With the old woollen sock about their three shoulders, they talked a little. '. . . Funny,' Arrietty remarked, 'to be wrapped in a sock and inside a boot.' But Pod, watching the candle flame, was worried about wastage and, when the clothes had steamed a little, he doused the flame. Tired out, they lay down at last among the borrowing-bags, cuddled together for warmth. The last sound Arrietty heard as she fell asleep was the steady drumming of the rain on the hollow leather of the boot.

CHAPTER SIX

'SUCH IS THE TREE, SUCH IS THE FRUIT'
End of great railway strike at Peoria, Ill., 1891
[*Extract from Arrietty's Diary and Proverb Book, August 26th.*]

ARRIETTY WAS the first to wake. 'Where am I!' she wondered. She felt warm—too warm, lying there between her mother and father—and when slightly she turned her head she saw three little golden suns, floating in the darkness; it was a second or two before she realized what they were, and with this knowledge memory flooded back—all that happened yesterday: the escape, the frenzied scramble across the orchard, the weary climb, the rain—the little golden suns, she realized, were the lace-holes of the boot!

Stealthily Arrietty sat up; a balmy freshness stole in upon her and, framed in the neck of the boot, she saw the bright day: grasses, softly stirring, tenderly sunlit: some were broken, where yesterday they had pushed through them dragging the borrowing-bags; there was a yellow buttercup, sticky and gleaming, it looked—like wet paint; on a tawny stalk of sorrel she saw an aphis—of a green so delicate that, against the sunlight, it looked transparent. 'Ants milk them,' Arrietty remembered, 'perhaps we could.'

She slid out from between her sleeping parents and, just as she was, with bare feet and in her vest and petticoat, she ventured out of doors.

It was a glorious day, sunlit and rain-washed—the earth

breathing out its scents. 'This,' Arrietty thought, 'is what I have longed for; what I have imagined; what I knew existed—what I knew we'd have!'

She pushed through the grasses and soft drops fell on her benignly, warmed by the sun. Downhill a little way she went, towards the hedge, out of the jungle of higher grass, into the shallow ditch where, last night, the rain and darkness had combined to scare her.

There was warm mud here, between the shorter grass blades, fast-drying now in the sun; a bank rose between her and the hedge: a glorious bank, it was, filled with roots; with grasses; with tiny ferns; with small sandy holes; with violet leaves and with pale scarlet pimpernel and, here and there, a globe of deeper crimson—wild strawberries!

She climbed the bank—leisurely and happily, feeling the warm sun through her vest, her bare feet picking their way more delicately than clumsy human feet. She gathered three strawberries, heavy with juice, and ate them luxuriously, lying full-length on a sandy terrace before a mouse-hole. From this bank she could see across the field, but to-day it looked different—as large as ever; as oddly tilted; but alight and alive with the early sunshine: now all the shadows ran a different way, dewy—they seemed —on the gleaming golden grass. She saw in the distance the lonely group of trees: they still seemed to float on

a grassy ocean. She thought of her mother's fear of open spaces. 'But I could cross this field,' she thought, 'I could go anywhere. . . .' Was this, perhaps, what Eggletina had thought? Eggletina—Uncle Hendreary's child—who, they said, had been eaten by the cat. Did enterprise, Arrietty wondered, always meet with disaster? Was it really better, as her parents had always taught her, to live in secret darkness underneath the floor?

The ants were out, she saw, and busy about their business —flurried, eager, weaving their anxious routes among the grass stems; every now and again, Arrietty noticed, waving its antennae, an ant would run up a grass stem and look around. A great contentment filled Arrietty: yes—here they were, for better or worse—there could be no going back!

Refreshed by the strawberries, she went on up the bank and into the shade of the hedge: here was sunflecked green-ness and a hollowness above her. Up and up as far as she could see there were layers and storeys of green chambers, crossed and recrossed with springing branches: cathedral-like, the hedge seemed from the inside.

Arrietty put her foot on a lower branch and swung herself up into the green shadows: quite easy, it was, with branches to her hand on all sides—easier than climbing a ladder; a ladder as high as this would mean a feat of endur-ance, and a ladder at best was a dull thing, whereas here was variety, a changing of direction, exploration of heights unknown. Some twigs were dry and rigid, shedding curls of dusty bark; others were lissom and alive with sap: on these she would swing a little (as so often she had dreamed of swinging in that other lifetime under the floor!).   'I will come here when it is windy,' she told herself, 'when the whole hedge is alive and swaying in the wind. . . .'

Up and up she went.   She found an old bird's-nest, the moss inside was straw-dry.   She climbed into it and lay for a while and, leaning over the edge, dropped crumbled pieces of dried moss through the tangled branches below her; to watch them plummet between the boughs gave her, she

found, an increased sense of height, a delicious giddiness which, safely in the nest, she enjoyed.   But having felt this safety made climbing out and on and up seem far more dangerous.   'Suppose I fell,' thought Arrietty, 'as those bits of moss fell, skimming down through the shadowy hollows and banging and bouncing as they go?'   But, as her hands closed round the friendly twigs and her toes spread a little to grip the bark, she was suddenly aware of her absolute safety—the ability (which for so long had been hidden deeply inside her) to climb.   'It's heredity,' she told herself, 'that's why borrowers' hands and feet are longer in proportion than the hands and feet of human beings; that's how my father can come down by a fold in the table-cloth; how he can climb a curtain by the bobbles; how he can swing on his name-tape from a desk to a chair, from a chair to the floor. Just because I was a girl, and not allowed to go borrowing, it doesn't say I haven't got the gift. . . .'

Suddenly, raising her head, she saw the blue sky above her, through the tracery of leaves—leaves which trembled and whispered as, in her haste, she swayed their stems. Placing her foot in a fork and swinging up, she caught her petticoat on a wild rose thorn and heard it rip. She picked the thorn out of the stuff and held it in her hand (it was the size to her of a rhinoceros-horn to a human being): it was light in proportion to its bulk, but very sharp and vicious looking. 'We could use this for something,' Arrietty thought. 'I must think . . . some kind of weapon. . . .' One more pull and her head and shoulders were outside the hedge; the sun fell hot on her hair, and dazzled by the brightness she screwed her eyes up as she gazed about her.

Hills and dales, valleys, fields and woods—dreaming in the sunshine; she saw there were cows in the next field but one. Approaching the wood, from a field on the lower side, she saw a man with a gun—very far away, he looked, very harmless. She saw the roof of Aunt Sophy's house and the kitchen chimney smoking. On the turn of a distant road, as it wound between the hedges, she saw a milk-cart: the sunlight flashed on the metal churn and she heard the faint fairy-like tinkle of the harness brasses. What a world—mile upon mile, thing after thing, layer upon layer of unimagined richness—and she might never have seen it! She might have lived and died as so many of her relations had done, in dusty twilight—hidden behind a wainscot.

Coming down, she found a rhythm: a daring swing, a letting go, and a light drop into thickly clustered leaves which her instinct told her would act as a safety net—a cage of lissom twigs, which sprang to hand and foot—lightly to be caught, lightly to be let go. Such leaves clustered more thickly towards the outside of the hedge, not in the bare hollows within, and her passage amongst them was almost like surf-riding—a controlled and bouncing slither. The last bough dropped her lightly on the slope of a grassy bank, springing back into place above her head, as lightly she let it go, with a graceful elastic shiver.

Arrietty examined her hands: one was slightly grazed. 'But they'll harden up,' she told herself. Her hair stood on end and was filled with bark dust and there in her white embroidered petticoat she saw a great tear.

Hurriedly she picked three more strawberries as a peace-offering and, wrapping them in a violet leaf so as not to stain her vest, she scrambled down the bank, across the ditch, and into the clump of long grass.

Homily, at the entrance to the boot, looked worried as usual.

'Oh, Arrietty, wherever have you been? Breakfast's been ready this last twenty minutes. Your father's out of his mind!'

'Why?' asked Arrietty, surprised.

'With worrying about you—with looking for you.'

'I was quite near,' Arrietty said. 'I was only in the hedge. You could have called me.'

Homily put her finger on her lip and glanced in a fearful way from one side to another: 'You can't *call*,' she said, dropping her voice to an angry whisper. 'We're not to make any noise at all, your father says. No calling or

shouting—nothing to draw attention. Danger, that's what he said there is—danger on all sides. . . .'

'I don't mean you have to whisper,' Pod said, appearing suddenly from behind the boot, carrying the half nail-scissor (he had been cutting a small trail through the thickest grass). But don't you go off, Arrietty, never again, without you say just where you're going, and what for, and for how long. Understand?'

'No,' said Arrietty, uncertainly, 'I don't quite. I mean I don't always know what I'm going *for*.' (For what, for instance, had she climbed to the top of the hedge?) 'Where is all this danger? I didn't see any. Excepting three cows two fields away.'

Pod looked thoughtfully to where a sparrow-hawk hung motionless in the clear sky.

'It's everywhere,' he said, after a moment. 'Before and Behind, Above and Below.'

CHAPTER SEVEN

'PUFF AGAINST THE WIND'
Oxford and Harvard Boat Race, 1869
[*Extract from Arrietty's Diary and Proverb Book, August 27th.*]

WHILE HOMILY and Arrietty were finishing breakfast, Pod got busy: he walked thoughtfully around the boot, surveying it from different angles; he would touch the leather with a practised hand, peer at it closely, and then stand back, half-closing his eyes; he removed the borrowing-bags, one by one, carefully stacking them on the grass outside, and then he crawled inside; they could hear him grunting and panting a little as he knelt, and stopped and measured—he was, they gathered, making a carefully calculated examination of seams, joins, floor space, and quality of stitching.

After a while he joined them as they sat there on the grass. 'Going to be a hot day,' he said thoughtfully, as he sat down, 'a real scorcher.' He removed his neck-tie and heaved a sigh.

'What was you looking at, Pod?' asked Homily, after a moment.

'You saw,' said Pod, 'that boot.' He was silent a moment, and then, 'That's no tramp's boot,' he said, 'nor that boot weren't made for no working man neither: that boot,' went on Pod, staring at Homily, 'is a gentleman's boot.'

'Oh,' breathed Homily in a relieved voice, half-closing her eyes and fanning her face with a limp hand, 'thank goodness for that!'

227

'Why, Mother,' asked Arrietty, irritated, 'what's wrong with a working man's boot? Papa's a working man, isn't he?'

Homily smiled and shook her head in a pitying way. 'It's a question,' she said, 'of quality.'

'Your mother's right there,' said Pod. 'Hand-sewn, that boot is, and as fine a bit of leather as ever I've laid me hand on.' He leaned towards Arrietty. 'And you see, lass, a gentleman's boot is well cared for, well greased and dubbined—years and years of it. If it hadn't been, don't you see, it would never have stood up—as this boot has stood up —to wind and rain and sun and frost. They pays dear for their boots, gentlemen do, but they sees they gets good value.'

'That's right,' agreed Homily, nodding her head and looking at Arrietty.

'Now, that hole in the toe,' Pod went on, 'I can patch that up with a bit of leather from the tongue. I can patch that up good and proper.'

'It's not worth the time nor the thread,' exclaimed Homily. 'I mean to say, just for a couple o' nights or a day or two; it's not as though we were going to *live* in a boot,' she pointed out, with an amused laugh.

Pod was silent a moment and then he said slowly: 'I bin thinking.'

'I mean to say,' Homily went on, 'we do know we got relations in this field and—though I wouldn't call a badgers' set a proper home, mind—at least it's somewhere.'

Pod raised solemn eyes. 'Maybe,' he said, in the same grave voice, 'but all the same, I bin thinking. I bin thinking,' he went on; 'relations or no relations, they're still borrowers, ain't they? And among human beings, for instance, who ever sees a borrower?' He gazed round challengingly.

'Well, that boy did,' began Arrietty, 'and——'

'Ah,' said Pod, 'because you, Arrietty, who wasn't no borrower—who hadn't even learned to borrow—went up and talked to him: sought him out, shameless—knowing no better. And I told you just what would happen; hunted out, I said we'd be, by cats and rat-catchers—by policemen and all. Now was I right or wasn't I?'

'Yes, you were right,' said Arrietty, 'but——'

'There ain't no buts,' said Pod. 'I was right. And if I was right then, I'm right now. See? I bin thinking and what I bin thinking is right—and, this time, there ain't going to be no nonsense from you. Nor from your mother, neither.'

'There won't be no nonsense from me, Pod,' said Homily in a pious voice.

'Now,' said Pod, 'this is how it strikes me: human beings stand high and move fast; when you stand higher you can see farther—do you get me? What I mean to say is—if, with them advantages, a human being can't never find a borrower . . . even goes as far as to say they don't believe borrowers *exist*, why should we borrowers—who stand lower and move slower, compared to them like—hope to do much better? Living in a house, say, with several families—well, of course, we know each other . . . stands to reason: we been brought up together. But come afield, to a strange place like this and—this is how it seems to me—borrowers is hid from borrowers.'

'Oh my——' said Homily unhappily.

'We don't move "slow" exactly,' said Arrietty.

'Compared to them, I said.   Our legs move *fast* enough —but theirs is longer: look at the ground they cover!'   He turned to Homily.   'Now don't upset yourself.   I don't say we won't find the Hendrearies—maybe we will . . . quite soon.   Or anyway before the winter——'

'The winter . . .' breathed Homily in a stricken voice.

'But we got to plan,' went on Pod, 'and act, as though there weren't no badgers' set.   Do you see what I mean?'

'Yes, Pod,' said Homily huskily.

'I bin thinking it out,' he repeated.   'Here we are, the three of us, with what we got in the bags, two hat-pins, and an old boot: we got to face up to it and, what's more,' he added solemnly, 'we got to live different.'

'How different?' asked Homily.

'Cold food, for instance.   No more hot tea.   No coffee. We got to keep the candle and the matches in hand for winter.   We got to look about us and see what there is.'

'Not caterpillars, Pod,' pleaded Homily, 'you promised! I couldn't never eat a caterpillar.'

'Nor you shall,' said Pod, 'not if I can help it.   There's other things, this time o'year, plenty.   Now, I want you to get up, the two of you, and see how this boot drags.'

'How do you mean?' asked Homily, mystified, but obediently they both stood up.

'See these laces?' said Pod, 'good and strong—been oiled, that's why . . . or tarred.   Now, you each take a lace over your shoulder and pull.   Turn your back to the boot—that's right—and just walk forward.'

Homily and Arrietty leaned on the traces and the boot came on with a bump and a slither so fast across the slippery grass that they stumbled and fell—they had not expected it would be so light.

'Steady on!' cried Pod, running up beside them. 'Take it steady, can't you? Up you get—that's the way ... steady, steady ... that's fine. You see,' he said, when they paused for breath, having dragged the boot to the edge of the long grass, 'how it goes—like a bird!' Homily and Arrietty rubbed their shoulders and said nothing; they even smiled slightly, a pale reflection of Pod's pride and delight. 'Now sit down, both of you. You was fine. Now, you'll see, this is going to be good.'

He stood beaming down at them as, meekly, they sat on the grass. 'It's like this,' he explained. 'I talked just now of danger—to you, Arrietty—and that's because, though brave we must be (and there's none braver than your mother when she's put to it), we can't never be foolhardy: we got to make our plans and we got to keep our heads; we can't afford to waste no energy—climbing hedges just for fun, and suchlike—and we can't afford to take no risks. We got to make our plan and we got to stick to it. Understand?'

'Yes,' said Arrietty, and Homily nodded her head. 'Your father's right,' she said.

'You got to have a main object,' went on Pod, 'and ours is there, ready-made—we got to find the badgers' set. Now how are we going to set about it? It's a big field—take us the best part of a day to get along one side of it, let alone have time to look down holes; and we'd be wore out, that's what we'd be. Say I went off looking by myself—well, your mother would never know a moment's peace all day long, till she had me safe back again: there's nothing bad enough for what she'd be imagining. *And* going on at you, Arrietty. Now, that's all wear and tear, and we can't afford too much of it. Folk get silly when they're fussed, if you see what I mean, and that's when accidents happen.'

'Now, my idea,' Pod went on, 'is this: we'll work our way all round this field, like I said last night, by the edges——'

'Hedges,' corrected Arrietty, under her breath, without thinking.

'I heard what you said, Arrietty,' remarked Pod quietly (he seldom grudged her superior education); 'there's hedges and edges, and I meant edges.'

'Sorry,' murmured Arrietty, blushing.

'As I was saying,' Pod went on, 'we'll work our way round, systematic-like, exploring the banks and'—he looked at Arrietty pointedly—'hedges—and camping as we go: a day here, a day or two there, just as we feel; or depending on the holes and burrows; there'll be great bits of bank where there couldn't be no badgers' set—we can skip those, as you might say. Now you see, Homily, we couldn't do this if we had a settled home.'

'You mean,' asked Homily sharply, 'that we've got to drag the boot?'

'Well,' said Pod, 'was it heavy?'

'With all our gear in it, it would be.'

'Not over grass,' said Pod.

'And uphill!' exclaimed Homily.

'*Level* here at the bottom of the field,' corrected Pod patiently, 'as far as them rushes; then uphill at the top of the field, alongside the stream; then across—*level* again; then the last lap of all, which brings us back to the stile again, and it's downhill all the way!'

'Um-m-m,' said Homily, unconvinced.

'Well,' said Pod, 'out with it—speak your mind: I'm open to suggestions.'

'Oh, Mother——' began Arrietty in a pleading voice, and then became silent.

'Has Arrietty and me got to drag all the time?' asked Homily.

'Now, don't be foolish,' said Pod, 'we take it in turns, of course.'

'Oh well,' sighed Homily, 'what can't be cured, needs must.'

'That's my brave old girl,' said Pod. 'Now about provender—*food*,' he explained, as Homily looked up bewildered, 'we better become vegetarian, pure and simple, one and all, and make no bones about it.'

'There won't be no bones to make,' remarked Homily grimly, 'not if we become vegetarian.'

'The nuts is coming on,' said Pod; 'nearly ripe they'll be down in that sheltered corner—milky like. Plenty of fruit—blackberries, them wild strawberries. Plenty of salad, dandelion, say, and sorrel. There's gleanings still in that cornfield t'other side of the stile. We'll manage—the thing is you got to get used to it: no hankering for boiled ham, chicken rissoles, and that kind of fodder. Now, Arrietty,' he went on, 'as you're so set on hedge-climbing, you and your mother had better go off and gather us some nuts, how's that, eh? And I'll get down to a bit of cobbling.' He glanced at the boot.

'Where do you find the nuts?' asked Arrietty.

'There, about half-way along'—Pod pointed to a thickening of pale green in the hedge—'before you get to the water. You climb up, Arrietty, and throw 'em down, and your mother can gather 'em up. I'll come down and join you later: we got to dig a pit.'

'A pit? Whatever for?' asked Arrietty.

'We can't carry that weight of nuts around,' explained Pod, 'not in a boot this size. Wherever we find provender, we got to make a cache like, and mark it down for winter.'

'Winter . . .' moaned Homily softly.

Nevertheless, as Arrietty helped her mother over the rough places in the ditch, which—because it was shallow, well drained, and fairly sheltered—could be used as a highway, she felt closer to Homily than she had felt for years: more like a sister, as she put it. 'Oh, look,' cried Homily, when they saw a scarlet pimpernel; she stooped and picked it by its hair-thin stalk. 'Int it lovely?' she said in a tender voice; touching the fragile petals with a work-worn finger, she tucked it into the opening of her blouse. Arrietty found a pale-blue counterpart in the delicate bird's-eye, and put it in her hair; and suddenly the day began to seem like a holiday. 'Flowers made for borrowers,' she thought, 'and humans don't realize. . . .'

At last they reached the nutty part of the hedge. 'Oh, Arrietty,' exclaimed Homily, gazing up at the spreading branches with mingled pride and fear, 'you can't never go up there.'

But Arrietty could and would: she was delighted to show off her climbing. In a workmanlike manner she stripped off her jersey, hung it on a grey-green spike of thistle, rubbed her palms together (in front of Homily she did not like to spit on them), and clambered up the bank.

Homily watched below, her two hands clasped and pressed against her heart, how the outer leaves shivered and shook as Arrietty, invisible, climbed up inside. 'Are you all right?' she kept calling. 'Oh, Arrietty, do be careful. Suppose you fell and broke your leg?' And then after a while the nuts

began to come down, and poor Homily, under fire, ran this way and that, in her panting efforts to retrieve them.

Not that they came down fast enough to be really dangerous. Nut-gathering was not quite so easy as Arrietty had imagined: for one thing, it was still a little early in the season and the nuts were not quite ripe; each was still encased in what to Arrietty looked something like a tough, green foxglove bell, and was fixed firmly to the tree. It was quite an effort, until she learned the trick of a sharp twist, for Arrietty to detach the clusters. And what was more, even to reach them was not easy: it meant climbing or swinging or edging her body along a perilously swaying branch tip (later Pod made her, with a piece of lead, some twine, and a supple dock root, a kind of swinging cosh with which she could strike them down); but she persevered, and soon there was a sizable pile in the ditch, neatly stacked up by the perspiring Homily.

'That'll do now,' Homily called out breathlessly after a while. 'No more or your poor pa will never get through with the digging,' and Arrietty, hot and dishevelled, with scratched face and smarting hands, thankfully climbed down. She flung herself full length in the speckled shade of a clump of cow-parsley and complained of feeling thirsty.

'Well, there's water farther along, so your pa says. Do you think you could walk it?'

Of course Arrietty could walk it. Tired she might be, but determined to foster this new-found spirit of adventure in her mother. She caught up her jersey and they set off along the ditch.

The sun was higher now and the round was hotter. They came to a place where some beetles were eating a long-dead mole. 'Don't look,' said Homily, quickening her step and averting her eyes, as though it were a street accident.

But Arrietty, more practical for once, said: 'But when they've finished, perhaps we ought to have the skin. It might come in useful,' she pointed out, 'for winter.'

'Winter . . .' breathed Homily. 'You say it to torment me,' she added in a sudden spurt of temper.

The stream when they reached it seemed less a stream than a small clear pond, disturbed as they approached by several plops and spreading silvery circles as the frogs, alarmed, dived in. It meandered out of a tangled wood beyond the hedge and, crossing the corner of the field, had spread into a small marsh of cresses, mud, and deep-sunk cattle-tracks. On the farther side of the stream the field was bounded, not by a junction of hedges but by several mildewed posts hung with rusty wire slung across the water; beyond this frail barrier the shadowed tree trunks of the wood seemed to crowd and glower as though they longed to rush forward across the strip of water into the sunlit field. Arrietty saw a powdery haze of wild forget-me-not, with here and there a solitary bulrush; the dry-edged cattle-tracks were water-filled chasms criss-crossed with dikes and there was a delicious smell of fragrant slime, lightly spiced with spearmint. A sinuous feathered current of clear ripples broke the still, sky-reflecting surface of the miniature lake. It was very beautiful, Arrietty thought, and strangely exciting; she had never seen so much water before.

'Watercress!' announced Homily in a flat voice. 'We'll take a bit o' that for tea. . . .'

They picked their way along the raised ridges of the cow craters whose dark pits of stagnant water reflected the cloudless sky. Arrietty, stooping over them, saw her own clear image sharply focused against the dreaming blue, but oddly tilted and somehow upside-down.

'Careful you don't fall in, Arrietty,' warned Homily, 'you only got one change, remember. You know,' she went on in an interested voice, pointing at a bulrush, 'I could have used one of those back home, under the kitchen. Just the thing for cleaning out the flues. Wonder your father never thought of it. And don't drink yet,' advised Homily, 'wait till we get where the water's running. Same with watercress, you don't want to pick it where the water's stagnant. You never know what you might get.'

At last they found a place from where it would be possible to drink: a solid piece of bark, embedded firmly in the mud yet stretching out into the stream forming a kind of landing stage or rough jetty. It was grey and nobbly and looked like a basking crocodile. Arrietty stretched her length on the corklike surface and cupping her hands took long draughts of the cool water. Homily, after some hesitation and arrangements of skirts, did the same. 'Pity,' she remarked, 'we don't have a jug nor a pail, nor some kind of bottle. We could do with some water in the boot.'

Arrietty did not reply; she was gazing happily down past the drifting surface into the depths below.

'Can vegetarians eat fish?' she asked, after a while.

'I don't rightly know,' said Homily; 'we'll have to ask

your father.' Then the cook in Homily reasserted itself. 'Are there any?' she asked, a trifle hungrily.

'Plenty,' Arrietty murmured dreamily, gazing down into the shifting depths: the stream, she thought, seemed to be gently breathing. 'About as long as my forearm. And some invisible things,' she added, 'like shrimps——'

'How do you mean—*invisible*?' asked Homily.

'Well,' explained Arrietty in the same absent voice, 'I mean you can see through them. And some black things,' she went on, 'like blobs of expanding velvet——'

'Leeches, I shouldn't wonder,' remarked Homily with a slight shudder, and added dubiously after a moment's thought: 'Might be all right stewed.'

'Do you think papa could make a fishing-net?' asked Arrietty.

'Your father can make anything,' asserted Homily loyally. 'No matter what—you've only got to name it.'

Arrietty lay quiet for a while, dozing she seemed on this sun-soaked piece of bark, and when at last she spoke Homily gave a startled jump—she, too, lulled for once into quietness, had begaun to float away. 'Never do,' she thought, 'to drop off to sleep on a log like this: you might turn over.'

And she roused herself by an inward shake and rapidly blinked her eyes.

'What did you say, Arrietty?' she asked.

'I said,' Arrietty went on after a moment in a lilting lazy voice (she spoke as though she too had been dreaming), 'couldn't we bring the boot down here?   Right beside the water?'

CHAPTER EIGHT

'EVERY MAN'S HOUSE IS HIS CASTLE'
Great Fire of London began 1666
[*Extract from Arrietty's Diary and Proverb Book, September 2nd.*]

AND THAT is just what they did do. Pod, consulted, had looked over the site, weighed the pros and cons, and rather ponderously, as though it was his own idea, decided they should move camp. They would choose a site farther along the hedge as near as was safe to the brook. 'Homily can do her washing. You got to have water,' he announced, but rather defensively as though he had only just thought of it. 'And I *might* make a fish-net, at that.'

The boot, though fully loaded, ran quite easily along the shallow ditch with all three of them in harness. The site Pod had chosen was a platform or alcove half-way up the steepish bank below the hedge.

'You want to keep fairly high,' he explained (as, to make it lighter for hauling, they unpacked the boot in the ditch), 'with rain like we had the other night and the brook so near. You got to remember,' he went on, selecting a sharp tool, 'that flood we had back home when the kitchen boiler burst.'

'What do you mean,' sniffed Homily, 'got to remember? Scalding hot, that one was, too.' She straightened her back and gazed up the slope at the site.

It was well chosen: a kind of castle, Arrietty had called it, in which they would live in the dungeons, but in their case the dungeon was more like an alcove, open to the sun and

241

air. A large oak-tree, at one time part of the hedge, had been sawn off at the base; solid and circular, it stood above the bank where the hedge thinned, like the keep of a fortress, its roots flung out below as flying buttresses. Some of these were not quite dead and had shot forth here and there a series of suckers like miniature oak-trees. One of these saplings overhung their cave, shading its lip with sun-flecked shadow.

The underside of a large root formed the roof of their alcove and other smaller roots supported the walls and floor. These, last, Pod pointed out, would come in handy as beams and shelves.

He was busy now (while the boot still lay in the ditch) extracting some nails from the heel.

'It seems a shame,' remarked Homily as she and Arrietty sorted out belongings for earlier transportation. 'You'll loosen the whole heel.'

'What good's the heel to us?' asked Pod, perspiring with effort; 'we ain't going to wear the boot. And I need the nails,' he added firmly.

The flat top of the tree-trunk, they decided, would come in useful as a look-out, a bleaching ground for washing, and a place for drying herbs and fruit. Or for grinding corn. Pod was urged to chip out foot-holes in the bank for easier climbing. (This he did later, and for years after these foot-holes were considered by naturalists to be the work of the greater spotted woodpecker.)

'We got to dig a cache for these nuts,' remarked Pod, straightening his aching back, 'but better we get all ship-shape here first and snug for the night, as you might

say. Then after the digging we can come home straight
to bed.'

Seven nails, Pod decided, were enough for the moment (it
was tough work extracting them). The idea had come to him
when he had been mending the hole in the toe. Heretofore
he had only worked on the softest of glove leathers and his
little cobbler's needle was too frail to pierce the tough hide of
the boot. Using the electric bell-clapper as a hammer, he
had pierced (with the help of a nail) a series of matching
holes—in the boot itself and the tongue which was meant to
patch it; then all he had to do was to thread in some twine.

By the same token, he had made a few eyelet holes round
the ankle of the boot so they could, if necessary, lash it up at
night—as campers would close a tent flap.

It did not take them long to drag the empty boot up the
slope, but wedging it firmly in the right position under the
main root of the alcove was a tricky business and took a
good deal of manœuvring. At last it was done—and they
left panting but relieved.

The boot lay on its side, sole against the rear wall and
ankle facing outwards, so that if disturbed at night they
could spot the intruder approaching, and when they woke
in the morning they would get the early sun.

Pod drove a series of nails along one shelf-like root on the
right wall of the alcove (the left wall was almost completely
taken up by the boot), on which he hung his tools: the half-
nail scissor, the fret-saw, the bell-clapper, and the piece of
razor-blade.

Above this shelf was a sandy recess which Homily could
use as a larder; it went in quite deep.

When Pod had placed the larger hat-pin in a place of strategic importance near the mouth of the alcove (the smaller one they were to keep in the boot in case, Pod said, 'of these alarms at night') they felt they had met the major demands of the moment and, though tired, they felt a pleasant sense of achievement and of effort well spent.

'Oh, my back,' exclaimed Homily, her hands in the small

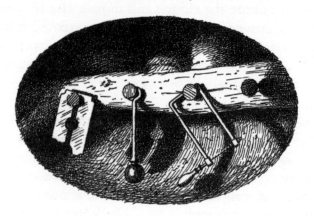

of it. 'Let's just sit down, Pod, for a moment and rest quietly and look at the view.' And it was worth looking at in the afternoon sunlight: they could see right away across the field. A pheasant flew out of the far group of trees and whirred away to the left.

'We can't sit for long,' said Pod, after a moment; 'we got to dig that cache.'

Wearily, they collected the half nail-scissor and a borrowing-bag for anything they might see on the way, and the three of them climbed down the bank.

'Never mind,' Pod comforted Homily as they made their

way along the ditch, 'we can go straight to bed after. And you haven't got no cooking,' he reminded her.

Homily was not comforted. As well as tired she realized suddenly she was feeling very hungry, but not—she reflected glumly—somehow, for nuts.

When they reached the place and Pod had removed the first sods in order to reach the soil (great shrubs these were to him, like uprooting clumps of pampas), Homily revived a little—determined to play her part: courageous helpmate, it was to-day. She had never dug before but the prospect faintly excited her. Strange things are possible in this odd world and she might (one never knew) discover a new talent.

They had to take it in turns with the half nail-scissor. ('Never mind,' Pod told them. 'I'll set to work to-morrow and rig us up a couple of spades.')

Homily screamed when she saw her first worm: it was as long as she was—even longer, she realized as the last bit wriggled free. 'Pick it up,' shouted Pod; 'it won't hurt you. You got to learn.' And before Arrietty (who was not too keen on worms herself) could volunteer to help, she saw her mother, with set face and tensed muscles, lay hold of the

writhing creature and drop it some inches beyond the hole, where gratefully it writhed away among the grasses. 'It was heavy,' Homily remarked—her only comment—as she went back to her digging; but Arrietty thought she looked a trifle pale.   After her third worm, Homily became slightly truculent—she handled it with the professional casualness of an experienced snake-charmer—almost bored, she seemed.   Arrietty was much impressed.   It was a different story, however, when her mother dug up a centipede—then Homily not only screamed but ran, clutching her skirts, half-way up the bank, where she stood on a flat stone, almost gibbering.   She only consented to rejoin them when Pod, tickling the squirming creature with the tip of the nail-scissor, sent it scuttling angrily into the 'bush.'

They carried a few nuts home for supper: these, and several wild strawberries, a leaf or two of watercress, washed down with cold water, made an adequate though dismal repast.   There seemed to be something lacking; a bit of digestive biscuit would have been nice, or a good cup of hot tea.   But the last piece of biscuit, Homily decided, must be kept for breakfast, and the tea (Pod had ordained) only for celebrations and emergencies.

But they slept well all the same; and felt safe, tucked away under their protecting root, with the boot laced up in front. It was a little airless, perhaps, but they were far less cramped for space because so many of their belongings could be stacked outside now in the sandy, root-filled annexe.

CHAPTER NINE

'AS YE SOW, SO SHALL YE REAP'
Oliver Cromwell, Protector of England, died 1658
[*Extract from Arrietty's Diary and Proverb Book, September 3rd.*]

'Now, TO-DAY,' said Pod, at breakfast next morning, 'we'd better go gleaning. There's a harvested cornfield yonder. Nuts and fruit is all right,' he went on, 'but for winter we're going to need bread.'

'Winter?' moaned Homily. 'Aren't we supposed to be looking for the badgers' set? And,' she went on, 'who's going to grind the corn?'

'You and Arrietty, couldn't you?' said Pod, 'between two stones.'

'You'll be asking us to make fire with two sticks next,' grumbled Homily, 'and how do you think I can make bread without an oven? And what about yeast? Now, if you ask me,' she went on, 'we don't want to go gleaning and trying to make bread and all that nonsense: what we want to do is to put a couple of nuts in our pockets, pick what fruit we see on the way, and have a real good look for the Hendrearies.'

'As you say,' agreed Pod, after a moment, and heaved a sigh.

They tidied away breakfast, put the more precious of their belongings inside the boot and carefully laced it up, and struck out uphill, beyond that water, along the hedge which lay at right angles to the bank in which they had passed the night.

It was a weary trapes. Their only adventure was at midday, when they rested after a frugal luncheon of rain-sodden, overripe blackberries. Homily, lying back against the bank, her drowsy eyes fixed on the space between a stone and a log, saw the ground begin to move; it streamed past the gap, in a limited but constant flow.

'Oh, my goodness, Pod,' she breathed, after watching a moment to make sure it was not an optical illusion, 'do you see what I see? There, by that log . . .' Pod, following the direction of her eyes, did not speak straight away, and when he did it was hardly above a whisper.

'Yes,' he said, seeming to hesitate, 'it's a snake.'

'Oh, my goodness . . .' breathed Homily again in a trembling voice, and Arrietty's heart began to beat wildly.

'Don't move,' whispered Pod, his eyes on the steady ripple: there seemed to be no end—the snake went on and on and on (unless it was, as Arrietty thought afterwards, that Time itself, in a moment of danger, has often been said to slow down), but just when they felt they could bear the sight not a moment longer, they saw the flick of a tail.

They all breathed again. 'What was it, Pod?' asked Homily weakly. 'An adder?'

'A grass snake, I think,' said Pod.

'Oh,' exclaimed Arrietty, with a relieved little laugh, 'they're harmless.'

Pod looked at her gravely; his currant-bunnish face seemed more doughy than usual. 'To humans,' he said slowly. 'And what's more,' he added, 'you can't talk to snakes.'

'Pity,' remarked Homily, 'that we did not bring one of the hat-pins.'

'What good would that have done?' asked Pod.

By about tea-time (rose-hips, this time: they were sick of sodden blackberries) they found, to their surprise, that they

were more than half-way along the third side of the field. There had been more walking than searching; none of the ground they had covered so far could have housed the Hendrearies, let alone a badger colony; the bank, as they made their way uphill beside the hedge, had become lower in proportion until, here where they sat drearily munching rose-hips, there was no bank at all.

'It's almost as far now,' said Pod, 'to go back the same way as we came as to keep on round. What do you say, Homily?'

'We better keep on round, then,' said Homily hoarsely, a hairy seed of a rose-hip being stuck in her throat. She began to cough. 'I thought you said you cleaned them?' she complained to Arrietty, when she could get back her breath.

'I must have missed one,' said Arrietty. 'Sorry,' and she passed her mother a new half-hip, freshly scoured; she had rather enjoyed opening the pale scarlet globes and scooping out the golden nest of close-packed seeds, and she liked the flavour of the hips themselves—they tasted, she thought, of apple-skins honeyed over with a dash of rose petal.

'Well, then,' said Pod, standing up, 'we better start moving.'

The sun was setting when they reached the fourth and last side of the field; but the hedge threw out a ragged carpet of shadow. Through a gap in the dark branches they could see a blaze of golden light on a sea of harvested stubble.

'As we're here,' suggested Pod, standing still and staring through the gap, 'and it's pretty well downhill most the way back now, what's the harm in an ear or two of corn?'

'None,' said Homily wearily, 'if it would walk out and follow us.'

'Corn ain't heavy,' said Pod; 'wouldn't take us no time to pick up a few ears. . . .'

Homily sighed. It was she who had suggested this trip, after all. In for a penny, she decided wanly, in for a pound.

'Have it your own way,' she said resignedly.

So they clambered through the hedge and into the cornfield.

And into a strange world (as it seemed to Arrietty), not like the Earth at all: the golden stubble, lit by the evening sun, stood up in rows like a blasted colourless forest; each separate bole threw its own long shadow and all the shadows, combed by the sun in one direction, lay parallel—a bizarre criss-cross of black and gold which flicked and fleckered with every footstep. Between the boles, on the dry straw-strewn earth, grew scarlet pimpernel in plenty, with here and there a ripened ear of wheat.

'Take a bit of stalk, too,' Pod advised them. 'Makes it easier to carry.'

The light was so strange in this broken, beetle-haunted forest that, every now and again, Arrietty seemed to lose sight of her parents but, turning panic-stricken, would find them again quite close, zebra-striped with sun and shadow.

At last they could carry no more and Pod had mercy; they forgathered on their own side of the hedge, each with two bunches of wheat ears, carried head downwards by a short length of stalks. Arrietty was reminded of Cramp-furl, back home in the big house, going past the grating with onions for the kitchen; they had been strung on strings and looked much like these corn grains but in a different proportion.

'Can you manage all that?' asked Pod anxiously of Homily as she started off ahead down the hill.

'I'd sooner carry it than grind it,' remarked Homily tartly, without looking back.

'There wouldn't be no badgers' sets along this side,' panted Pod (he was carrying the heaviest load), coming abreast of Arrietty. 'Not with all the ploughing, sowing, dogs, men, horses, tractors, and what-not as there must have been——'

'Where could one be, then?' asked Arrietty, setting down

her corn for a moment to rest her hands. 'We've been all round.'

'There's only one place to look now,' said Pod; 'them trees in the middle,' and standing still in the deep shadow, he gazed across the stretch of pasture land. The field looked in this light much as it had on that first day (could that only be the day before yesterday?). But from this angle they could not see the trail of dusky shadow thrown by the island of trees.

'Open ground,' said Pod, staring; 'your mother would never make it.'

'I'd go,' said Arrietty. 'I'd like to go. . . .'

Pod was silent. 'I got to think,' he said, after a moment. 'Come on, lass. Take up your corn, else we won't get back before dark.'

They didn't. Or, rather, it was deep dusk along the ditch of their home stretch and almost dark when they came abreast of their cave. But even in the half-light there seemed something suddenly home-like and welcoming about the sight of their laced-up boot.

Homily sank down at the foot of the bank, between her bunches of corn. 'Just a breather,' she explained weakly, 'before that next pull up.'

'Take your time,' said Pod. 'I'll go ahead and undo the

laces.' Panting a little, half-dragging his ears of corn, he started up the bank. Arrietty followed.

'Pod,' called Homily from the darkness below, without turning, 'you know what?'

'What?' asked Pod.

'It's been a long day,' said Homily; 'suppose, to-night, we made a nice cup of tea?'

'Please yourself,' said Pod, unlacing the neck of the boot and feeling cautiously inside. He raised his voice, shouting down at her: 'What you have now, you can't have later. Bring the half-scissor, Arrietty, will you? It's on a nail in the store-room.' After a moment he added impatiently: 'Hurry up. No need to take all day, it's just there to your hand.'

'It isn't,' came Arrietty's voice, after a moment.

'What do you mean—it isn't?'

'It isn't here. Everything else is, though.'

'Isn't there!' exclaimed Pod unbelievingly. 'Wait a minute, let *me* look.' Their voices sounded muffled to Homily, listening below; she wondered what the fuss was about.

'Something or someone's been mucking about in here,' she heard Pod say, after what seemed a distressed pause; and picking up her ears of wheat Homily scrambled up the bank: heavy going, she found it, in the half-light.

'Get a match, will you,' Pod was saying in a worried voice, 'and light the candle,' and Arrietty foraged in the boot to find the wax-vestas.

As the wick guttered, wavered, then rose to a steady flame, the little hollow, half-way up the bank, became illumined like a scene on a stage; strange shadows were cast on the sandy walls of the annexe. Pod and Homily and little Arrietty appeared as they passed back and forth curiously unreal, like characters in a play. There were the borrowing-bags, stacked neatly together as Pod had left them, their mouths tied up with twine; there hung the tools from their beam-like root, and, leaning beside them—as Pod had left it this morning—the purple thistle-head with which he had swept the floor. He stood there now, white-faced in the candlelight, his hand on a bare nail. 'It was here,' he was saying, tapping the nail; 'that's where I left it.'

'Oh, goodness!' exclaimed Homily, setting down her wheat ears. 'Let's just look again.' She pulled aside the borrowing-bags and felt behind them. 'And you, Arrietty,' she ordered, 'could you get round to the back of the boot?'

But it was not there, nor, they discovered suddenly, was the larger hat-pin. 'Anything but them two things,' Pod kept on saying in a worried voice as Homily, for the third or fourth time, went through the contents of the boot. 'The smaller hat-pin's here all right,' she kept repeating, 'we still got one. You see no animal could unlace a boot——'

'But what kind of animal,' asked Pod wearily, 'would take a half nail-scissor?'

'A magpie might,' suggested Arrietty, 'if it looked kind of shiny.'

'Maybe,' said Pod. 'But what about the hat-pin? I don't see a magpie carrying the two. No,' he went on thoughtfully, 'it doesn't look to me like no magpie, nor like any other race of bird. Nor no animal neither, if it comes to that. Nor I wouldn't say it was any kind of human being. A human being, like as not, finding a hole like this smashes the whole place up. Kind of kick with their feet, human beings do out walking 'fore they touch a thing with their hands. Looks to me,' said Pod, 'like something more in the style of a borrower.

'Oh,' cried Arrietty joyfully, 'then we've found them!'

'Found what?' asked Pod.

'The cousins . . . the Hendrearies. . . .'

Pod was silent a moment. 'Maybe,' he said uneasily again.

'Maybe!' mimicked Homily, irritated. 'Who else could it be? They live in this field, don't they? Arrietty, put some water on to boil, there's a good girl; we don't want to waste the candle.'

'Now see here——' began Pod.

'But we can't fix the tin-lid,' interrupted Arrietty, 'without the ring part of the nail-scissor.'

'Oh, goodness me,' complained Homily, 'use your head and think of something! Suppose we'd never had a nail-scissor! Tie a piece of twine round an aspirin lid and hang it over the flame from a nail or bit of root or something. What were you saying, Pod?'

'I said we got to go careful on the tea, that's all. We was only going to make tea to celebrate like, or in what you might call a case of grave emergency.'

'Well, we are, aren't we?'

'Are what?' asked Pod.

'Celebrating. Looks like we've found what we come for.'

Pod glanced uneasily towards Arrietty who, in the farther corner of the annexe, was busily knotting twine round a ridged edge of a screw-on lid. 'You don't want to go so fast, Homily,' he warned her, lowering his voice, 'nor you don't want to jump to no conclusions. Say it was one of the Hendrearies. All right then, why didn't they leave a word or sign or stay a while and wait for us? Hendreary knows our gear all right—that Proverb book of Arrietty's, say, many's the time he's seen it back home under the kitchen.'

'I don't see what you're getting at,' said Homily in a puzzled voice, watching Arrietty anxiously as gingerly she suspended the water-filled aspirin lid from a root above the candle. 'Careful,' she called out, 'you don't want to burn the twine.'

'What I'm getting at is this,' explained Pod. 'Say you look at the nail-scissor as a blade, a sword, as you might say, and the hat-pin as a spear, say, or a dagger. Well, whoever took them things has armed himself, see what I mean? And left us weaponless.'

'We got the other hat-pin,' said Homily in a troubled voice.

'Maybe,' said Pod, 'but he doesn't know that. See what I mean?'

'Yes,' whispered Homily, subdued.

'Make tea, if you like,' Pod went on, 'but I wouldn't call it a celebration. Not yet, at any rate.'

Homily glanced unhappily towards the candle: above the aspirin lid (she noticed longingly) already there rose a welcome haze of steam. 'Well,' she began, and hesitated, then suddenly she seemed to brighten, 'it comes to the same thing.'

'How do you mean?' asked Pod.

'About the tea,' explained Homily, perking up. 'Going by what you said, stealing our weapons and such—this looks to be something you might call serious. Depends how it strikes you. I mean,' she went on hurriedly, 'there's some I know as might even name it a state of grave emergency.'

'There's some as might,' agreed Pod wanly. Then, suddenly, he sprang aside, beating the air with his hands. Arrietty screamed and Homily, for a second, thought they had both gone mad. Then she saw.

A great moth had lumbered into the alcove, attracted by the candle; it was fawn-coloured and (to Homily) hideous, drunk, and blinded with light. 'Save the tea!' she cried, panic-stricken, and seizing the purple thistle-head, beat wildly about the air. Shadows danced every way and, in their shouting and scolding, they hardly noticed a sudden, silent thickening of night swerve in on the dusk; but they felt the wind of its passing, watched the candle gutter, and saw the moth was gone.

'What was that?' asked Arrietty at last, after an awed silence.

'It was an owl,' said Pod. He looked thoughtful.

'It ate the moth?'

'As it would eat you,' said Pod, 'if you went mucking about after dusk. We're living and learning,' he said. 'No more candles after dark. Up with the sun and down with the sun: that's us, from now on.'

'The water's boiling, Pod,' said Homily.

'Put the tea in,' said Pod, 'and douse the light: we can drink all right in the dark,' and turning away he propped the broom handle back against the wall and, while Homily was making the tea, he tidied up the annexe, stacking the

ears of wheat alongside the boot, straightening the borrowing-bags, and generally seeing all was shipshape for the night. When he had finished he crossed to the recessed shelf and ran a loving hand along his neatly hanging row of tools. Just before they doused the light, he stood for a long time, deep in thought—a quiet hand on a grimly empty nail.

CHAPTER TEN

' LIKE TURNS TO LIKE '
Republic declared in France, 1870
[*Extract from Arrietty's Diary and Proverb Book, September 4th.*]

THEY SLEPT well and woke next morning bright and early.
The sun poured slantwise into the alcove and, when Pod had
unlaced it, into the neck of the boot.   For breakfast Arrietty
gathered six wild strawberries and Homily broke up some
wheat grains with Pod's small bell-clapper which, sprinkled
with water, they ate as cereal.   'And, if you're still hungry,
Arrietty,' remarked Homily, 'you can get yourself a nut.'
Arrietty was and did.

The programme for the day was arranged as follows: Pod,
in view of last night's happening, was to make a solitary
expedition across the field to the island of trees in the centre
in one last bid to find the badgers' set.   Homily, because of
her fear of open spaces, would have to stay behind, and
Arrietty, Pod said, must keep her company.   'There's
plenty of jobs about the house,' he told them.   'To start with
you can weather-proof one of the borrowing-bags, rub it all
over hard with a bit of candle, and it'll do for carting water.
Then you can take the fret-saw and saw off a few hazel-nuts
for drinking out of, and while you're about it you can gather
a few extra nuts and store them in the annexe, seeing as we
don't have a spade.   There's a nice bit o' horse-hair I saw,
in the hedge going towards the stile, caught on a bramble
bush; you can fetch a bit o' that along, if you feel like it, and

I'll see about making a fish-net. And a bit more corn-crushing wouldn't come amiss . . .'

'Oh, come on, Pod,' protested Homily. 'Oblige you we'd like to, but we're not black slaves. . . .'

'Well,' said Pod, gazing thoughtfully across the ocean of tussocky grass, 'it'll take me pretty near all day—getting there, searching around, and getting back: I don't want you fretting. . . .'

'I knew it would end like this,' said Homily later, in a depressed voice, as she and Arrietty were waxing the borrowing-bag. 'What did I tell you always, back home, when you wanted to emigrate? Didn't I tell you just how it would be—draughts, moths, worms, snakes, and what not? And you saw how it was when it rained? What's it going to be like in winter? You tell me that. No one can say I'm not trying,' she went on, 'and no one won't hear a word of grumble pass my lips, but you mark my words, Arrietty; we won't none of us see another spring.' And a round tear fell on the waxed cloth and rolled away like a marble.

'What with the rat-catcher,' Arrietty pointed out, 'we wouldn't have if we'd stayed back home.'

'And I wouldn't be surprised,' Homily persisted, 'if that boy wasn't right. Remember what he said about the end of the race? Our time is come, I shouldn't wonder. If you ask me, we're dying out.'

But she cheered up a bit when they took the bag down to the water to fill it up and a sliver of soap to wash with: the drowsy heat and the gentle stir of ripples past their landing-stage of bark seemed always to calm her; and she even encouraged Arrietty to have a bath and let her splash about

a little in the shallows.   For a being so light the water was
incredibly buoyant and it would not be very long, Arrietty
felt, before she would learn to swim.   Where she had used
the soap the water went cloudy and softly translucent, the
shifting colour of moonstones.

After her bath Arrietty felt refreshed and left Homily in
the annexe to 'get the tea' and went on up the hedge to
collect the horse-hair (not that there was anything to 'get,'
Homily thought irritably, setting out a few hips and haws,
some watercress, and, with the bell-clapper, she cracked a
couple of nuts).

The horse-hair, caught on a bramble, was half-way up the
hedge, but Arrietty, refreshed by her dip, was glad of a
chance to climb.   On the way down, seeking a foothold,
she let out a tiny scream; her toes had touched, not the cool
bark, but something soft and warm.   She hung there,
grasping the horse-hair and staring through the leaves: all
was still—nothing but tangled branches, flecked with sunlight.   After a second or two, in which she did not dare to
move, a flicker of movement caught her eye, as though the
tip of a branch had moved.   Staring she saw, like a bunch
of budding twigs, the shape of a brownish hand.   It could
not be a hand, of course, she told herself, but that's what it
looked like, with tiny, calloused fingers no larger than her
own.   Picking up courage, she touched it with her foot and
the hand grasped her toes.   Screaming and struggling, she
lost her balance and came tumbling through the few
remaining branches on to the dead leaves below.   With her
had fallen a small laughing creature no taller than herself.
'That frighted you,' it said.

Arrietty stared, breathing quickly. He had a brown face, black eyes, tousled dark hair, and was dressed in what she guessed to be shabby moleskin, worn smooth side out. He seemed so soiled and earth-darkened that he matched not only the dead leaves into which they had fallen but the blackened branches as well. 'Who are you?' she asked.

'Spiller,' he said cheerfully, lying back on his elbows.

'You're filthy,' remarked Arrietty disgustedly after a moment; she still felt breathless and very angry.

'Maybe,' he said.

'Where do you live?'

His dark eyes became sly and amused. 'Here and there,' he said, watching her closely.

'How old are you?'

'I don't know,' he said.

'Are you a boy or a grown-up?'

'I don't know,' he said.

'Don't you ever wash?'

'No,' he said.

'Well,' said Arrietty, after an awkward silence, twisting the coarse strands of greyish horse-hair about her wrist, 'I'd better be going——'

'To that hole in the bank?' he asked—the hint of a jeer in his voice.

Arrietty looked startled. 'Do you know it?' When he smiled, she noticed, his lips turned steeply upwards at the corners making his mouth a 'V': it was the most teasing kind of smile she had ever seen.

'Haven't you ever seen a moth before?' he asked.

'You were watching last night?' exclaimed Arrietty.

'Were it private?' he asked.

'In a way; it's our home.'

But he looked bored suddenly, turning his bright gaze away as though searching the more distant grasses. Arrietty opened her mouth to speak but he silenced her with a peremptory gesture, his eyes on the field below. Very curious, she watched him rise cautiously to his feet and then, in a single movement, spring to a branch above his head, reach for something out of sight, and drop again to the ground. The object, she saw, was a taut, dark bow strung with gut and almost as tall as he was; in the other hand he held an arrow.

Staring into the long grass he laid the arrow to the bow, the gut twanged, and the arrow was gone. There was a faint squeak.

'You've killed it,' cried Arrietty, distressed.

'I meant to,' he replied, and sprang down the bank into

the field. He made his way to the tussock of grass and returned after a moment with a dead field-mouse swinging from his hand. 'You got to eat,' he explained.

Arrietty felt deeply shocked, she did not know quite why —at home, under the kitchen, they had always eaten meat; but borrowed meat from the kitchen upstairs; she had seen it raw but she had never seen it killed.

'We're vegetarians,' she said primly. He took no notice: this was just a word to Spiller, one of the noises which people made with their mouths. 'Do you want some meat?' he asked casually. 'You can have a leg.'

'I wouldn't touch it,' cried Arrietty indignantly. She rose to her feet, brushing down her skirt. 'Poor thing,' she said, referring to the field-mouse, 'and I think you're horrid,' she said, referring to him.

'Who isn't?' remarked Spiller, and reached above his head for his quiver.

'Let me look,' begged Arrietty, turning back, suddenly curious.

He passed it to her. It was made, she saw, of a glove finger—the thickish leather of a country glove; the arrows were dry pine-needles, weighted, and tipped with black-thorn.

'How do you stick the thorns to the shaft?' she asked.

'Wild-plum-gum,' sang out Spiller, all in one word.

'Wild-plum-gum?' repeated Arrietty. 'Are they poisoned?' she asked.

'No,' said Spiller, 'fair's fair. Hit or miss. They got to eat—I got to eat. And I kill 'em quicker than an owl does. Nor I don't eat so many.' It was quite a long speech for Spiller. He slung his quiver over his shoulder and turned away. 'I'm going,' he said.

Arrietty scrambled quickly down the bank. 'So am I,' she told him.

They walked along in the dry ditch together. Spiller, she noticed, as he walked glanced sharply about him: the bright black eyes were never still. Sometimes, at a slight rustle in grass or hedge, he would become motionless: there would be no tensing of muscles—he would just cease to move; on such occasions, Arrietty realized, he exactly matched his background. Once he dived into a clump of dead bracken and came out again with a struggling insect.

'Here you are,' he said, and Arrietty, staring, saw some kind of angry beetle.

'What is it?' she asked.

'A cricket. They're nice. Take it.'

'To eat?' asked Arrietty, aghast.

'Eat? No. You take it home and keep it. Sings a treat,' he added.

Arrietty hesitated. 'You carry it,' she said, without committing herself.

When they came abreast of the alcove, Arrietty looked up and saw that Homily, tired of waiting, had dozed off: she was sitting on the sunlit sand and had slumped against the boot.

'Mother,' she called softly from below, and Homily woke at once. 'Here's Spiller . . .' Arrietty went on, a trifle uncertainly.

'Here's what?' asked Homily, without interest. 'Did you get the horse-hair?'

Arrietty, glancing sideways at Spiller, saw that he was in

one of his stillnesses and had become invisible. 'It's my mother,' she whispered. 'Speak to her. Go on.'

Homily, hearing a whisper, peered down, screwing her eyelids against the setting sun.

'What shall I say?' asked Spiller. Then, clearing his voice, he made an effort. 'I got a cricket,' he said. Homily screamed. It took her a moment to add the dun-coloured patches together into the shapes of face, eyes, and hands; it was to Homily as though the grass had spoken.

'Whatever is it?' she gasped. 'Oh, my goodness gracious, whatever have you got there?'

'It's a cricket,' said Spiller again, but it was not to this insect Homily referred.

'It's Spiller,' Arrietty repeated more loudly, and in an aside she whispered to Spiller: 'Drop that dead thing and come on up . . .'

Spiller not only dropped the field-mouse but a fleeting echo of some dim, half-forgotten code must have flicked his memory, and he laid aside his bow as well. Unarmed, he climbed the bank.

Homily stared at Spiller rather rudely when he stepped on to the sandy platform before the boot. She moved right forward, keeping him at bay. 'Good afternoon,' she said coldly; it was as though she spoke from the threshold.

Spiller dropped the cricket and propelled it towards her with his toe. 'Here you are,' he said. Homily screamed again, very loudly and angrily, as the cricket scuttled knee high past her skirts and made for the darker shadow behind the boot. 'It's a present, Mother,' Arrietty explained indignantly. 'It's a cricket: it sings——'

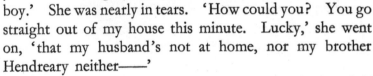

But Homily would not listen. 'How dare you! How dare you! How dare you! You naughty, dirty, unwashed boy.' She was nearly in tears. 'How could you? You go straight out of my house this minute. Lucky,' she went on, 'that my husband's not at home, nor my brother Hendreary neither——'

'Uncle Hendreary——' began Arrietty, surprised, and, if looks could kill, Arrietty would have died.

'Take your beetle,' Homily went on to Spiller, 'and go! And never let me see you here again!' As Spiller hesitated, she added in a fury: 'Do you hear what I say?'

Spiller threw a swift look towards the rear of the boot and a somewhat pathetic one towards Arrietty. 'You better keep it,' he muttered gruffly, and dived off down the bank.

'Oh, Mother!' exclaimed Arrietty reproachfully. She stared at the 'tea' her mother had set out, and even the fact that her mother had filled the half-hips with clover honey milked from the blooms failed to comfort her. 'Poor Spiller! You were rude——'

'Well, who is he? What does he want here? Where did you find him? Forcing his way on respectable people and flinging beetles about! Wouldn't be surprised if we all woke up one day with our throats cut. Did you see the dirt! Ingrained! I wouldn't be surprised if he hadn't left a flea,' and she seized the thistle-broom and briskly swept the spot where the miserable Spiller had placed his unwelcome feet. 'I never had such an experience as this. Never. Not in all my born days. Now, that's the type,' she concluded fiercely, 'who would steal a hat-pin!'

Secretly Arrietty thought so too but she did not say so, using her tongue instead to lick a little of the honey out of the split rose-hip. She also thought, as she savoured the sun-warmed honey, that Spiller, the huntsman, would make better use of the hat-pin than either her mother or father could. She wondered why he wanted the half nail-scissor. 'Have you had your tea?' she asked Homily after a moment.

'I've eaten a couple of wheat grains,' admitted Homily in a martyred voice. 'Now I must air the bedding.'

Arrietty smiled, gazing out across the sunlit field: the bedding was one piece of sock—poor Homily with practically no housework had little now on which to vent her energy. Well, now she'd had Spiller and it had done her good—her eyes looked brighter and her cheeks pinker. Idly, Arrietty watched a small bird picking its way amongst the grasses—no, it was too steady for a bird. 'Here comes Papa,' she said after a moment.

They ran down to meet him. 'Well?' cried Homily eagerly, but as they drew closer, she saw by his face that the news he brought was bad. 'You didn't find it?' she asked in a disappointed voice.

'I found it all right,' said Pod.

'What's the matter then? Why do you look so down? You mean—they weren't there? You mean—they've left?'

'They've left, all right. Or been eaten.' Pod stared unhappily.

'What can you mean, Pod?' stammered Homily.

'It's full o' foxes,' he told them ponderously, his eyes still round with shock. 'Smells awful . . .' he added after a moment.

CHAPTER ELEVEN

'MISFORTUNES MAKE US WISE'
Louis XIV of France born 1638
[*Extract from Arrietty's Diary and Proverb Book, September 5th.*]

HOMILY CARRIED on a bit that evening. It was under-standable—what were they faced with now? This kind of Robinson Crusoe existence for the rest of their lives? Raw food in the summer was bad enough but in the stark cold of winter, Homily protested, it would not sustain life. Not that they had the faintest chance of surviving the winter, anyway, without some form of heat. A bit of wax candle would not last for ever. Nor would their few wax-vestas. And supposing they made a fire of sticks, it would have to be colossal—an absolute conflagration it would appear to a borrower—to keep alight at all. And the smoke of this, she pointed out, would be seen for miles. No, she concluded gloomily, they were in for it now and no two ways about it, as Pod and Arrietty would see for themselves, poor things, when the first frosts came.

It was the sight of Spiller, perhaps, which had shaken Homily, confirming her worst premonitions—uncouth, unwashed, dishonest, and ill-bred, that's what she summed him up to be, everything she most detested and feared. And this was the level (as she had often warned them back home) to which borrowers must sink if ever, for their sins, they took to the open fields.

To make matters worse, they were awakened that night

by a strange sound—a prolonged and maniac bellow, it sounded to Arrietty, as she lay there trembling, breath held and heart racing. 'What was it?' she whispered to Pod, when at last she dare speak.

The boot creaked as Pod sat up in bed. 'It's a donkey,' he said, 'but close.' After a moment he added: 'Funny—I ain't ever seen a donkey hereabouts.'

'Nor I,' whispered Arrietty. But she felt somehow relieved and was just preparing to settle down again when another sound, closer, caught her ear. 'Listen!' she said sharply, sitting up.

'You don't want to lie awake listening,' Pod grumbled, turning over and pulling after him an unfair share of the sock. 'Not at night, you don't.'

'It's in the annexe,' whispered Arrietty.

The boot creaked again as Pod sat up. 'Keep quiet, Pod, do,' grumbled Homily, who had managed to doze off.

'Quiet yourself,' said Pod, trying to concentrate. It was a small whirring sound he heard, very regular. 'You're right,' he breathed to Arrietty, 'it's in the annexe.' He threw off the sock, which Homily clutched at angrily, pulling it back about her shoulders. 'I'm going out,' he said.

'No, Pod, you don't!' implored Homily huskily. 'We're all right here, laced up. Stay quiet——'

'No, Homily, I got to see.' He felt his way along the ankle of the boot. 'Stay quiet, the two of you, I won't be long.'

'Oh dear,' exclaimed Homily in a scared voice. 'Then take the hat-pin,' she implored nervously as she saw him begin to unthread the laces. Arrietty, watching, saw the boot fall open and her father's head and shoulders appear suddenly against the night sky; there was a scrabbling, a rustling, and a skittering—and Pod's voice shouting—'Dang you . . . dang you . . . dang you!' Then there was silence.

Arrietty crept along the ankle of the boot and put her head out into the air; the alcove was filled with bright moonlight, and every object could be plainly seen. Arrietty stepped out and looked about her. A silvery Pod stood on the lip of the alcove, staring down at the moon-drenched field.

'What was it?' called Homily from the depths of the boot.

'Danged field-mice,' called Pod, 'been at the corn.'

And Arrietty saw in that pale, friendly light that the sandy floor of the annexe was strewn with empty husks.

'Well, that's that,' said Pod, turning back and kicking the scattered husks. 'Better get the thistle,' he added, 'and sweep up the mess.'

Arrietty did so, almost dancing. Enchanted, she felt, by this friendly radiance which lent an unfamiliar magic to even the most matter-of-fact objects—such as Pod's bell-clapper hanging from its nail and the whitened stitching on the boot. When she had made three neat piles of husks she joined Pod at the lip of the alcove and they sat silent for a while on the still warm sand, listening to the night.

An owl called from the spinney beside the brook—a fluting, musical note which was answered, at great distance, by a note as haunting in a slightly higher key, weaving a shuttle of sound back and forth across the sleeping pasture, linking the sea of moonlight and the velvet shadowed woods.

'Whatever the danger,' Arrietty thought, sitting there at peace beside her father, 'whatever the difficulty, I am still glad we came!'

'What we need in this place,' said Pod at last, breaking the long silence, 'is some kind of tin.'

'Tin?' repeated Arrietty vaguely, not sure she had understood.

'Or a couple of tins. A cocoa tin would do. Or one of them they use for baccy.' He was silent awhile, and then he added: 'That pit we dug weren't deep enough; bet them danged field-mice have been at the nuts.'

'Couldn't you learn to shoot a bow and arrow?' asked Arrietty after a moment.

'Whatever for?' asked Pod.

Arrietty hesitated, then, all in a breath, she told him about Spiller: the well-sprung bow, the thorn-tipped, deadly arrows. And she described how Spiller had been watching them from the darkness when they played out their scene with the moth on the stage of the lighted alcove.

'I don't like that,' said Pod after a moment's thought, 'not neighbours watching I don't like. Can't have that, you know. Not by night nor by day neither, it ain't healthy, if you get my meaning.'

Arrietty did get his meaning. 'What we want here is some kind of shutter or door. A piece of chicken wire might do. Or that cheese-grater, perhaps—the one we had at home. It would have to be something that lets the light in, I mean,' she went on. 'We can't go back to living in the dark.'

'I got an idea,' said Pod suddenly. He stood up and,

turning about, craned his neck upwards to the overhang above. The slender sapling, silvery with moonlight, leaned above their bank. Pod stared a moment at the leaves against the sky as though calculating distances; then, looking down, he kicked about the sand with his feet.

'What is it?' whispered Arrietty, thinking he had lost something.

'Ah,' said Pod, in a pleased voice, and went down on his knees, 'this 'ould do.' And he shovelled about with his hands, uncovering, after a moment, a snaking loop of tough root—seemingly endless. 'Yes,' he repeated, 'this'll do fine.'

'What for?' asked Arrietty, wildly curious.

'Get me the twine,' said Pod. 'There on that shelf, where the tools are. . . .'

Arrietty, standing on tiptoe, reached her hand into the sandy recess and found the ball of twine.

'Give it here,' said Pod, 'and get me the bell-clapper.'

Arrietty watched her father tie a length of twine on to the bell-clapper and, balancing a little perilously on the very edge of their terrace, take careful aim and, with a violent effort, fling the clapper up into the branches above; it caught hold, like an anchor, among a network of twigs.

'Now, come on,' said Pod to Arrietty, breathing steadily, 'take hold and pull. Gently does it . . . steady now. Gently . . . gently . . .' and leaning together their full weight on the twine, hand over hand they drew down the stooping branch. The alcove became dark suddenly with broken shadow, cut and trembling with filtered moonlight.

'Hold on,' panted Pod, guiding the twine to the loop of

root, 'while I make her fast.'   He gave a grunt.   'There,'
he said, and stood up, rubbing the strain out of his hands
(he was flecked all over, Arrietty noticed, with trembling
blobs of silver), 'get me the half-scissor.   Dang it, I forgot
—the fret-saw will do.'

It was hard to lay hands on the fret-saw in this sudden

darkness, but at last she found it and Pod cut his halyard.
'There,' he said again in a satisfied voice.   'She's fast—
and we're covered.   How's that for an idea?   You can let
her up or down, depending on what goes on, wind, weather,
and all the rest of it. . . .'

He removed the bell-clapper and made the twine fast to
the main branch.   'Won't keep the field-mice out, nor them
kind of cattle—but,' he gave a satisfied laugh, 'there won't
be no more watching.'

'It's wonderful,' said Arrietty, her face among the
leaves, 'and we can still see out.'

'That's the idea,' said Pod. 'Come on now: time we got back to bed!'

As they felt their way towards the mouth of the boot, Pod tripped against a pile of wheat-husks and stumbled, coughing, into their dusty scatter. As he stood up and brushed himself down, he remarked thoughtfully: 'Spiller— you said his name was?' He was silent a moment and then added thoughtfully: 'There's a lot worse food, when you come to think of it, than a piping-hot, savoury stew made of corn-fed field-mouse.'

CHAPTER TWELVE

'OUT OF SIGHT, OUT OF MIND'
H.M.S. *Captain* lost, 1870
[*Extract from Arrietty's Diary and Proverb Book, September 7th.*]

HOMILY WAS in a worried mood next morning. 'What's all this?' she grumbled when, a little tousled, she crept out of the boot and saw that the alcove was filled with a greenish, underwater light.

'Oh, Mother,' exclaimed Arrietty reproachfully, 'it's lovely!' A faint breeze stirred the clustered leaves which, parting and closing, let pass bright spears and arrows of dancing light. A delightful blend of mystery and gaiety (or so it seemed to Arrietty). 'Don't you see,' she went on as its inventor preserved a hurt silence, 'Papa made it: it's quick cover—lets in the light but keeps out the rain; and we can see out but they can't see in.'

'Who's they?' asked Homily.

'Anything . . . anybody passing. Spiller,' she added on a gleam of inspiration.

Homily relented. 'H'mm,' she vouchsafed in a non-committal tone, but she examined the uncovered root in the floor, noted the running clove-hitch, and ran a thoughtful finger down the taut twine.

'The thing to remember,' Pod explained earnestly, aware of her tardy approval, 'is—when you let her go—keep hold of the halyard: you don't want this here halyard ever to leave the root. See what I mean?'

Homily saw. 'But you don't want to waste the sun-shine,' she pointed out, 'not while it's summer, you don't. Soon it will be——' She shuddered slightly and tightened her lips, unable to say the word.

'Well, winter ain't here yet,' exclaimed Pod lightly. 'Sufficient unto the day, as they say.' He was busy with the halyard. 'Here you are—up she goes!' and, as the twine ran squeaking under the root, the leaves flew up out of sight and the alcove leapt into sudden sunlight.

'See what I mean?' said Pod again in a satisfied voice.

During breakfast the donkey brayed again, loud and long, and was answered almost at once by the neigh of a horse.

'I don't like it,' said Homily suddenly, setting down her half hazel-shell of honey and water. Even as she spoke a dog yelped—too close for comfort. Homily started—and over went the honey and water, a dark stain on the sandy floor. 'Me nerves is all to pieces,' Homily wailed, clapping her hands to her temples and looking from side to side with wild eyes.

'It's nothing, Mother,' Arrietty explained, irritated. 'There's a lane just below the spinney: I saw it from the top of the hedge. It's people passing, that's all; they're bound to pass sometimes——'

'That's right,' agreed Pod, 'you don't want to worry. You eat up your grain——'

Homily stared distastefully at the bitten-into grain of corn, dry and hard as a breakfast roll three days after a picnic. 'Me teeth ain't up to it,' she said unhappily.

'According to Arrietty,' explained Pod, holding up the spread fingers of his left hand and knocking each back in turn, 'between us and that lane we got five barriers: the stream down at the corner—one; them posts with rusty wire across the stream—two; a fair-sized wood—three; another hedge—four; and a bit o' rough grazing ground—five.' He turned to Arrietty. 'Ain't that right, lass? You been up the hedge?'

Arrietty agreed. 'But that bit of grazing ground belongs to the lane—a kind of grass verge.'

'There you are then,' exclaimed Pod triumphantly, slapping Homily on the back, 'Common land! And someone's tethered a donkey there. What's wrong with that? Donkeys don't eat you—no more don't horses.'

'A dog might,' said Homily. 'I heard a dog.'

'And what of it?' exclaimed Pod. 'It wasn't the first time and it won't be the last. When I was a lad, down at the big house, the place was awash with setters, as you might say. Dogs is all right: you can talk to dogs.'

Homily was silent a moment, rolling the wheat grain backwards and forwards on the flat piece of slate which they used as a table.

'It's no good,' she said at last.

'What's no good?' asked Pod, dismayed.

'Going on like this,' said Homily. 'We got to do something before winter.'

'Well, we are doing something, aren't we?' said Pod. He nodded towards Arrietty. 'Like it says in her book—Rome weren't built in a day.'

'Find some kind of human habitation,' went on Homily,

'that's what we've got to do—where there's fires and pickings and proper sort of cover.' She hesitated. 'Or,' she went on in a set, determined voice, 'we got to go back home.'

There was a stunned silence. 'We got to do what?' asked Pod weakly, when he could find his voice; and Arrietty, deeply upset, breathed: 'Oh, Mother——'

'You heard me, Pod,' said Homily; 'all these hips and haws and watercress and dogs barking and foxes in the badgers' set and creeping in the night and stealing and rain coming up and nothing to cook on. You see what I mean? Back home, in the big house, it wouldn't take us no time to put a few partitions up and get kind of straight again under the kitchen. We did it once, that time the boiler burst: we can do it again.'

Pod stared across at her and when he spoke he spoke with the utmost gravity. 'You don't know what you're saying, Homily. It's not just that they'll be waiting for us; that they've got the cat, set traps, laid down poison, and all that caper: it's just that you don't *go back*, Homily, not once you've come out, you don't. And we ain't *got* a home. That's all over and done with. Like it or not, we got to go on now. See what I mean?' When Homily did not reply, he turned his grave face to Arrietty.

'I'm not saying we're not up against it; we are—right up against it. More than I like to let on. And if we don't stick together, we're finished—see? And it will be the end —like you once said, Arrietty—the end of our race! Never let me hear another word from either one of you, you or your mother, about——' with great solemnity he slightly raised his voice, stressing each word, 'going back anywhere—let alone under the floor!'

They were very impressed; they both stared back at him, unable, for the moment, to speak.

'Understand?' asked Pod sternly.

'Yes, Papa,' whispered Arrietty; and Homily swallowed, nodding her head.

'That's right,' Pod told them more gently. 'Like it says in your book, Arrietty, "A Word is enough to the Wise."

'Now get me the horse-hair,' he went on more jovially. 'It's a nice day. And while you two clear breakfast, I'll start on the fish-net. How's that?' Homily nodded again. She did not even ask him (as on any other occasion she would immediately have) how, when they had caught the fish, he proposed that they should cook it. 'There's a nice lot of dry bark about. Do fine,' said Pod, 'for floats.'

But Pod, though good at knots, had quite a bit of trouble with the horse-hair: the long tail-strands were springy and would slide from the eye of the needle. When the chores were done, however, and Arrietty sent off to the brook with two borrowing-bags—the waxed one for water and the other for bark, Homily came to Pod's rescue and, working together, they evolved a close mesh on the spider-web principle, based on Homily's knowledge of tatting.

'What about this Spiller?' Pod asked uneasily after a while, as he sat beside Homily, watching her fingers.

Homily snorted, busy with her knots. 'Don't talk to me of that one,' she said after a moment.

'Is he a borrower, or what?' asked Pod.

'I don't know what he is,' cried Homily, 'and what's more, I don't care neither. Threw a beetle at me, that's all I know. And stole the pin and our nail-scissor.'

'You know that for sure?' asked Pod, on a rising note.

'Sure as I'm sitting here,' said Homily. 'You ain't seen him.'

Pod was silent a moment. 'I'd like to meet him,' he said after a while, staring out across the sunlit field.

The net grew apace and the time went by almost without their noticing. Once when, each taking an end, they held the work out for inspection, a grasshopper sprang from the bank below, bullet-like, into the meshes; and it was only after—with infinite care for the net—they had freed the struggling creature that Homily thought of luncheon.

'Goodness,' she cried, staring across the field, 'look at them shadows! Must be after two. What can have happened to Arrietty?'

'Playing down there with the water, I shouldn't wonder,' said Pod.

'Didn't you tell her "there and back and no dawdling"?'

'She knows not to dawdle,' said Pod.

'That's where you're wrong, Pod, with Arrietty. With Arrietty you got to say it every time!'

'She's going on for fourteen now,' said Pod.

'No matter,' Homily told him, rising to her feet, 'she's young for her age. You always got to tell her, else she'll make excuses.'

Homily folded up the net, brushed herself down, and bustled across the annexe to the shelf above the tool rack.

'You hungry, Pod?' (It was a rhetorical question: they were always hungry, all of them, every hour of the day. Even after meals they were hungry.)

'What is there?' he asked.

'There's a bunch of haws, a couple of nuts, and a mildewed blackberry.'

Pod sighed. 'All right,' he said.

'But which?' asked Homily.

'The nut's more filling,' said Pod.

'But what can I do, Pod?' cried Homily unhappily. 'Any suggestions? Do you want to go and pick us a couple of wild strawberries?'

'That's an idea,' said Pod, and he moved towards the bank.

'But you got to look careful,' Homily told him, 'they've

got a bit scarce now. Something's been at them. Birds maybe. Or,' she added bitterly, 'more likely that Spiller.'

'Listen!' cried Pod, raising a warning hand. He stood quite still at the edge of their cave, staring away to his left.

'What was it?' whispered Homily, after a moment.

'Voices,' said Pod.

'What kind of voices?'

'Human,' said Pod.

'Oh, my——' whispered Homily fearfully.

'Quiet,' said Pod.

They stood quite still, ears attuned. There was a faint hum of insects from the grasses below and the buzzing of a fly which had blundered into the alcove; it flew jerkily about between them and settled greedily at last on the sandy floor where at breakfast Homily had spilled the honey. Then suddenly, uncomfortably close, they heard a different sound, a sound which drove the colour from their cheeks and which filled their hearts with dread—and it was, on the face of it, a cheerful sort of sound: the sound of a human laugh.

Neither moved; frozen, they stood—pale and tense with listening. There was a pause and, nearer now, a man's voice cursed—one short, sharp word and, immediately after, they heard the yelp of a dog.

Pod stooped; swiftly, with a jerk of the wrist, he released the halyard and, hand over steady hand, he pulled on the swaying tree: this time he used extra strength, drawing the branches lower and closer until he had stuffed the mouth of their cave with a close-knit network of twigs.

'There,' he gasped, breathing hard, 'take some getting through, that will.'

Homily, bewildered by the dappled half-light, could not make out his expression, but somehow she sensed his calm. 'Will it look all right from outside?' she asked evenly, matching her tone to his.

'Should do,' said Pod. He went up to the leaves and peered out between them, and with steady hands and sure grip tried the set of the branches. 'Now,' he said, stepping back and drawing a deep breath, 'hand me that other hat-pin.'

Then it was that a further strange thing happened. Pod put out his hand—and there at once was the hat-pin, but it had been put in his grasp too quietly and too immediately to have been put there by Homily: a shadowy third shared their dim-lit cavern, a dun-coloured creature of invisible stillness. And the hat-pin was the hat-pin they had lost.

'Spiller!' gasped Homily hoarsely.

CHAPTER THIRTEEN

'MEAT IS MUCH, BUT MANNERS ARE MORE'
New Style introduced into Britain, 1752
[*Extract from Arrietty's Diary and Proverb Book, September 11th.*]

HE MUST have slid in with the lowering of the leaves—a shadow among shadows. Now she could see the blob of face, the tangled thatch of hair, and that he carried two borrowing-bags, one empty and one full. And the bags, Homily realized with a sinking of the heart, were the bags which that morning she had handed to Arrietty.

'What have you done with her?' Homily cried, distraught. 'What have you done with Arrietty?'

Spiller jerked his head towards the back of the alcove. 'Coming up over yon field,' he said, and his face remained quite expressionless. 'I floated her off down the current,' he added carelessly. Homily turned wild eyes towards the back of the alcove as though she might see through the sandy walls and into the field beyond: it was the field through which they had trapsed on the day of their escape.

'You what?' exclaimed Pod.

'Floated her off down the river,' said Spiller, 'in half of a soap-box,' he explained irritably, as though Pod were being dense.

Pod opened his mouth to reply, then, staring, remained silent: there was a sound of running footsteps in the ditch below; as they came abreast of the alcove and thundered past outside, the whole of the bank seemed to tremble and

286

the bell-clapper fell off its nail—they heard the steady rasp of men's harsh breathing and the panting of a dog.

'It's all right,' said Spiller, after a tense pause, 'they cut off left, and across. Gipsies,' he added tersely, 'out rabbiting.'

'Gipsies?' echoed Pod dully, and he wiped his brow with his sleeve.

'That's right,' said Spiller, 'down there by the lane; coupla caravans.'

'Gipsies . . .' breathed Homily in a blank kind of wonderment, and for a moment she was silent—her breath held and her mouth open, listening.

'It's all right,' said Spiller, listening too, 'they gone across now, alongside the cornfield.'

'And what's this now about Arrietty?' stammered Pod.

'I told you,' said Spiller.

'Something about a soap-dish?'

'Is she all right?' implored Homily, interrupting. 'Is she safe? Tell us that——'

'She's safe,' said Spiller, 'I told you. Box, not dish,' he corrected, and glanced interestedly about the alcove. 'I slept in that boot once,' he announced conversationally, nodding his head towards it.

Homily repressed a shudder. 'Never mind that now,' she said, hurriedly dismissing the subject, 'you go on and tell us about Arrietty. This soap-dish, or box, or whatever it was. Tell us just what happened.'

It was difficult to piece the story together from Spiller's terse sentences, but at last some coherence emerged. Spiller, it seemed, owned a boat—the bottom half of an aluminium soap-case, slightly dented; in this, standing up, he would propel himself about the stream. Spiller had a summer camp (or hunting lodge) in the sloping field behind—an old blackened tea kettle it was—wedged sideways in the silt of the stream (he had several of these bases it appeared, of which, at some time, the boot had been one)—and he would borrow from the caravans, transporting the loot by water; this boat gave him a speedy getaway, and one which left no scent. Coming up against the current was slower, Spiller explained, and for this he was grateful for the hat-pin, which not only served as a sharp and pliable punt-pole, but as a harpoon as well. He became so lyrical about the hat-pin that Pod and Homily began to feel quite pleased with themselves, as though, out of the kindness of their hearts, they had achieved some benevolent gesture. Pod longed to ask to what use Spiller had put the half nail-scissor but could not bring himself to do so, fearing to strike a discordant note in so bland a state of innocent joy.

On this particular afternoon, it seemed, Spiller had been transporting two lumps of sugar, a twist of tea, three leaden hair-curlers, and one of those plain gold earrings for pierced ears known as sleepers across the wider part of the brook where, pond-like, it spread into their field, when (he told them) he had seen Arrietty at the water's edge, barefoot in the warm mud, playing some kind of game. She had a quill-

like leaf of bulrush in her hand and seemed to be stalking frogs: she would steal up behind her prey, where innocently it sat basking in the sun, and—when she was close enough— she would tap the dozing creature smartly in the small of its back with her swaying length of wand; there would then be a croak, a plop, a splash—and it was one up to Arrietty. Sometimes she was seen approaching—then, of course, it was one up to the frog. She challenged Spiller to a match, completely unaware (he said) that she had another interested spectator—the gipsies' dog, a kind of mongrel greyhound, which stared with avid eyes from the woodland edge of the pond. Nor (he added) had she heard the crackling in the underbrush which meant that its masters were close behind.

Spiller, it seemed, had just had time to leap ashore, push Arrietty into the shallow soap-box and, with a few hurried directions about the whereabouts of the kettle, shove her off down-stream.

'But will she ever find it?' gasped Homily. 'The kettle, I mean?'

'Couldn't miss it,' said Spiller, and went on to explain that the current fetched up close against the spout, in a feathery pile-up of broken ripples—and there the soap-box always stuck. 'All she got to do,' he pointed out, 'is make fast, tip the stuff out, and walk on back up.'

'Along the ridge of the gas-pipe?' asked Pod. Spiller threw him a startled glance, shrewd but somehow closed. 'She could do,' he said shortly.

'Half a soap-box . . .' murmured Homily wonderingly, trying to picture it, '. . . hope she'll be all right.'

'She'll be all right,' said Spiller, 'and there b'aint no scent on the water.'

'Why didn't you get in too,' asked Pod, 'and go along with her, like?'

Spiller looked faintly uncomfortable. He rubbed his dark hand on the back of his moleskin trousers; he frowned slightly, glancing at the ceiling. 'There b'aint room for two,' he said at last, 'not with cargo.'

'You could have tipped the cargo out,' said Pod.

Spiller frowned more deeply, as though the subject bored him. 'Maybe,' he said.

'I mean,' Pod pointed out, 'there you were, weren't you? out in the open, left without cover. What's a bit of cargo compared to that?'

'Yes,' said Spiller, and added uncomfortably, referring to his boat: 'She's shallow—you ain't seen her: there b'aint room for two.'

'Oh, Pod——' cried Homily, suddenly emotional.

'Now what?' asked Pod.

'This boy,' went on Homily in ringing tones, 'this—well, anyway, there he stands!' and she threw out an arm towards Spiller.

Pod glanced at Spiller. Yes, indeed, there he stood, very embarrassed and indescribably grubby.

'He saved her life,' went on Homily, throaty with gratitude, 'at the expense of his own!'

'Not expense,' Pod pointed out after a moment, staring thoughtfully at Spiller. 'I mean he's here, isn't he?' And added reasonably in surprised afterthought: 'And she's not!'

'She will be,' said Homily, suddenly confident, 'you'll

see; everything's all right. And he's welcome to the hat-pin. This boy's a hero.' Suddenly herself again, she began to bustle about. 'Now you sit here, Spiller,' she urged him hospitably, 'and rest yourself. It's a long pull up from the water. What'll you take? Could you do with a nice half a rose-hip filled with something or other? We haven't much,' she explained with a nervous laugh, 'we're newcomers, you see. . . .'

Spiller put a grubby hand into a deep pocket. 'I got this,' he said, and threw down a sizable piece of something heavy which bounced juicily as it hit the slate table. Homily moved forward; curiously, she stooped. 'What is it?' she asked in an awed voice. But even as she spoke she knew: a faint gamy odour rose to her nostrils—gamy, but deliciously savoury, and for one fleeting, glorious second she felt almost faint with greed: it was a roast haunch of——

'Meat,' said Spiller.

'What kind of meat?' asked Pod. He too looked rather glassy-eyed—an exclusive diet of hips and haws might be non-acid-forming but it certainly left corners.

'Don't tell me,' Homily protested, clapping her hands to her ears. And, as they turned towards her surprised, she looked apologetic but added eagerly: 'Let's just eat it, shall we?'

They fell to, slicing it up with the sliver of razor-blade. Spiller looked on surprised: surfeited with regular protein, he was not feeling particularly hungry. 'Lay a little by for Arrietty,' Homily kept saying, and every now and again she remembered her manners and would press Spiller to eat.

Pod, very curious, kept throwing out feelers. 'Too big

for field-mouse,' he would say, chewing thoughtfully, 'yet too small for rabbit.   You couldn't eat stoat . . . might be a bird, of course.'

And Homily, in a pained voice, would cry: 'Please, Pod . . .' and would turn coyly to Spiller.   'All *I* want to know is how Spiller cooks it.   It's delicious and hung just right.'

But Spiller would not be drawn.   'It's easy,' he admitted once (to Homily's bewilderment: how could it be 'easy' out here in a grateless wilderness devoid of coke or coal? And, natural gratitude apart, she made more and more fuss of Spiller: she had liked him, she was convinced now, from the first).

Arrietty returned in the middle of this feast.   She staggered a little when she had pushed her way through the tight-packed screen of leaves, swayed on her two feet, and sat down rather suddenly in the middle of the floor.

Homily was all concern.   'What have they done to you, Arrietty?   What's the matter?   Are you hurt?'

Arrietty shook her head.   'Seasick,' she said weakly, 'my head's all awhirl.'   She glanced reproachfully across at Spiller.   'You spun me out in the current,' she told him accusingly.   'The thing went round and round and round and round and round and round and——'

'Now, that's enough, Arrietty,' interrupted Homily, 'or you'll have us all whirling.   Spiller was very kind.   You should be grateful.   He gave his life for yours——'

'He didn't give his life,' explained Pod again, slightly irritated.

But Homily took no notice.   'And then came on up here
with the borrowing-bags to say you were all right.   You
should thank him.'

'Thank you, Spiller,' said Arrietty, politely but wanly,
looking up from her place on the floor.

'Now get up,' said Homily, 'that's a good girl.   And
come to the table.   Not had a bite since breakfast—that's

all that's the matter with you.   We've saved you a nice
piece of meat——'

'A nice piece of what?' asked Arrietty in a dazed voice,
not believing her ears.

'Meat,' said Homily firmly, without looking at her.

Arrietty jumped up and came across to the table; she
stared blankly down at the neat brown slices.   'But I
thought we were vegetarians. . . .'   After a moment she
rasied her eyes to Spiller: there was a question in them.   'Is
it——?' she began, unhappily.

Spiller shook his head quickly; it was a firm negative and
settled her misgivings.   'We never ask,' put in Homily
sharply, tightening her lips and creating a precedent; 'let's
just call it a bit of what the gipsies caught and leave it at
that.'

'Not leave it . . .' murmured Arrietty dreamily. Quite recovered she seemed suddenly; and arranging her skirts she joined them at the low table round which they sat picnic-wise on the floor. Tentatively she took up a slice in two fingers, took a cautious bite, then closed her eyes and almost shuddered, so welcome and downright was the flavour. '*Did* the gipsies catch it?' she asked incredulously.

'No,' said Pod, 'Spiller did.'

'I thought so,' Arrietty said. 'Thank you, Spiller,' she added. And this time her voice sounded heartfelt—alive and ringing with proper gratitude.

CHAPTER FOURTEEN

'LOOK HIGH, AND FALL LOW'
First Balloon Ascent in England, 1784
[*Extract from Arrietty's Diary and Proverb Book, September 15th.*]

MEALS BECAME different after that—different and better—
and this had something to do, Arrietty decided, with their
stolen half nail-scissor. Stolen? An unpleasant-sounding
word, seldom applied to a borrower. 'But what else can
you call it?' Homily wailed as she sat one morning on the
edge of the alcove while Pod sewed a patch on her shoe,
'or expect even? Of a poor, homeless, ignorant boy
dragged up, as they say, in the gutter——'

'Ditch, you mean,' put in Arrietty drowsily, who was
lying below on the bank.

'I mean gutter—' repeated Homily, but she looked a little
startled: she had not known Arrietty was near, 'it's a
manner of speaking. No,' she went on primly, adjusting
the hem of her skirt to hide her stockinged foot (there was a
slight hole, she had noticed, in the toe), 'you can't blame the
lad. I mean, with that sort of background, what could he
learn about ethics?'

'About whatticks?' asked Pod. Homily, poor ignorant
soul, occasionally hit on a word which surprised him and,
what surprised him still more, sometimes she hit on its
meaning.

'Ethics,' repeated Homily coolly and with perfect con-
fidence. 'You know what ethics are, don't you?'

'No, I don't,' Pod admitted simply, sewing away on his patch; 'sounds to me like something you pick up in the long grass.'

'Them's ticks,' said Homily.

'Or,' Pod went on, smoothing the neat join with a licked thumb, 'that thing that horses get from drinking too quick.'

'It's funny . . .' mused Arrietty, 'that you can't have just one.'

'One what?' asked Homily sharply.

'One ethic,' said Arrietty.

'That's where you're wrong,' snapped Homily. 'As a matter of fact there is only one. And Spiller's never learned it. One day,' she went on, 'I'm going to have a nice, quiet, friendly talk with that poor lad.'

'What about?' asked Arrietty.

Homily ignored the question: she had composed her face to a certain kind of expression and was not going to change it. '"Spiller," I'll say, "you never had a mother——"'

'How do you know he never had a mother?' asked Pod. 'He must have had,' he added reasonably, after a moment's reflection.

'Yes,' put in Arrietty, 'he did have a mother. That's how he knows his name.'

'How?' asked Homily, suddenly curious.

'Because his mother told him, of course! Spiller's his surname. His first name's Dreadful.'

There was a pause.

'What is it?' asked Homily then, in an awed voice.

'Dreadful!'

'Never mind,' snapped Homily, 'tell us: we're not children.'

'That's his name: Dreadful Spiller. He remembers his mother saying it one day, at table. "A Dreadful Spiller, that's what you are," she said, "aren't you?" It's about all he does remember about his mother.'

'All right,' said Homily, after a moment, composing her features back to gentle tolerance, 'then I'll say to him' (she smiled her sad smile), '"Dreadful," I'll say, "dear boy, my poor orphan lad——"'

'How do you know he's orphaned?' interrupted Pod. 'Have you ever asked him if he's orphaned?'

'You can't ask Spiller things,' put in Arrietty quickly. 'Sometimes he tells you, but you can't ask him. Remember when you tried to find out how he did the cooking? He didn't come back for two days.'

'That's right,' agreed Pod glumly, 'couple o' days without meat. We don't want that again in a hurry. Look here, Homily,' he went on, turning suddenly towards her, 'better leave Spiller alone.'

'It's for his own good,' protested Homily angrily, 'and it's *telling*, not *asking*! I was only going to say——' (again she smiled her smile) '"Spiller, my poor lad . . ." or "Dreadful" or whatever his name is——'

'You can't call him Dreadful, Mother,' put in Arrietty, 'not unless he asks you——'

'Well, "Spiller" then! Homily threw up her eyes. 'But I got to tell him.'

'Tell him what?' asked Pod, irritated.

'This *ethic*!' Homily almost shouted, 'this what we all

been brought up on! That you don't never borrow from a borrower!'

Impatiently Pod snapped off his thread. 'He knows that,' he said. He handed the shoe to Homily. 'Here you, put it on.'

'Then what about the hat-pin?' persisted Homily.

'He give it back,' Pod said.

'He didn't give back the nail-scissor!'

'He skins the game with it,' said Arrietty quickly. 'And we get the meat.'

'Skins the game?' pondered Homily. 'Well, I never.'

'That's right,' agreed Pod, 'and cuts it up. See what I mean, Homily?' He rose to his feet. 'Better leave well alone.'

Homily was struggling absent-mindedly with the laces of her shoe. 'Wonder how he does cook?' she mused aloud after a moment.

'Wonder away,' said Pod. He crossed to the shelf to replace his tools. 'No harm in that, so long as you don't ask.'

'Poor orphaned lad . . .' said Homily again. She spoke quite lightly but her eye was thoughtful.

CHAPTER FIFTEEN

'NO JOY WITHOUT ALLOY'
Columbus discovered New World, 1492
[*Extract from Arrietty's Diary and Proverb Book, September 25th.*]

THE NEXT six weeks (according to Tom Goodenough) were the happiest Arrietty ever spent out of doors. Not that they could be called halcyon exactly: they ran, of course, the usual gamut of English summer weather—days when the fields were drowned in opal mist and spiders' webs hung jewelled in the hedges; days of breathless heat and stifling closeness; thundery days with once a searing strike of lightning across the woods when Homily, terrified, had buried the razor-blade saying that 'steel attracts'; and one whole week of dismal, steady rain with scarcely a let-up, when the ditch below their bank became a roaring cataract on which Spiller, guiding his tin soap-case with uncanny speed and skill, intrepidly shot the rapids; during this week Homily and Arrietty were kept house-bound in case, Pod told them, they should slip on the mud and fall in: it would be no joke, he explained, to be swept along down the ditch to the swollen stream at the corner and on and on through the lower fields until they met the river and eventually, he concluded, be carried out to sea.

'Why not say "across to America" and have done with it?' Homily had remarked tartly, remembering Arrietty's *Gazetteer of the World*. But she got ahead with her winter knitting, saw the men had hot drinks, and dried out poor

299

Spiller's clothes over the candle while he huddled naked, but clean for once, in the boot.   The rain never actually beat into the alcove but there was an unpleasant dampness all over everything, white mildew on the leather of the boot, and, once, a sudden crop of yellow toadstools where none had been before.   Another morning, when Homily crept forth shivering to get breakfast, a silvery track of slime

wound ribbon-like across the floor and, putting her hand on the tool shelf for the matches, she gave a startled scream—stuffed, the shelf was, and flowing over with a heaving mass of slug.   A slug that size cannot be easily tackled by a borrower, but luckily this one shrunk up and feigned dead: once they had prized it out of its close-fitting retreat, they could bowl it over across the sandy floor and roll it away down to the bank.

After this, towards the end of September, there did come some halcyon days—about ten of them: sun and butterflies and drowsy heat; and a second burst of wild flowers.   There was no end to Arrietty's amusements out of doors.   She would climb down the bank, across the ditch, and into the long grass, and stretched between the stems would lie there watching.   Once she became used to the habits of the insects she no longer feared them: her world, she realized, was not their world and for them hers had little interest; except, perhaps for that bug-like horror (an ethic to Pod) which, crawling sluggishly across bare skin, would bury its head and cling.

Grasshoppers would alight like prehistoric birds on the grasses above her head; strange, armour-plated creatures, but utterly harmless to such as she. The grass stems would sway wildly beneath their sudden weight, and Arrietty, lying

watchful below, would note the machine-like slicing of the mandibles as the grasshopper munched its fill.

Bees, to Arrietty, were as big as birds are to humans; and if honey-bees were pigeon-sized, a bumble-bee in weight and girth could be compared to a turkey. These too she found, if unprovoked, were harmless. A quivering bumble-bee, feeding greedily on clover, became strangely still all at once when, with gentle fingers, she stroked his fur. Benignity met with benignity: and anger, she found, was only roused through fear. Once she was nearly stung when, to tease it, she imprisoned a bee in that bloom called wild snapdragon by closing the lip with her hands. The trapped bee buzzed like a dynamo and stung, not Arrietty this time, but the enclosing calyx of the flower.

A good deal of time she would spend by the water—paddling, watching, learning to float. The frogs fought shy of her: at Arrietty's approach, they would plop away with bored bleats of distaste, their bulging eyes resigned but nervous; 'look where it comes again . . .'[1] they seemed to croak.

After bathing, before putting on her clothes, sometimes she would dress up: a skirt of violet leaves, stalks uppermost, secured about the waist with a twist of faded columbine, and, aping the fairies, a foxglove bell for a hat. This, Arrietty thought as she stared at her bright reflection in the stagnant water of a hoof crater, might look all right on gnomes, elves, brownies, pixies, and what not, but she had to admit that it looked pretty silly on a common or garden borrower: for one thing, if the lip fitted the circumference of her head, the whole thing stood up too high like some kind of pinkish sausage or a very drawn-out chef's cap. Yet if, on the other hand, the lip of the bell flowed out generously in a gentle, more hat-like curve, the whole contraption slid down past her face to rest on her shoulders in a Ku-Klux-Klan effect.

And to get hold of these bells at all was not easy: foxglove plants were high. Fairies, Arrietty supposed, just flew up to them with raised chins and neatly pointed toes, trailing a wisp of gauze. Fairies did everything so gracefully:

[1] Tom Thumb edition of Shakespeare's Tragedies, with foreword on the Author.

Arrietty, poor girl, had to hook down the plant with a forked stick and sit on it as heavily as she could while she plucked any bells within reach. Sometimes the plant would escape her and fly up again. But usually, by shifting her weight along the stalk, she would manage to get five or six bells—sufficient anyway to try some out for size.

Spiller, gliding by in his cleverly loaded boat, would stare with some surprise: he was not altogether approving of Arrietty's games; having spent all his life out of doors, fending for himself against nature, he had no picture of what such freedom could mean to one who had spent her childhood under a kitchen floor; frogs were just meat to Spiller; grass was 'cover'; and insects a nuisance, especially gnats; water was there to drink, not to splash in; and streams were highways which held fish. Spiller, poor harried creature, had never had time to play.

But he was a fearless borrower; that even Pod conceded; as skilful in his own way as ever Pod had been. The two gentlemen would have long discussions of an evening after supper, on the finer points of a multiplex art. Pod belonged to a more moderate school: the daily sortie and modest loot—a little here, a little there— nothing to rouse suspicion. Spiller preferred a make- hay-while-the-sun- shines technique: a swift whip-round

of whatever he could lay hands on and a quick getaway. This difference in approach was understandable, Arrietty thought, as listening she helped her mother with the dishes: Pod was a house-borrower, long established in traditional routine; whereas Spiller dealt exclusively with gipsies—here to-day and gone to-morrow—and must match his quickness with theirs.

Sometimes a whole week would elapse without their seeing Spiller, but he would leave them well stocked with cooked food: a haunch of this or that, or a little stew flavoured with wild garlic which Homily would heat over the candle. Flour, sugar, tea, butter—even bread—they had now in plenty. Spiller, in his nonchalant way, would sooner or later provide almost anything they asked for—a piece of plum-coloured velvet out of which Homily made a new skirt for Arrietty, two whole candles to augment their stub, four empty cotton-reels on which they raised their table, and, to Homily's joy, six mussel shells for plates.

Once he brought them a small glass medicine bottle, circular in shape. As he uncorked it, Spiller said: 'Know what this is?'

Homily, wry-faced, sniffed at the amber liquid. 'Some kind of hair-wash?' she asked, grimacing.

'Elder-flower wine,' Spiller told her, watching her expression. 'Good, that is.'

Homily, about to taste, suddenly changed her mind. 'When wine is in,' she told Spiller—quoting from Arrietty's *Diary and Proverb Book*, 'wit is out. Besides, I was brought up teetotal.'

'He makes it in a watering-can,' explained Spiller, 'and pours it out of the spout.'

'Who does?' asked Homily.

'Mild Eye,' said Spiller.

There was a short silence, tense with curiosity. 'And who might Mild Eye be?' asked Homily at last. Airily pinning up her back hair, she moved slightly away from Spiller and began softly to hum below her breath.

'He that had the boot,' said Spiller carelessly.

'Oh?' remarked Homily. She took up the thistle-head and began to sweep the floor—without seeming to be rude she managed to convey a gentle dismissal of the now-I-must-get-on-with-the-housework kind—'What boot?'

'This boot,' said Spiller, and kicked the toe.

Homily stopped sweeping; she stared at Spiller. 'But this was a gentleman's boot,' she pointed out evenly.

'"Was" is right,' said Spiller.

Homily was silent a moment. 'I don't understand you,' she said at last.

'Afore Mild Eye pinched 'em,' explained Spiller.

Homily laughed. 'Mild Eye . . . Mild Eye . . . who is this Mild Eye?' she asked airily, determined not to be rattled.

'I told you,' said Spiller, 'the gipsy as took up the boots.'

'Boots?' repeated Homily, raising her eyebrows and stressing the plural.

'They was a pair. Mild Eye picked 'em up outside the scullery door . . .' Spiller jerked his head, 'that big house down yonder. Went there selling clothes-pegs and there they was, set out on the cobbles, pairs of 'em—all shapes and sizes, shined up nice, set out in the sunshine . . . brushes and all.'

'Oh,' said Homily thoughtfully—this sounded a good 'borrow,' 'and he took the lot?'

Spiller laughed. 'Not Mild Eye. Took up the pair and closed up the gap.'

'I see,' said Homily. After a moment she asked: 'And who borrowed this one? You?'

'In a manner of speaking,' said Spiller, and added, as though in part explanation: 'He's got this piebald cat.'

'What's the cat got to do with it?' asked Homily.

'A great tom comes yowling round the place one night and Mild Eye ups and heaves a boot at it—this boot.' Again Spiller kicked at the leather. 'Good and watertight this boot was afore a weasel bit into the toe. So I gets hold of her, drags her through the hedge by the laces, heaves her into the water, jumps aboard, sails downstream to the corner, brings her aground on the mud and dries her out after, up in the long grass.

'Where we found it?' asked Homily.

'That's right,' said Spiller. He laughed. 'You should have heard old Mild Eye in the morning. Knew just where he'd heaved the boot, cussin' and swearin'. Couldn't make it out.' Spiller laughed again. 'Never passes that way,' he went on, 'but he has another look.'

Homily turned pale. 'Another look?' she repeated nervously.

Spiller shrugged. 'What's the difference? Wouldn't think to look this side of the water. Knows where he heaved the boot, Mild Eye does: that's what he can't fathom.

'Oh, my,' faltered Homily unhappily.

'You've no call to worry,' said Spiller. 'Anything you'm wanting?'

'A bit of something woollen, I wouldn't mind,' said Homily; 'we was cold last night in the boot.'

'Like a bit of sheep's fleece?' asked Spiller. 'There's plenty down to the lane along them brambles.'

'Anything,' agreed Homily, 'providing it's warm. And providing—' she added, suddenly struck by a horrid thought, 'it ain't a sock.' Her eyes widened. 'I don't want no sock belonging to Mild Eye.'

Spiller dined with them that night (cold boiled minnow with sorrel salad). He had brought them a splendid wad of cleanish fleece and a strip of red rag off the end of a blanket. Pod, less teetotal than Homily, poured him out a half hazel-shell of elderberry wine. But Spiller would not touch it. 'I've things to do,' he told them soberly, and they guessed he was off on a trip.

'Be away long?' asked Pod casually as, just to sample it, he took a sip of wine.

'A week,' said Spiller, 'ten days, maybe . . .'

'Well,' said Pod, 'take care of yourself.' He took another sip of wine. 'It's nice,' he told Homily, proffering the hazel-shell, 'you try it.'

Homily shook her head and tightened her lips. 'We'll miss you, Spiller,' she said, batting her eyelids and ignoring Pod, 'and that's a fact——'

'Why have you got to go?' asked Arrietty suddenly.

Spiller, about to push his way through the screen of leaves, turned back to look at her.

Arrietty coloured. 'I've asked him a question,' she realized unhappily, 'now he'll disappear for weeks.' But this time Spiller seemed merely hesitant.

'Me winter clothes,' he said at last.

'Oh!' exclaimed Arrietty, raising her head—delighted. 'New?'

Spiller nodded.

'Fur?' asked Homily.

Spiller nodded again.

'Rabbit?' asked Arrietty.

'Mole,' said Spiller.

There was a sudden feeling of gaiety in the candle-lit alcove: a pleasant sense of something to look forward to. All three of them smiled at Spiller and Pod raised his 'glass.' 'To Spiller's new clothes,' he said, and Spiller, suddenly embarrassed, dived quickly through the branches. But before the living curtain had stopped quivering they saw his face again; amused and shy, it poked back at them framed in leaves. 'A lady makes them,' he announced self-consciously, and quickly disappeared.

CHAPTER SIXTEEN

'EVERY TIDE HAS ITS EBB'
Burning of the Tower of London, 1841
[*Extract from Arrietty's Diary and Proverb Book, October 30th.*]

NEXT MORNING early Pod, on the edge of the alcove, summoned Arrietty from the boot. 'Come on out,' he called, 'and see this.'

Arrietty, shivering, pulled on a few clothes, and wrapping the piece of red blanket around her shoulders she crept out beside him. The sun was up and the landscape shimmered, dusted over with what, to Arrietty, looked like powdered sugar.

'This is it,' said Pod, after a moment, 'the first frost.'

Arrietty pushed her numbed fingers under her arm-pits, hugging the blanket closer. 'Yes,' she said soberly, and they stared in silence.

After a bit Pod cleared his throat. 'There's no call to wake your mother,' he said huskily; 'like as not, with this sun, it'll be clear in less than an hour.' He became silent again, thinking deeply. 'Thought you'd like to see it,' he said at last.

'Yes,' said Arrietty again, and added politely: 'It's pretty.'

'What we better do,' said Pod, 'is get the breakfast quietly and leave your mother sleeping. She's all right,' he went on, 'deep in that fleece.'

'I'm perished,' grumbled Homily at breakfast, her hands wrapped round a half hazel-shell filled with piping hot tea (there was less need, now they had Spiller, to economize on candles). 'It strikes right through to the marrow. You know what?' she went on.

'No,' said Pod (it was the only reply). 'What?'

'Say we went down to the caravan site and had a look round? There won't be no gipsies: when Spiller goes, it means they've moved off. Might find something,' she added, 'and in this kind of weather there ain't no sense in sitting around. What about it, Pod? We could wrap up warm.'

Arrietty was silent, watching their faces: she had learned not to urge.

Pod hesitated. Would it be poaching, he wondered— was this Spiller's preserve? 'All right,' he agreed uncertainly, after a moment.

It was not a simple expedition. Spiller having hidden his boat, they had to ferry themselves across the water on a flat piece of bark, and it was rough going when, once in the wood, they tried to follow the stream by land: both banks were thickly grown with brambles, ghastly forests of living barbed wire which tore at their hair and clothes; by the time they had scrambled through the hedge on to the stretch of grass beside the lane, they were all three dishevelled and bleeding.

Arrietty looked about her at the camping site and was depressed by what she saw: this wood through which they had scrambled now shut off the last pale gleams of sun; the shadowed grass was bruised and yellow; here and there were odd bones, drifting feathers, bits of rag, and every now and again a stained newspaper flapped in the hedge.

'Oh dear,' muttered Homily, glancing from side to side, 'somehow, now, I don't seem to fancy that bit o' red blanket.'

'Well,' said Pod, after a pause, 'come on. We may as

well take a look round. . . .' And he led the way down the bank.

They poked about rather distastefully and Homily thought of fleas. Pod found an old iron saucepan without a bottom: he felt it might do for something but could not think for what; he walked around it speculatingly and, once or twice, he tapped it sharply with the head of his hatpin, which made a dull clang. Anyway, he decided at last as he moved away, it was no good to him here and was far too heavy to shift.

Arrietty found a disused cooking-stove: it was flung into the bank below the hedge—so sunk it was in the grasses and so thickly engrained with rust that it must have been there for years. 'You know,' she remarked to her mother, after studying it in silence, 'you could live in a stove like this.'

Homily stared. 'In that?' she exclaimed disgustedly. The stove lay tilted, partially sunk in earth; as stoves went it was a very small one, with a barred grate and a miniature oven of the kind which are built into caravans. Beside it, Arrietty noticed, lay a small pile of fragile bones.

'Not sure she isn't right,' agreed Pod, tapping the bars of the grate, 'you could have a fire in here, say, and live in the oven like.'

'Live!' exclaimed Homily. 'Be roasted alive, you mean.'

'No,' exclaimed Pod, 'needn't be a big fire. Just enough to warm the place through like. And there you'd be'— he looked at the brass latch on the door of the oven—'safe as houses. Iron, that is,' he rapped the stove with his hat-pin; 'nothing couldn't gnaw through that.'

'Field-mice could slip through them bars,' said Homily.

'Maybe,' said Pod, 'but I wasn't thinking so much about field-mice as about'—he paused uneasily—'stoats and foxes and them kind of cattle.'

'Oh, Pod,' exclaimed Homily, clapping her hands flat to her cheeks and making her eyes tragic, 'the things you do bring up! Why do you do it?' she implored him tearfully. 'Why? You know what it does to me!'

'Well, there are such things,' Pod pointed out stolidly. 'In this life,' he went on, 'you got to see what *is*, as you might say, and then face up to what you wish there wasn't.'

'But foxes, Pod,' protested Homily.

'Yes,' agreed Pod, 'but there they are; you can't deny 'em. See what I mean?'

'I see all right,' said Homily, eyeing the stove more kindly, 'but say you lit it, the gipsies would see the smoke.'

'And not only the gipsies,' admitted Pod, glancing aside at the lane, 'anyone passing would see it. No,' he sighed, as he turned to go, 'this stove ain't feasible. Pity—because of the iron.'

The only really comforting find of the day was a piping-hot blackened potato: Arrietty found it on the site of the gipsies' fire. The embers were still warm, and, when stirred with a stick, a line of scarlet sparks ran snakewise through the ash. The potato steamed when they broke it open, and comforted they ate their fill, sitting as close as they dared to the perilous warmth.

'Wish we could take a bit of this ash home,' Homily remarked. 'This is how Spiller cooks, I shouldn't wonder—borrows a bit of the gipsies' fire. What do you think, Pod?'

Pod blew on his crumb of hot potato. 'No,' he said, taking a bite and speaking with his mouth full, 'Spiller cooks regular-like whether the gipsies are here or not. Spiller's got his own method.   Wish I knew what it was.'

Homily leaned forward, stirring the embers with a charred stick. 'Say we kept this fire alight,' she suggested, 'and brought the boot down here?'

Pod glanced about uneasily. 'Too public,' he said.

'Say we put it in the hedge,' went on Homily, 'alongside that stove? What about that? Say we put it *in* the stove?' she added suddenly, inspired but fearful.

Pod turned slowly and looked at her. 'Homily——' he began and paused, as though stumped for words.   After a moment he laid a hand on his wife's arm and looked with some pride towards his daughter. 'Your mother's a wonderful woman,' he said in a moved voice. 'And never you forget it, Arrietty.'

Then it was 'all hands to the plough': they gathered sticks like maniacs, and wet leaves to keep up the smoulder.   Backwards and forwards they ran, up into the hedges, along the banks, into the spinney . . . they tugged and wrenched

and tripped and stumbled . . . and soon a white column of smoke spiralled up into the leaden sky.

'Oh my,' panted Homily, distressed, 'folks 'll see this for miles!'

'No matter,' gasped Pod, as he pushed on a lichen-covered branch, 'they 'll think it's the gipsies. Pile on some more of them leaves, Arrietty, we got to keep this going till morning.'

A sudden puff of wind blew the smoke into Homily's eyes and the tears ran down her cheeks. 'Oh my,' she exclaimed—again distressed. 'This is what we 'll be doing all winter, day in, day out, till we 're wore to the bone and run out of fuel. It ain't no good, Pod. See what I mean?'

And she sat down suddenly on a blackened tin-lid and wept in earnest. 'You can't spend the rest of your life,' she whimpered, 'tending an open fire.'

Pod and Arrietty had nothing to say: they knew suddenly that Homily was right: borrowers were too little and weak to create a full-sized blaze. The light was fading and the wind sharpening, a leaden wind which presaged snow.

'Better we start for home,' said Pod, at last. 'We tried anyway. Come on, now,' he urged Homily, 'dry your eyes: we 'll think of something else. . . .'

But they didn't think of anything else. And the weather became colder. There was no sign of Spiller and, after ten days, they ran out of meat and started (their sole source of warmth) on the last bit of candle.

'I don't know,' Homily would moan unhappily, as at night they crept under the fleece, 'what we 're going to do,

I'm sure. We won't see Spiller again, that's one thing certain. Dare say he's met with an accident.'

Then came the snow. Homily, tucked up in the boot, would not get up to see it. To her it presaged the end. 'I'll die here,' she announced, 'tucked up comfortable. You and father,' she told Arrietty, 'can die as you like.'

It was no good Arrietty assuring her that the field looked very pretty, that the cold seemed less severe, and that she had made a sledge of the blackened tin-lid which Pod had retrieved from the ashes: she had made her grave and was determined to lie in it.

In spite of this, and rather heartlessly, Arrietty still enjoyed her toboggan runs down the bank with a wide sweep into the ditch at the bottom. And Pod, brave soul, still went out to forage—though there was little left to eat in the hedgerows and for this little, a few remaining berries, they had to compete with the birds. Though appreciably thinner, none of them felt ill and Arrietty's snow-tanned cheeks glowed with healthy colour.

But five days later it was a different story: intense cold and a second fall of snow—snow which piled up in air-filled drifts, too light and feathery to support a matchstick, let alone a borrower. They became house-bound and, for most of the time, joined Homily in the boot. The fleece was warm but, lying there in semi-darkness, the time passed slowly and the days were very boring. Homily would revive occasionally and tell them stories of her childhood: she could be as long-winded as she liked with this audience which could not get away.

They came to an end of the food. 'There's nothing left,'

announced Pod, one evening, 'but one lump of sugar and a quarter inch of candle.'

'I couldn't never eat that,' complained Homily, '—not paraffin wax.'

'No one's asking you to,' said Pod. 'And we've still that drop of elderberry wine.'

Homily sat up in bed. 'Ah!' she said, 'put the sugar in the wine and heat it up over the quarter inch of candle.'

'But, Homily,' protested Pod, surprised, 'I thought you was teetotal.'

'Grog's different,' explained Homily. 'Call me when it's ready,' and she lay down again, piously closing her eyes.

'She will have her way,' muttered Pod, aside to Arrietty. He eyed the bottle dubiously. 'There's more there than I thought there was. I hope she'll be all right. . . .'

It was quite a party: so long it had been since they had lit the candle; and it was pleasant to gather round it and feel its warmth.

When at last, warmed and befuddled, they snuggled down in the fleece, a curious contentment filled Arrietty—a calmness akin to hope. Pod, she noticed, drowsed with wine, had forgotten to lace up the boot . . . well, perhaps it didn't matter—if it was their last night on earth.

CHAPTER SEVENTEEN

'WHAT HEAVEN WILL, NO FROST CAN KILL'
Great Earthquake at Lisbon, 50,000 killed, 1755
[*Extract from Arrietty's Diary and Proverb Book, November 1st.*]

IT WAS NOT their last night on earth: it seldom is, somehow; it was, however, their last night *in* earth.

Arrietty was the first to wake. She woke tired, as though she had slept badly, but it was only later (as she told Tom) that she remembered her dream of the earthquake. She not only woke tired but she woke cramped, and in a most uncomfortable position. There seemed more light than was usual, and then she remembered the unlaced opening. But why, she wondered, as she roused a little, did the daylight seem to come in from above, as from a half-concealed skylight? And suddenly she understood—the boot, which lay always on its side, for some extraordinary reason was standing upright. Her first thought (and it made her heart beat faster) was that her dream of an earthquake had been fact. She glanced at Pod and Homily: from what she could see of them, so enmeshed they were in fleece, they appeared to be sleeping soundly, but not, she thought, quite in the same positions as when they had gone to bed. Something had happened—she was sure of it—unless she still was dreaming.

Stealthily Arrietty sat up; although the boot was open, the air felt surprisingly warm—almost stuffy; it smelt of wood smoke and onions and of something else—a smell she could not define—could it be the scent of a human being?

318

Arrietty crept along the sole of the boot until she stood under the opening. Staring up she saw, instead of the sandy roof of the annexe, a curious network of wire springs and some kind of striped ceiling. They must be under some bed, she realized (she had seen this view of beds back home); but what bed? And where?

Trembling a little, but too curious not to be brave, she put her foot as high as she could into an eyelet hole and pulled herself erect on a loop of shoe-lace; another step up, a harder pull—and she found she could see out: the first thing she saw, standing close beside her—so close that she could see into it—was a second boot exactly like their own.

That was about all she could see from her present position: the bed was low, stretching up she could almost touch the springs with her hands. But she could hear things—the liquid purr of a simmering kettle, the crackle of a fire, and a deeper, more rhythmic, sound—the sound of a human snore.

Arrietty hesitated: she was in half a mind to wake her parents, but, on second thoughts, she decided against it. First to find out a bit more. She unloosed a couple of lace-holes and eased out through the gap and, via the boot's instep, she walked out to the toe. Now she could really see.

As she had guessed, they were in a caravan. The boots stood under a collapsible bed which ran along one side of it's length; and facing her on the opposite side, parallel to this bed, she saw a miniature coal range very like the one in the hedge, and a light-grained overmantel. The shelves of the overmantel, she saw, were set with pieces of looking-glass and adorned with painted vases, old coronation mugs, and trails of paper flowers. Below and on each side were set-in drawers and cupboards. A kettle simmered gently on the flat of the stove and a fire glowed redly through the bars.

At right angles, across the rear end of the caravan, she saw a second bunk, built in more permanently above a locker, and the locker, she noted, thinking of cover, was not set in flush with the floor: there was space below into which, if crouching, a borrower might creep. In the bunk above the locker she saw a heaving mountain of patchwork which she knew must contain, by the sound of the snoring, a human being asleep. Beside the head of the bunk stood a watering-can, a tin mug balanced on the spout. Elder-flower wine, she thought—that last night had been their undoing.

To her left, also at right angles, was the door of the caravan, the top half open to the winter sunshine; it faced, she knew, towards the shafts. A crack of sunlight ran down the latch side of this door—a crack through which, if she dared approach it, she might perhaps see out.

She hesitated. It was only a step to the crack—a yard and a half at most: the human mountain was still heaving, filling the air with sound. Lightly, Arrietty slid from the toe of the boot to the worn piece of carpet and, soundless in her stockinged feet, she tiptoed to the door. For a moment the sunlight striking brightly through the crack almost seemed to blind her, then she made out a stretch of dirty grass, sodden with melting snow, a fire smoking sulkily between two stones, and beyond that, some way distant below the hedge, she saw a familiar object—the remains of a disused stove. Her spirits rose: so they were still at the same old caravan site—they had not, as she had feared at first, been travelling in the night.

As, her nose in the crack, she stood there staring, a sudden silence behind her caused her to turn; and, having turned, she froze: the human being was sitting up in bed. He was a huge man, fully dressed, dark-skinned, and with a mass of curling hair; his eyes were screwed up, his fists stretched, and his mouth wide open in a long-drawn, groaning yawn.

Panic-stricken, she thought about cover. She glanced at the bed to her right—the bed under which she had awakened. Three strides would do it; but better to be still, that's what Pod would say: the shadowed part of the door against which she stood would seem still darker because of that opened half above, filled so brightly with winter sunshine. All Arrietty did was to move aside from the crack of light against whose brightness she might be outlined.

The human being stopped yawning and swung his legs down from the bunk and sat there a moment, pensively, admiring his stockinged feet. One of his eyes, Arrietty noticed, was dark and twinkling, the other paler, hazel-yellow, with a strangely drooping lid. This must be Mild Eye—this great, fat, terrifying man, who sat so quietly smiling at his feet.

As Arrietty watched, the strange eyes lifted a little and the smile broadened: Mild Eye, Arrietty saw, was looking at the boots.

She caught her breath as she saw him lean forward and

(a stretch of the long arm was enough) snatch them up from below the other bed.   He examined them lovingly, holding them together as a pair, and then, as though struck by some discrepancy in the weight, he set one down on the floor. He shook the other gently, turning its opening towards his palm and, as nothing fell out, he put his hand inside.

The shout he gave, Arrietty thought afterwards, must have been heard for miles.   He dropped the boot, which fell on its side, and Arrietty, in an anguish of terror, saw Homily and Pod run out and disappear between his legs (but not, she realized, before he had glimpsed them) into the shallow space between his bunk and the floor.

There was a horrified pause.

Arrietty was scared enough, but Mild Eye seemed even more so: his two strange eyes bulged in a face which had turned the colour of putty.   Two tiny words hung in the silence, a thread-thin echo, incredible to Mild Eye: someone . . . something . . . somewhere . . . on a note of anguish, had stammered out 'Oh dear!'

And that was controlled enough, Arrietty thought, for what Homily must be feeling: to be woken from a deep sleep and shaken out of the boot; to have seen those two strange eyes staring down at her; to have heard that

thunderous shout. The space between the locker and the floor, Arrietty calculated, could not be more than a couple of inches; it would be impossible to stand up in there and, although safe enough for the moment, there they would have to stay: there seemed no possible way out.

For herself—glued motionless against the shadows—she was less afraid: true enough she stood face to face with Mild Eye; but he would not see her, of this she felt quite sure, providing she did not move: he seemed too shaken by those half-glimpsed creatures which so inexplicably had appeared between his feet.

Stupefied, he stared for a moment longer; then awkwardly he got down on all fours and peered under the locker; as though disappointed, he got up again, found a box of matches, struck a light, and once again explored the shadows as far as the light would carry. Arrietty took advantage of his turned back to take her three strides and slip back under the bed. There was a cardboard box under here, which she could use as cover, some ends of rope, a bundle of rabbit snares, and a slimy saucer which once had contained milk.

She made her way between these objects until she reached the far end—the junction of the bed with the locker below the bunk. Peering out through the tangle of rabbit snares she saw that Mild Eye—despairing of matchlight—had armed himself with a hefty knobkerrie stick which he was now running back and forth in a business-like manner along the space between the bunk and the floor. Arrietty, her hands pressed tight against her heart, once thought she heard a strangled squeak and a muttered: 'Oh, my gracious——!'

At that moment the door of the caravan opened, there was a draught of cold air, and a wild-eyed woman looked in. Wrapped in a heavy shawl against the cold, she was carrying a basket of clothes-pegs. Arrietty, crouching among the rabbit snares, saw the wild eyes open still more wildly, and a flood of questions in some foreign tongue was aimed at Mild Eye's behind. Arrietty saw the woman's breath smoke in the clear sunshine and could hear her earrings jangle.

Mild Eye, a little shamefaced, rose to his feet; he looked very big to Arrietty and, though she could no longer see his face, his hanging hands looked helpless. He replied to the woman in the same language: he said quite a lot; sometimes his voice rose on a curious squeak of dismayed excitement.

He picked up the boot, showed it to the woman, said a lot about it, and—somewhat nervously, Arrietty noticed—he put his hand inside; he pulled out the wad of fleece, the unravelled sock, and—with some surprise because it had once been his—the strip of coloured blanket. As he showed these to the woman, who continued to jeer, his voice became almost tearful. The woman laughed then—a thin, high peal of raucous laughter. Completely heartless, Arrietty thought, completely unkind. She wanted almost for Mild Eye's sake to run out and show this doubting creature that there were such things as borrowers ('it's so awful and sad,' she once admitted to Tom Goodenough, 'to belong to a race that no sane person believes in'). But tempting as this thought was she thought better of it, and instead she edged herself out from the end of the bed into the darker space below the bunk.

And only just in time: there was a faint thud on the carpet, and there, not a foot from where she had stood, she saw the four paws of a cat—three black and one white; she saw him stretch, roll over, and rub his whiskered face on the sun-warmed carpet: he was black, she saw, with a white belly. He or she? Arrietty did not know: a fine beast anyway, sleek and heavy as cats are who hunt for themselves out of doors.

Sidling crab-wise into the shadows, her eyes on the basking cat, she felt her hand taken suddenly, held, and squeezed tight. 'Oh, thank goodness . . .' Homily breathed in her ear, 'thank heavens you're safe.'

Arrietty put a finger to her lips. 'Hush,' she whispered, barely above her breath, staring towards the cat.

'It can't get under here,' whispered Homily. Her face, Arrietty saw, looked pallid in the half-light, grey and streaked with dust. 'We're in a caravan,' she went on, determined to tell the news.

'I know,' said Arrietty, and pleaded: 'Mother, we'd better be quiet.'

Homily was silent a moment, then she said: 'He caught your father's back with that stick. The soft part,' she added reassuringly.

'Hush,' whispered Arrietty again. She could not see much from where she was, but Mild Eye, she gathered, was struggling into a coat; after a moment he stooped, and his hand came near when he felt under the settee for the bundle of rabbit snares; the woman was still out of doors busy about the fire.

After a while, her eyes growing used to the dimness,

she saw her father sitting some way back, leaning against the wall. She crawled across to him, and Homily followed.

'Well, here we are,' said Pod, barely moving his lips, 'and not dead yet,' he added, with a glance at Homily.

CHAPTER EIGHTEEN

'HIDDEN TROUBLES DISQUIET MOST'
Gun Powder Plot, 1605
[*Extract from Arrietty's Diary and Proverb Book, November 5th.*]

THEY CROUCHED there listening, holding their breaths as Mild Eye unlatched the door, relatched it, and clumped off down the steps.

There was a pause.

'We're alone now,' remarked Homily at last in her ordinary speaking voice, 'I mean, we could get out, I shouldn't wonder, if it weren't for that cat.'

'Hush——' whispered Pod. He had heard the woman shoot some mocking question at Mild Eye and, at Mild Eye's mumbled reply, the woman had laughed her laugh. Arrietty, too, was listening.

'*He* knows we're here,' she whispered, 'but *she* won't believe him . . .'

'And that cat'll know we're here, too, soon enough,' replied Pod.

Arrietty shivered. The cat, she realized, must have been asleep on the bed, while she, Arrietty, had been standing unprotected beside the door.

Pod was silent a while, thinking deeply. 'Yes,' he said at last, 'it's a rum go: he must have come round at dusk last night, seeing after his snares . . . and there he finds his lost boot in our hollow.'

'We should have pulled down the screen,' whispered Arrietty.

'We should that,' agreed Pod.

'We didn't even lace up the boot,' went on Arrietty.

'Yes,' said Pod, and sighed. 'A bottle at night and you're out like light. That how it goes?' he asked.

'More or less,' agreed Arrietty in a whisper.

They sat waist-high in dusty trails of fluff. 'Disgusting,' remarked Homily, suppressing a sneeze. 'If I'd built this caravan,' she grumbled, 'I'd have set the bunk in flush with the floor.'

'Then thank goodness you didn't build it,' remarked Pod, as a whiskered shadow appeared between them and the light: the cat had seen them at last.

'Don't panic,' he went on calmly, as Homily gave a gasp, 'this bunk's too low, we're all right here.'

'Oh my goodness,' whispered Homily, as she saw a luminous eye. Pod squeezed her hand to silence her.

The cat, having sniffed his way along the length of the opening, lay down suddenly on its side and ogled them through the gap: quite friendly, it looked, and a little coy, as though coaxing them out to play.

'They don't *know*,' whispered Homily then, referring to cats in general.

'You keep still,' whispered Pod.

For a long time nothing much happened: the shaft of sunshine moved slowly across the worn carpet, and the cat, motionless, seemed to doze.

'Well,' whispered Homily, after a while, 'in a way, it's kind of nice to be indoors.'

Once the woman came in and fumbled in the dresser for a wooden spoon and took away the kettle; they heard her

swearing as she tended the outdoor fire, and once a gust of
acrid smoke blew in through the doorway, making Arrietty
cough.   The cat woke up at that and cocked an eye at them.

Towards midday, they smelt a savoury smell—the gamy
smell of stew: it would drift towards them as the wind
veered and then, tormentingly, would drift away.

Arrietty felt her mouth water.

'*Oh*, I'm hungry . . .' she sighed.

'I'm thirsty,' said Homily.

'I'm both,' said Pod.   'Now be quiet, the two of you,'
he told them, 'shut your eyes and think of something else.'

'Whenever I shut my eyes,' protested Homily, 'I see a nice
hot thimbleful of tea, or I think of that teapot we had back
home: that oak-apple teapot, with a quill spout.'

'Well, think of it,' said Pod; 'no harm in that, if it does
you good. . . .'

The man came back at last.   He unlatched the door and
threw a couple of snared rabbits down on the carpet.   He
and the woman ate their meal on the steps of the caravan,
using the floor as a table.

At this point the smell of food became unbearable; it
drew the three borrowers out of the shadows to the very

edge of their shelter: the tin plates, filled with savoury stew, were at eye level; they had a splendid view of the floury potatoes and the richly running gravy. 'Oh my . . .' muttered Homily unhappily, 'pheasant—and what a way to cook it!'

Once Mild Eye threw a morsel on the carpet. Enviously they watched the cat pounce and leisurely fall to, crunching up the bones like the hunter it was. 'Oh my . . .' muttered Homily again, 'those teeth!'

At length Mild Eye pushed aside his plate. The cat stared with interest at the pile of chewed bones to which here and there clung slivers of tender meat. Homily stared too: the plate was almost in range. 'Dare you, Pod?' she whispered.

'No,' said Pod—so loudly and firmly that the cat turned round and looked at him; gaze met gaze with curious mutual defiance; the cat's tail began slowly to swish from side to side.

'Come on,' gasped Pod, as the cat crouched, and all three dodged back into the shadows in the split half-second before the pounce.

Mild Eye turned quickly. Staring, he called to the woman, pointing towards the bunk, and both man and woman stooped their heads to floor-level, gazing across the carpet . . . and gazing, it seemed to Arrietty, crouched with her parents against the back wall of the caravan, right into their faces. It seemed impossible that they could not be seen: but—'It's all right,' Pod told them, speaking with still lips in the lightest of whispers, 'don't panic—just you keep still.'

There was silence: even the woman now seemed uneasy—the cat, padding and peering, back and forth along the length of the locker, had aroused her curiosity. 'Don't you move,' breathed Pod again.

A sudden shadow fell across the patch of sunlight on the carpet: a third figure, Arrietty noted with surprise, loomed up behind the crouching gipsies in the doorway; someone less tall than Mild Eye. Arrietty, rigid between her parents, saw three buttons of a stained corduroy waistcoat and, as its wearer stopped, she saw a young face, and a tow-coloured head of hair. 'What's up?' asked a voice which had a crack in it.

Arrietty saw Mild Eye's expression change: it became all at once sulky and suspicious. He turned slowly and faced the speaker, but before he did so he slid his right hand inconspicuously across the floor of the caravan, pushing the two dead rabbits out of sight.

'What's up, Mild Eye?' asked the boy again. 'Looks like you'm seeing ghosties.'

Mild Eye shrugged his great shoulders. 'Maybe I am,' he said.

The boy stooped again, staring along the floor, and Arrietty could see that, under one arm, he carried a gun. 'Wouldn't be a ferret by any chance?' he asked slily.

The woman laughed then. 'A ferret!' she exclaimed, and laughed again. 'You're the one for ferrets. . . .' Pulling her shawl more tightly about her she moved away towards the fire. 'You think the cat act *kind* like that for a ferret?'

The boy stared curiously past the cat across the floor,

screwing his eyelids to see beyond the pacing cat and into the shadows. 'The cat bain't acting so kind,' he remarked thoughtfully towards the fire.

'A couple of midgets he's got in there,' the woman told him, '—dressed up to kill—or so he says,' and she went off again into screams of jeering laughter.

The boy did not laugh; his expression did not change: calmly he stared at the crack below the bunk. 'Dressed up to kill . . .' he repeated and, after a moment, he added: 'Only two?'

'How many do you want?' asked the woman. 'Half a dozen? A couple's enough, ain't it?'

'What do you reckon to do with them?' asked the boy.

'Do with them?' repeated the woman, staring stupidly.

'I mean, when you catch them?'

The woman gave him a curious look, as though doubting his reason. 'But there ain't nothing there,' she told him.

'But you just said——'

The woman laughed, half angry, half bewildered. 'Mild Eye sees 'em—not me. Or so he makes out. There ain't nothing there, I tell you——'

'I seen 'em all right,' said Mild Eye. He stretched his first finger and thumb. 'This high, I'd say—a bit of a woman, it looked like, and a bit of a man.'

'Mind if I look?' asked the boy, his foot on the steps. He laid down his gun, and Arrietty, watching, saw him put his hand in his pocket; there was a stealthiness about his move-ment which drove the blood from her heart. 'Oh,' she gasped, and grabbed her father's sleeve.

'What is it?' breathed Pod, leaning towards her.

'His pocket——' stammered Arrietty.   'Something alive in his pocket!'

'A ferret,' cried Homily, forgetting to whisper.   'We're finished.'

'Hush——' implored Pod.   The boy had heard something; he had seated himself on the top step and was now leaning forward gazing towards them across the strip of faded carpet.   At Homily's exclamation, Pod had seen his eyes widen, his face become alert.

'What's the good of whispering?' complained Homily, lowering her voice all the same.   'We're for it now. Wouldn't matter if we sang——'

'Hush——' said Pod again.

'How would you think to get 'em out?' the boy was asking, his eyes on the gap; his right hand, Arrietty saw, still feeling in his pocket.

'Easy,' explained Mild Eye; 'empty the locker and take up them boards underneath.'

'You see?' whispered Homily, almost in triumph, 'it doesn't matter what we do now!'

Pod gave up.   'Then sing,' he suggested wearily.

'Nailed down, them boards are, aren't they?' asked the boy.

'No,' said Mild Eye.   'I've had 'em out after rats; they comes out in a piece.'

The boy, his head lowered, was staring into the gap. Arrietty, from where she crouched, was looking straight into his eyes: they were thoughtful eyes, bland and blue.

'Say you catch them,' the boy went on, 'what then?'

'What then?' repeated Mild Eye, puzzled.

'What do you want to do with 'em?'

'Do with 'em? Cage 'em up. What else?'

'Cage 'em up in what?'

'In that.' Mild Eye touched the bird cage, which swung slightly. 'What else?'

('And feed us on groundsel, I shouldn't wonder,' muttered Homily below her breath.)

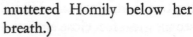

'You want to keep 'em?' asked the boy, his eyes on the shadowed gap.

'Keep 'em, naow! Sell 'em!' exclaimed Mild Eye. 'Fetch a pretty penny, that lot would—cage and all complete.'

'Oh, my goodness,' whimpered Homily.

'Quiet,' breathed Pod, 'better the cage than the ferret.'

'No,' thought Arrietty, 'better the ferret.'

'What would you feed 'em on?' the boy was asking; he seemed to be playing for time.

Mild Eye laughed indulgently. 'Anything. Bits o' left-overs. . . .'

('You hear that?' whispered Homily, very angry.

'Well, to-day it was pheasant,' Pod reminded her; but he was glad she was angry: anger made her brave.)

Mild Eye had climbed right in now—blotting out the sunshine. 'Move over,' he said to the boy, 'we got to get at the locker.'

The boy shifted, a token shift. 'What about the cat?' he said.

'That's right,' agreed Mild Eye, 'better have the cat out. Come on, Tiger——'

But the cat, it seemed, was as stubborn as the boy and shared his interest in borrowers: evading Mild Eye's hand, it sprang away to the bed, and (Arrietty gathered from a slight thud immediately above their heads) from the end of the bed to the locker. Mild Eye came after it: they could see his great feet close against the gap—their own dear boot was there just beside them, with the patch which Pod had sewn! It seemed incredible to see it worn, and by such a hostile foot.

'Better cart it out to the missus,' suggested the boy, as Mild Eye grabbed the cat; 'if it bain't held on to it'll only jump back in.'

('Don't you dare,' moaned Homily, just below her breath.

Pod looked amazed. 'Who are you talking to?' he asked in a whisper.

'Him—Mild Eye; the minute he leaves this caravan that boy'll be after us with the ferret.'

'Now, see here——' began Pod.

'You mark my words,' went on Homily in a panic-stricken whisper. 'I know who he is now. It's all come back to me: young Tom Goodenough. I heard speak of that one many a time back home under the kitchen. And I wouldn't be surprised if it wasn't him we saw at the window —that day we made off, remember? Proper devil he's reckoned to be with that ferret——'

'Quiet, Homily!' implored Pod.

'Why? For heaven's sake—they know we're here: quiet or noisy—what's the difference to a ferret?')

Mild Eye swore suddenly as though the cat had scratched him. 'Cart him right out,' said the boy again, 'and see she holds him.'

'Don't fret,' said Mild Eye, 'we can shut the door.'

'That bain't no good,' said the boy; 'we can't shut the top half; we got to have light.'

On the threshold Mild Eye hesitated. 'Don't you touch nothin',' he said, and stood there a moment, waiting, before he clumped off down the steps. On the bottom rung he seemed to slip: the borrowers could hear him swearing. 'This blamed boot,' they heard him say, and something about the heel.

'You all right?' called out the boy carelessly. The answer was an oath.

'Block your ears,' whispered Homily to Arrietty. 'Oh, my goodness me, did you hear what he said?'

'Yes,' began Arrietty obligingly, 'he said——'

'Oh, you wicked, heathen girl,' cried Homily angrily, 'shame on yourself for listening!'

'Quiet, Homily,' begged Pod again.

'But you know what happened, Pod?' whispered Homily excitedly. 'The heel came off the boot! What did I tell you, up in the ditch, when you would take out them nails!' For one brief moment she forgot her fears and gave a tiny giggle.

'Look,' breathed Arrietty suddenly, and reached for her mother's hand. They looked.

The boy, leaning towards them on one elbow, his steady gaze fixed on the slit of darkness between the locker and floor, was feeling stealthily in the right-hand pocket of his coat—it was the deep, pouched pocket common to game-keepers.

'Oh, my . . .' muttered Homily, as Pod took her hand.

'Shut your eyes,' said Pod. 'No use running and you won't know nothing: a ferret strikes quick.'

There was a pause, tense and solemn, while three small hearts beat quickly. Homily broke it.

'I've tried to be a good wife to you, Pod,' she announced tearfully, one eye screwed obediently shut, the other cautiously open.

'You've been first-rate,' said Pod, his eyes on the boy. Against the light it was hard to see, but something moved in his hand: a creature he had taken from his pocket.

'A bit sharp sometimes,' went on Homily.

'It doesn't matter now,' said Pod.

'I'm sorry, Pod,' said Homily.

'I forgive you,' said Pod absently. A deeper shadow now had fallen across the carpet: Mild Eye had come back up the steps. Pod saw the woman had sneaked up behind him, clasping the cat in her shawl.

The boy did not start or turn. 'Make for my pocket . . .' he said steadily, his eyes on the gap.

'What's that?' asked Mild Eye, surprised.

'Make for my pocket,' repeated the boy, 'do you hear what I say?' And suddenly he loosed on the carpet the thing he had held in his hand.

'Oh, my goodness——' cried Homily, clutching on to Pod.

'Whatever is it?' she went on, after a moment, both eyes suddenly open. Some kind of living creature it was, but

certainly not a ferret . . . too slow . . . too angular . . . too
upright . . . too——

Arrietty let out a glad cry: 'It's Spiller!'

'What?' exclaimed Homily, almost crossly—tricked, she
felt, when she thought of those grave 'last words.'

'It's Spiller,' Arrietty sang out again, 'Spiller . . .
Spiller . . . Spiller!'

'Looking quite ridiculous,' remarked Homily; and indeed
he did look rather odd and sausage-like, stuffed out in his
stiff new clothes; he would render them down gradually
to a wearable suppleness.

'What are you waiting for?' asked Spiller. 'You heard
what he said. Come on now. Get moving, can't you?'

'That boy?' exclaimed Homily, 'was he speaking to
us?'

'Who else?' snapped Spiller. 'He don't want Mild Eye
in his pocket. Come on——'

'His pocket!' exclaimed Homily in a frantic whisper.
She turned to Pod. 'Now let's get this right: young Tom
Goodenough wants me'—she touched her own chest—'to
run out there, right in the open, get meself over his trouser-
leg, across his middle, up to his hip, and potter down all
meek and mild into his pocket?'

'Not you only,' explained Pod, 'all of us.'

'He's crazy,' announced Homily firmly, tightening her
lips.

'Now, see here, Homily——' began Pod.

'I'd sooner perish,' Homily asserted.

'That's just what you will do,' said Pod.

'Remember that peg-bag?' she reminded him. 'I

couldn't face it, Pod.   And where's he going to take us?
Tell me that?'

'How should I know?' exclaimed Pod.   'Now, come on,
Homily, you do what he says, there's me brave old girl . . .
take her by the wrist, Spiller, she's got to come . . . ready
Arrietty?   Now for it——' and suddenly there they were,
the whole group of them—out in the open.

CHAPTER NINETEEN

'FORTUNE FAVOURS THE BRAVE'
Sherman's March to the Coast began, 1864
[*Extract from Arrietty's Diary and Proverb Book, November 13th.*]

THE WOMAN screeched when she saw them: she dropped the cat, and ran for her life, making hell for leather towards the main road. Mild Eye, too, was taken aback: he sat down on the bed with his feet in the air as though a contaminated flood were swirling across the carpet: the cat, unnerved by the general uproar, made a frantic leap for the overmantel, bringing down two mugs, a framed photograph, and a spray of paper rosebuds.

Pod and Arrietty made their own slithering way across the folds of trouser-leg to the rising slope of hip; but poor Spiller, pulling and pushing a protesting Homily, was picked up and dropped in. For one awful moment, attached by the wrist to Spiller, Homily dangled in air, before the boy's quick fingers gathered her up and tidied her neatly away. Only just in time—for Mild Eye, recovering, had made a sudden grab, missing her by inches ('Torn us apart, he would have,' she said later, 'like a couple of bananas!'). Deep in the pocket, she heard his angry shout of 'Four of 'em you got there. Come on: fair's fair—hand over them first two!'

They did not know what happened next: all was darkness and jumble. Some sort of struggle was going on—there was the sound of heavy breathing, muttered swear words, and the pocket swayed and bounced. Then, by the bumping, they knew the boy was running and Mild Eye, shouting behind him, was cursing his heelless boot. They heard these shouts grow fainter, and the crackle of breaking branches as the boy crashed through a hedge.

There was no conversation in the pocket: all four of them

felt too dazed. At last Pod, wedged upside-down in a corner, freed his mouth from fluff. 'You all right, Homily?' he gasped. Homily, tightly interwoven with Spiller and Arrietty, could not quite tell. Pod heard a slight squeak. 'Me leg's gone numb,' said Homily unhappily.

'Not broken, is it?' asked Pod anxiously.

'Can't feel nothing in it,' said Homily.

'Can you move it?' asked Pod.

There was a sharp exclamation from Spiller as Homily said 'No.'

'If it's the leg you're pinching,' remarked Spiller, 'stands to reason you can't move it.'

'How do you know?' asked Homily.

'Because it's mine,' he said.

The boy's steps became slower: he seemed to be going uphill; after a while he sat down. The great hand came down amongst them. Homily began to whimper, but the fingers slid past her; they were feeling for Spiller. The coat was pulled round and the pocket flap held open, so the boy could peer at them. 'You all right, Spiller?' he asked.

Spiller grunted.

'Which is Homily?' asked the boy.

'The noisy one,' said Spiller. 'I told you.'

'You all right, Homily?' asked the boy.

Homily, terrified, was silent.

The great fingers came down again, sliding their way into the pocket.

Spiller, standing now with legs apart and back supported against the upright seam, called out tersely: 'Leave 'em be.'

The fingers stopped moving. 'I wanted to see if they were all right,' said the boy.

'They're all right,' said Spiller.

'I'd like to have 'em out,' the boy went on. 'I'd like to have a look at 'em.' He peered downwards at the open pocket. 'You're not dead, are you?' he inquired anxiously. 'You bain't none of you dead?'

'How could we say, if we was?' muttered Homily irritably.

'You leave 'em be,' said Spiller again; 'it's warm in here: you don't want to bring 'em out sudden into the cold.

You'll see 'em often enough,' he consoled the boy, 'once we get indoors.'

The fingers withdrew and they were in the dark again; there was a rocking and the boy stood up. Pod, Homily, and Arrietty slid the length of the bottom seam of the pocket, fetching up against the opposite corner; it was full of dried breadcrumbs, jagged and hard as concrete. 'Ouch!' cried Homily, unhappily. Spiller, Arrietty noticed, though he swayed on his feet, managed to keep upright. Spiller, she guessed, had travelled by pocket before: the boy was walking again now, and the coat swayed with a more predictable rhythm. 'After a while,' Arrietty thought, 'I'll have a go at standing myself.'

Pod experimentally broke off a jagged piece of breadcrumb which, after patient sucking, slowly began to dissolve. 'I'll try a bit of that,' said Homily, holding out her hand; she had revived a little and was feeling peckish.

'Where's he taking us?' she asked Spiller after a while.

'Round the wood and over the hill.'

'Where he lives with his grandpa?'

'That's right,' admitted Spiller.

'I ain't ever heard tell much about gamekeepers,' said Homily, 'nor what they'd be apt to do with—a borrower, say. Nor what sort of boy this is neither. I mean,' she went on in a worried voice, 'my mother-in-law had an uncle once who was kept in a tin box with four holes in the lid and fed twice a day by an eye-dropper. . . .'

'He ain't that sort of boy,' said Spiller.

'Whatever's an eye-dropper?' asked Pod. He took it to be some strange sort of craft or profession.

'Then there was Lupy's cousin, Oggin, you remember,' went on Homily. 'They made a regular kind of world for him in the bottom of an old tin bath in the outhouse; grass, pond, and all. And they gave him a cart to ride in and a lizard for company. But the sides of the bath were good and slippery: they knew he couldn't get out. . . .'

'Lupy?' repeated Spiller wonderingly. 'Wouldn't be two called that?'

'This one married my brother Hendreary,' said Homily. 'Why,' she exclaimed with sudden excitement, 'you don't say you know her!'

The pocket had stopped swaying: they heard some metallic sound and the sliding squeak of a latch.

'I know her all right,' whispered Spiller. 'She makes my winter clothes.'

'Quiet,' urged Pod; 'we've arrived.' He had heard the sound of an opening door and could smell an indoor smell.

'You know *Lupy*?' Homily persisted, unaware even that the pocket had become darker. 'But what are they doing? And where are they living—she and Hendreary? We thought they was eaten by foxes, children and all. . . .'

'Quiet, Homily,' implored Pod. Strange movements seemed to be going on, doors were opening and shutting; so stealthily the boy was walking the pocket now hung still.

'Tell us, Spiller, quick,' went on Homily; but she dropped her voice to an obedient whisper. 'You must know! Where are they living now?'

Spiller hesitated—in the semi-darkness he seemed to smile.

'They're living here,' he said.

The boy now seemed to be kneeling.

As the fingers came down again, feeling amongst them, Homily let out a cry. 'It's all right,' whispered Pod, as she burrowed back among the crumbs. 'Keep your head—we got to come out some time.'

Spiller went first; he sailed away from them—nonchal-

antly astride a finger, without even bothering to glance back. Then it was Arrietty's turn. 'Oh my goodness me . . .' muttered Homily, 'wherever will they put her?'

Pod's turn next; but Homily went with him. She scrambled aboard at the last moment by creeping under the thumb. There was hardly time to feel sick (it was the swoosh through the empty air which Homily always dreaded), so deftly and gently they found themselves set down.

A gleam of firelight struck the tiny group as they stood beside the hearth, against a high, wooden wall: it was, they discovered later, the side of the log-box. They stood together—close and scared, controlling their longing to run. Spiller, they noticed, had disappeared.

The boy, on one knee, towered above them—a terrifying mountain of flesh. The firelight flickered on his down-turned face: they could feel the draught of his breathing.

'It's all right,' he assured them, 'you'll be all right now.' He was staring with great interest, as a collector would stare at a new-found specimen. His hand hovered above them as though he longed to touch them, to pick one of them up, to examine each more closely.

Nervously Pod cleared his throat. 'Where's Spiller?' he asked.

'He'll be back,' said the boy. After a moment he added: 'I got six altogether in there.'

'Six what?' asked Homily nervously.

'Six borrowers,' said the boy. 'I reckon I got the best collection of borrowers in two counties. And,' he added, 'me grandad ain't seen one. His eyes is sharp enough, yet he ain't ever seen a borrower.'

Pod cleared his throat again. 'He ain't supposed to,' he said.

'Some I got in there'—the boy jerked his head towards the log-box—'I never sees neither. Scared. Some folks say you can't never tame 'em. You can give 'em the earth, 'tis said, but they'll never come out and be civil.'

'I would,' said Arrietty.

'Now you behave yourself,' snapped Homily, alarmed.

'Spiller would, too,' said Arrietty.

'Spiller's different,' replied Homily, with a nervous glance towards the boy—Spiller, she felt, was the boy's curator: the go-between of this rare collection. 'Gets so much a head, I wouldn't wonder?'

'Here he is,' said Arrietty, looking towards the corner of the log-box.

Noiselessly he had come upon them.

'She won't come out,' said Spiller to the boy.

'Oh,' exclaimed Homily, 'does he mean Lupy?'

No one answered. Spiller stood silent, looking up at the boy. The boy frowned thoughtfully; he seemed disappointed. He looked them over once more, examining each of them from head to foot as though loath to see them go; he sighed a little. 'Then take 'em in,' he said.

CHAPTER TWENTY

'LONG LOOKED FOR COMES AT LAST'
Vasco da Gama rounded Cape of Good Hope, 1497
[*Extract from Arrietty's Diary and Proverb Book, November 20th.*]

THEY FILED in through the Gothic-shaped hole in the wainscot, a little nervous, a little shy. It was shadowy inside like a cave; disappointingly it felt uninhabited and smelled of dust and mice. 'Oh dear,' muttered Homily incredulously, 'is this how they live . . .?' She stopped suddenly and picked up some object from the floor. 'My goodness,' she whispered aside excitedly to Pod, 'do you know what this is?' and she brandished a whitish object under his nose.

'Yes,' said Pod, 'it's a bit of quill pipe-cleaner. Put it down, Homily, and come on, do. Spiller's waiting.'

'It's the spout of our old oak-apple tea-pot,' persisted Homily, 'that's what it is. I'd know it anywhere and it's no good telling me any different. So they *are* here . . .' she mused wonderingly as she followed Pod into the shadows to where Spiller with Arrietty stood waiting.

'We go up here,' said Spiller, and Homily saw that he stood with his hand on a ladder. Glancing up to where the rungs soared away above them into dimness, she gave a slight shudder: the ladder was made of matchsticks, neatly glued and spliced to two lengths of split cane, such as florists use to support potted plants.

'I'll go first,' said Pod. 'We better take it one at a time.'

Homily watched fearfully until she heard his voice from above.

'It's all right,' he whispered from some invisible eyrie; 'come on up.'

Homily followed, her knees trembling, and emerged at last on to the dim-lit platform beside Pod—an aerial landing stage, that was what it seemed like—which creaked a little when she stepped on it and almost seemed to sway. Below lay hollow darkness; ahead an open door. 'Oh my goodness,' she muttered, 'I do hope it's safe . . . don't look down,' she advised Arrietty, who came up next.

But Arrietty had no temptation to look down: her eyes were on the lighted doorway and the moving shadows within; she heard the faint sound of voices and a sudden high-pitched laugh.

'Come on,' said Spiller, slipping past her, and making towards the door.

Arrietty never forgot her first sight of that upstairs room: the warmth, the sudden cleanliness, the winking candle-light, and the smell of home-cooked food.

And so many voices . . . so many people. . . .

Gradually, in a dazed way, she began to sort them out: that must be Aunt Lupy embracing her mother—Aunt Lupy so round and glowing, her mother so smudged and lean. Why did they cling and weep, she wondered, and squeeze each others' hands? They had never liked each other—all the world knew that. Homily had thought Lupy stuck-up because, back in the big house, Lupy had lived in the drawing-room and (she had heard it rumoured) changed for dinner at night. And Lupy despised Homily for living under the kitchen and for pronouncing parquet 'parkett.'

And here was Uncle Hendreary, his beard grown thinner, telling her father that this could not be Arrietty, and her father, with pride, telling Uncle Hendreary it could. Those must be the three boy cousins—whose names she had not caught—graduated in size but as like as peas in a pod. And this thin, tall, fairylike creature, neither old nor young,

who hovered shyly in the background with a faint uneasy smile, who was she?

Homily screamed when she saw her and clapped her hand to her mouth. 'It can't be Eggletina!'

It evidently could. Arrietty stared too, wondering if she had heard aright: Eggletina, that long lost cousin who one fine day escaped from under the floor and was never seen again? A kind of legend she had been to Arrietty and a life-long cautionary tale. Well, here she was, safe and sound, unless they all were dreaming.

And well they might be.

There was something strangely unreal about this room—

furnished with doll's-house furniture of every shape and size, none of it matching or in proportion. There were chairs upholstered in rep or velvet, some of them too small to sit in and some too steep and large; there were chiffoniers which were too tall and occasional tables far too low; and a toy fire-place with coloured plaster coals and its fire-irons stuck down all-of-a-piece with the fender; there were two make-believe windows with curved pelmets and red satin curtains, each hand-painted with an imitation view—one looked out on a Swiss mountain scene, the other a Highland glen ('Eggletina did them,' Aunt Lupy boasted in her rich society voice. 'We're going to have a third when we get the curtains—a view of Lake Como from Monte S. Primo'); there were table lamps and standard lamps, flounced, festooned, and tasselled, but the light in the room, Arrietty noticed, came from humble, familiar dips like those they had made at home.

Everybody looked extraordinarily clean and Arrietty became even shyer. She threw a quick glance at her father and mother and was not reassured: none of their clothes had been washed for weeks nor, for some days, had their hands and faces. Pod's trousers had a tear in one knee and Homily's hair hung down in snakes. And here was Aunt Lupy, plump and polite, begging Homily please to take off her things in the kind of voice, Arrietty imagined, usually reserved for feather boas, opera cloaks, and freshly cleaned white kid gloves.

But Homily, who back at home had so dreaded being 'caught out' in a soiled apron, knew one worth two of that. She had, Pod and Arrietty noticed with pride, adopted her woman-tried-beyond-endurance role backed up by one called yes-I've-suffered-but-don't-let's-speak-of-it-now; she had invented a new smile, wan but brave, and had—in the same good cause—plucked the two last hair-pins out of her dust-filled hair. 'Poor dear Lupy,' she was saying, glancing wearily about, 'what a lot of furniture! Whoever helps you with the dusting?' And swaying a little, she sank on a chair.

They rushed to support her, as she hoped they might. Water was brought and they bathed her face and hands. Hendreary stood with the tears in his brotherly eyes. 'Poor valiant soul,' he muttered, shaking his head, 'your mind kind of reels when you think of what she's been through. . . .'

Then, after a quick wash and brush up all round and a brisk bit of eye-wiping, they all sat down to supper. This they ate in the kitchen, which was rather a come-down except that, in here, the fire was real: a splendid cooking-range made of a large, black door-lock; they poked the fire through the keyhole, which glowed handsomely, and the smoke, they were told, went out through a series of pipes to the cottage chimney behind.

The long, white table was richly spread: it was an eighteenth-century finger-plate off some old drawing-room door—white-enamelled and painted with forget-me-nots, supported firmly on four stout pencil stubs where once the screws had been; the points of the pencils emerged slightly through the top of the table; one was copying-ink and they were warned not to touch it in case it stained their hands.

There was every kind of dish and preserve—both real and false; pies, puddings, and bottled fruits out of season—all cooked by Lupy, and an imitation leg of mutton and a dish of plaster tarts borrowed from the dolls' house. There were three real tumblers as well as acorn cups and a couple of green glass decanters.

Talk, talk, talk. . . . Arrietty, listening, felt dazed: she saw now why they had been expected. Spiller, she gathered, having found the alcove bootless and its inmates flown, had salvaged their few possessions and had run and told young Tom. Lupy felt a little faint suddenly when they mentioned this person by name, and had to leave the table. She sat awhile in the next room on a frail gilt chair placed just inside the doorway—'between draughts' as she put it—fanning her round red face with a lark's feather.

'Mother's like this about humans,' explained the eldest cousin. 'It's no good telling her he's tame as anything and wouldn't hurt a fly!'

'You never know,' said Lupy darkly, from her seat in the doorway. 'He's nearly full grown! And that, they say, is when they start to be dangerous. . . .'

'Lupy's right,' agreed Pod, 'I'd never trust 'em meself.'

'Oh, how can you say that?' cried Arrietty. 'Look at the way he snatched us up right out of the jaws of death!'

'Snatched you up?' screamed Lupy from the next room. 'You mean—*with his hands*?'

Homily gave her brave little laugh, listlessly chasing a globule of raspberry around her too slippery plate. 'Naturally. . . .' She shrugged. 'It was nothing really.'

'Oh dear...' stammered Lupy faintly, 'oh, you poor thing . . . imagine it! I think,' she went on, 'if you'll excuse me a moment, I'll just go and lie down . . .' and she heaved her weight off the tiny chair, which rocked as she left it.

'Where did you get all this furniture, Hendreary?' asked Homily, recovering suddenly now that Lupy had gone.

'It was delivered,' her brother told her, 'in a plain white pillow-case. Someone from the big house brought it down.'

'From our house?' asked Pod.

'Stands to reason,' said Hendreary, 'It's all stuff from that doll's house, remember, they had upstairs in the school-room. Top shelf of the toy cupboard, on the right-hand side of the door.'

'Naturally I remember,' said Homily, 'seeing that some of it's mine. Pity,' she remarked aside to Arrietty, 'that we didn't keep that inventory,' she lowered her voice, 'the one you made on blotting-paper, remember.'

Arrietty nodded: there were going to be fireworks later—

she could see that. She felt very tired suddenly; there seemed too much talk and the crowded room felt hot.

'Who brought it down?' Pod was asking in a surprised voice. 'Some kind of human being?'

'We reckon so,' agreed Hendreary. 'It was lying there t'other side of the bank. Soon after we got turned out of the badgers' set and had set up house in the stove——'

'What stove was that?' asked Pod. 'Not the one by the camping site?'

'That's right,' Hendreary told him; 'two years we lived there, off and on.'

'A bit too close to the gipsies for my liking,' said Pod. He cut himself a generous slice of hot boiled chestnut and spread it thickly with butter. He remembered suddenly that pile of fragile bones.

'You got to be close,' Hendreary explained, 'like it or not, when you got to borrow.'

Pod, about to bite, withdrew the chestnut: he seemed amazed. 'You borrowed from caravans?' he exclaimed. 'At your age!'

Hendreary shrugged slightly and was modestly silent.

'Well I never,' said Homily admiringly, 'there's a brother for you! You think what that means, Pod——'

'I am thinking,' said Pod. He raised his head. 'What did you do about smoke?'

'You don't have none,' Hendreary told him, 'not when you cook on gas.'

'On gas!' exclaimed Homily.

'That's right. We borrowed a bit o' gas from the gas company: they got a pipe laid all along that bank. The stove was resting on its back, like, you remember? We dug down behind through a flue, a good six weeks we spent in that tunnel. Worth it in the end, though: three pin-hole burners, we had down there.'

'How did you turn 'em on and off?' asked Pod.

'We didn't—once lit, we never let them out. Still burning they are to this day.'

'You mean that you still go back there?'

Hendreary, yawning slightly, shook his head (they had eaten well and the room felt very close). 'Spiller lives there,' he said.

'Oh,' exclaimed Homily, 'so that's how Spiller cooked! He might have told us,' she went on, looking about in a hurt way, 'or, at any rate, asked us in——'

'He wouldn't do that,' said Hendreary. 'Once bitten, twice shy, as you might say.'

'How do you mean?' asked Homily.

'After we left the badgers' set——' began Hendreary, and broke off: slightly shamefaced, he seemed, in spite of his smile. 'Well, that stove was one of his places: he asked us in for a bite and a sup and we stayed a couple o' years——'

'Once you'd struck gas, you mean,' said Pod.

'That's right,' said Hendreary. 'We cooked and Spiller borrowed.'

'Ah!' said Pod. 'Spiller borrowed? Now I under-stand. . . . You and me, Hendreary; we got to face up to it—we're not as young as we was. Not by a long chalk.'

'Where is Spiller now?' asked Arrietty suddenly.

'Oh, he's gone off,' said Hendreary vaguely; he seemed a little embarrassed and sat there frowning and tapping the table with a pewter spoon (one of a set of six, Homily remembered angrily: she wondered how many were left).

'Gone off where?' asked Arrietty.

'Home, I reckon,' Hendreary told her.

'But we haven't thanked him,' cried Arrietty. 'Spiller saved our lives!'

Hendreary threw off his gloom. 'Have a drop of blackberry cordial,' he suggested suddenly to Pod. 'Lupy's own make? Cheer us all up. . . .'

'Not for me,' said Homily firmly, before Pod could speak. 'No good never comes of it, as we've found out to our cost.'

'But what will Spiller think?' persisted Arrietty, and there were tears in her eyes. 'We haven't even thanked him.'

Hendreary looked at her, surprised. 'Spiller? He don't hold with thanks. He's all right. . . .' and he patted Arrietty's arm.

'Why didn't he stay for supper?'

'He don't ever,' Hendreary told her; 'doesn't like company. He'll cook something on his own.'

'Where?'

'In his stove.'

'But that's miles away!'

'Not for Spiller—he's used to it. Goes part way by water.'

'And it must be getting dark,' Arrietty went on unhappily.

'Now don't you fret about Spiller,' her uncle told her. 'You eat up your pie. . . .'

Arrietty looked down at her plate (pink celluloid, it was, part of a tea-service which she seemed to remember);

somehow she had no appetite.   She raised her eyes.   'And
when will he be back?' she asked anxiously.

'He don't come back much.   Once a year for his new
clothes.   Or if young Tom sends 'im special.'

Arrietty looked thoughtful.   'He must be lonely,' she
ventured at last.

'Spiller?   No, I wouldn't say he was lonely.   Some
borrowers is made like that.   Solitary.   You get 'em now
and again.'   He glanced across the room to where his
daughter, having left the table, was sitting alone by the fire.
'Eggletina's a bit like that . . . pity, but you can't do
nothing about it.   Them's the ones as gets this craze for
humans—kind of man-eaters, they turns out to be. . . .'

When Lupy returned, refreshed from her rest, it all began
again: talk, talk, talk . . . and Arrietty slipped unnoticed
from the table.   But, as she wandered away towards the
other room, she heard it going on: talk about living arrangements; about the construction of a suite of rooms upstairs;
about what pitfalls there were in this new way of life and the
rules they had made to avoid such pitfalls—how you always
drew the ladder up last thing at night but that it should
never be moved while the men were out borrowing; that
the young boys went out as learners, each in turn, but that,
true to borrowing tradition, the women would stay at
home; she heard her mother declining the use of the kitchen.
'Thank you, Lupy,' Homily was saying; 'it's very kind of
you but we'd better begin as we mean to go on, don't you
think? quite separate.'

'And so it starts again,' thought Arrietty, as entering the
next room she seated herself in a stiff arm-chair.   But no

longer quite under the floor—up a little, they would be now, among the lath and plaster: there would be ladders instead of dusty passages, and that platform, she hoped, might do instead of her grating.

She glanced about her at the over-furnished room: the doll's-house left-overs suddenly looked silly—everything for show and nothing much for use; the false coals in the fire-place looked worn as though scrubbed too often by Lupy, and the painted view in the windows had finger-marks round the edge.

She wandered out to the dim-lit platform; this, with it's dust and shadows, had she known of such things, was something like going back-stage. The ladder was in place, she noticed—a sign that someone was out—but in this case, not so much 'out' as 'gone.' Poor Spiller . . . solitary, they had called him. 'Perhaps,' thought Arrietty self-pityingly, 'that's what's the matter with me. . . .'

There was a faint light, she saw now, in the chasm below her; what at first had seemed a lessening of darkness seemed now a welcoming glow. Arrietty, her heart beating, took hold of the ladder and set her foot on the first rung. 'If I don't do it now,' she thought desperately, 'this first evening —perhaps, in the future, I should never dare again.' There seemed too many rules in Aunt Lupy's house, too many people, and the rooms seemed too dark and too hot. 'There may be compensations,' she thought, her knees trembling a little as rung after rung she started to climb down, 'but I'll have to discover them myself.'

Soon she stood once again in the dusty entrance hall; she glanced about her and then nervously she looked up;

she saw the top of the ladder outlined against the light and the jagged edge of the high platform. It made her feel suddenly dizzy and more than a little afraid: suppose someone, not realizing she was below, decided to pull it up?

The faint light, she realized, came from the hole in the wainscot: the log-box, for some reason, was not laid flush against it—there might well be room to squeeze through. She would like to have one more peep at the room in which, some hours before, young Tom had set them down—to have some little knowledge, however fleeting, of this human dwelling which from now on would compose her world.

All was quiet as she stole towards the Gothic-shaped opening. The log-box, she found, was a good inch and a half away. It was easy enough to slip out and ease her tiny body along the narrow passage left between the side of the box and the wall. Again a little frightening: suppose some human being decided suddenly to shove the log-box into place. She would be squashed, she thought, and found long afterwards, glued to the wainscot, like some strange, pressed flower. For this reason she moved fast, and reaching the box's corner, she stepped out on the hearth.

She glanced about the room. She could see the rafters of the ceiling, the legs of a Windsor chair, and the underside of its seat. She saw a lighted candle on a wooden table, and, by its leg, a pile of skins on the floor—ah this, she realized, was the secret of Spiller's wardrobe.

Another kind of fur lay on the table, just beyond the candle above a piece of cloth—tawny yellow and somehow rougher. As she stared it seemed to stir. A cat? A fox? Arrietty froze to stillness, but she bravely stood her ground.

Now the movement became unmistakable: a roll over and a sudden lifting up.

Arrietty gasped—a tiny sound, but it was heard.

A face looked back at her, candle-lit and drowsed with sleep, below its thatch of hair.   There was a long silence. At last the boy's lips curved softly into a smile—and very young he looked after sleeping, very harmless.   The arm on which he had rested his head lay loosely on the table and Arrietty, from where she stood, had seen his fingers relax.   A clock was ticking somewhere above her head; the candle flame rose, still and steady, lighting the peaceful room; the coals gave a gentle shudder as they settled in the grate.

'Hallo,' said Arrietty.

'Hallo,' replied young Tom.